January stood th   crowd, every word and emotion they had ever shared and not shared but thought about was there, glittering on her flesh for him to see alone. She considered walking over to him as he sat there expecting her, waiting for her, calling to her with his eyes, pulling at every part of her with his mind, but she just couldn't. Her pain kept her still. Unsteady but still. She stood locked onto the wooded floors of the old bar, as the dulcimer-laden lullaby played on.

Then, she raised her finger to her lips and blew him a kiss. Mouthing the words, "Goodbye." She turned around and walked out of the bar, deciding it best to just let it all go. All of it. He would not run after her and she did not want him to.

It simply could not be sustained. Someone had to make the choice to stop it. To end the connection, break away from its desperate pull. Its interruption. Its never-ending distraction.

It was an unfilled and unspoken promise. Years of hanging on to something that was too unreal to ever be real. It was time to stop drinking the wine. Stop partaking in even a sip of what was not hers to consume. It was never hers.

After all, wine made her judgment hazy, her mind heady.

And she had always been more of a whiskey kind of girl.

Muse

by

Melanie Snow

This is a work of fiction. Names, characters, places, and incidents are either the product of the author's imagination or are used fictitiously, and any resemblance to actual persons living or dead, business establishments, events, or locales, is entirely coincidental.

Muse

COPYRIGHT © 2019 by Melanie Snow

Cover Art by *Tina Lynn Stout*

The Wild Rose Press, Inc.
PO Box 708
Adams Basin, NY 14410-0708
Visit us at www.thewildrosepress.com

Publishing History
First Vintage Rose Edition, 2019
Print ISBN 978-1-5092-2203-2
Digital ISBN 978-1-5092-2204-9

Published in the United States of America

Dedication

To the muse who inspires me every day. Always.

Miami 2010

"I'm going to have to find a different way to love you," he said flatly. His eyes darting away as he forced himself to look at anything else but her. He could feel those steel gray eyes penetrating him, regardless of his attempt to avoid them.

January agreed. "You're right. I know you're right." She ran her long fingers through her hair and sank deeper into the worn leather chair. "I just never imagined it would come to this. We've had something so special for so long, for so many years, Alexander. How do you suppose we are going to just pretend we are regular people who once knew each other in college?"

Alexander did not have a plan. For more than fifteen years, they had known each other. January was only seventeen the first time he had noticed her standing in a line to sign up for classes on campus. She was a freshman. He could never shake that day from his memory. It wasn't anything extraordinary, just another first day back on campus after summer break. Being a senior, it was only natural to peek at the new blood. There she had been. Standing in line as the rain began to fall, oblivious to it as she refused to take her nose out of the book she was reading. Proust, it had been. Students were jumping out of line, giving up because of the falling rain, and there she stood like a stone. Later she would tell him it was because she absolutely would not miss out on taking the infamous literature class called *Stories*. It was tough to get into, and every English major wanted in. This was before signing up for classes on the Internet, so waiting in line was how it was done. January described the rain as "good fortune." She later counted the number of people who had been before her in line and concluded the class would have been filled by the time it was her turn had all those people not run away from the rain. Alexander remembered her signing the papers, dripping from the rain, and smiling at the highly-irritated school advisor. She walked, no, glided, away, beaming into the light as it filtered through the clouds. He did not know who she was or where she was going, but at that moment, he only knew he had to meet her.

That was 1995.

It was now 2010. Much had changed. One thing had not gone away in all those years, and that was his intense connection to her. They had shared letters. Phone calls. Text messages. Emails. Thoughts intertwined in the dead of night.

For fifteen years.

They had married other people.

Lived on opposite sides of the earth.

Held down careers.

They had watched each other grow and change through ink on paper and blinking letters on a computer screen.

A few brief meetings in person.

Not nearly enough.

Yet they still felt something for each other. Regardless of the separation, regardless of the vast differences in their lives, they could not escape each other. They never cheated on their spouses. They never fulfilled the desires which burned within them. They didn't even know what those desires were exactly. What they had was something beyond words. It was a thought in the middle of the night which shuddered one of them awake and the other, thousands of miles away, woke up to feel it, too, and lay awake for hours confused and unable to return to sleep.

For Alexander, it was that moment in the rain in 1995. Always that same moment, repeating in his head, like a record on repeat, scratching only as it started over. For January, it was a slow torture. It was also bliss. Alexander was her muse, her secret. She had always believed a woman should have, at least, one secret she kept just for herself. Alexander was hers. The thoughts of him were hers. The words he wrote belonged to her. Her moments with him inside her head were hers and hers alone.

Now it had come to this. Something unexpected and completely unplanned. Alexander had been offered a job in the city where January lived. January did not believe in coincidences. She knew everything in their strange parallel lives had been building up to this for years.

"Love me differently?" she asked, amused. "How have you loved me at all?"

Alexander shrugged. "I don't want to feel uncomfortable around my wife when I think of you anymore. It's not right."

"You chose to feel that way." January's blonde hair fell into her face as it loosened from the ponytail she had hurriedly put together.

Alexander was here for an interview. He was *here*. In her town. He had not only interviewed but tentatively accepted the offer. He would become the associate dean of the university. How could he say no? "So why did you ask me to meet you here?"

The hotel was old, a boutique remodel from the 1920s decorated in stark white and bold greens. They sat in the lobby, too afraid to go into his room, and talked in subdued tones.

"I had to tell you. You needed to know I was moving here. That *we* are moving here."

January sighed, sinking deeper into the chair. The warm breeze filtered through the open lobby with the smell of salted Florida air clinging to it, just like humidity sticks to skin. "I mean, what are we supposed to do? Introduce our spouses? Have dinner parties together? Talk about our college days like we were drinking buddies?"

Alexander smiled. "We were."

"You know what I mean." January rolled her eyes.

"I just didn't want you to be on social media and see that I'd moved here. I wanted to tell you face to face. If you think this is a bad idea, I will go right back to the campus and tell them I changed my mind. I won't mess up our marriages, January."

January stood up, indignant. "You think we are going to start messing around now just because you moved here? We each had the chance for that a long time ago. Several times, if I recall. We both backed off." She could feel the hot tears swelling behind her eyes.

Alexander put his hands on her shoulders. "No, that's not what I thought at all. It's not that I didn't want you that way. I won't deny it. It used to be my first thought in the morning and my last at night, and then when I slept…oh, that's when I did get to have you. But, no, we have never actually made love." He gave a small smirk.

"Not physically." She looked up at him, the tears now running down her cheeks. "I wasn't ready for this, Alexander. I liked having you as my little secret. My 'could've been.' You and me, this has always been sacred to me. Now you will be here. I could feasibly run into you at a grocery store. What the hell is that going to feel like?"

Alexander laughed. "I really don't know. Maybe I will help you reach the coffee on the top shelf."

January laughed as the tears kept falling. "We are not 'run into each other at the grocery store' kind of people, Alexander. We are something else."

"That we are, baby. But we must make some decisions right now. Today. Here." He looked at his watch. "I am taking a plane home to Arizona tonight to begin making moving plans…with my wife. Whether you and I ever thought this could happen or not, it is. We are moving to Miami. So I go back to my original statement. I need to find a different way to love you."

Alexander lifted January's chin up, so their eyes locked on to each other. They wanted to kiss. The urge was there, just hanging in the air above them, luring them to push into each other like waves crashing onto the sand.

Alexander had kissed January twice when they were in college. The first time, January had consumed a few too many shots at a bar. She was so young but held her own with the guys quite well. Not that night, though. Alexander had been able to see the eyes on her at the bar as she fell into her inebriation. They had wanted to take her. Instead, he took her to his car where they sat in the backseat until their other friends were ready to leave. She had kissed him then. Liquor on her lips, but even so. She had kissed him deeply and intensely and had wrapped herself around him like a withering leaf, and he had not been the same since. Alexander had decided gentlemanly behavior was the best choice that night and ensured her safety back to her dorm. He was never entirely sure she recalled that kiss which was more than a kiss to him. Fifteen years later, as she stared into his eyes with that same wanton look, he had to catch himself before succumbing to it.

He looked down at her and wrapped his arms around her. "Oh, my love. Why could this not be another time for us? Why could our personal lives not be horrible, making this an easy escape?"

"Yeah, maybe I live in a trailer park and my husband is just a terrible, abusive man and you could come rescue me? That would make it easy. To just walk away. But it's not like that, Alex. Our lives are amazing outside of one another. It's just nice having you be a part of my life in whatever way I can have you. It just never was our time. But you *can* still love me, you know." January pushed out of his hold on her. "You living here, it's just too close. But I guess we can figure it out. I just think we should back off on our communications a bit."

Alexander did not like this response. "But…"

"No." January smoothed out her red dress and wiped the tears from her cheeks. "We live in the same town, but Miami is a big city. This doesn't have to get…familiar." She picked up her purse and smiled her white, toothy grin. The one she gave when she was fighting sadness. "You are still going to love me. I will still love you in my way. But if you think we need to have couples' nights and watch your wife and my husband have their hearts ripped out, I can't be a part of it. There is no safe love for us, my dear. Not one that is public. And the one that isn't, well, that's just outright infidelity. You and I are bigger than that."

With that, January turned around and walked through the lobby and out of the hotel. Her heels clicking against the tile, which still echoed after she had departed. Her perfume, a mix of gardenia and magnolia flower, still hung hot and heavy in the air. He breathed it in. For years, he had waited to smell that scent again.

So it began.

The trying not to love her anymore while being closer to her than ever.

Alexander felt a familiar numbness rush over his body. He knew she was thinking of him even seconds after her departure. Surely, she felt the same tingling.

****

January left the hotel, feeling numb and dumbfounded by what had just occurred. She had always known their paths would cross again but not quite like this and not in such a potentially permanent way. Her phone was buzzing. Alexander could not accept even a moment of not communicating with her.

"I spontaneously called you 'baby.' Sigh." Alexander texted.

January was defeated and responded because she knew she always would. *"I like it when you call me 'baby.'"*

7

"I was just caught up in the vignette I had imagined before you arrived. Us, in one of those hotel rooms, after dinner. Drinks, laughing. A kind of intimacy we've not ever had with each other. My inability to keep from holding your hand. So I spontaneously called you 'baby.' And it felt great."

"Then call me 'baby' again sometime. I promise not to protest." January smiled in the way only he could make her smile.

"I love this."

"Me, too. Probably a bit too much." January felt the air escape her lungs.

"Just let me be yours tonight as you sleep. We can worry another day about what is too much."

"You always belong to me in my dreams. But you moving here changes everything." January turned off her phone. It was too much to bare.

****

When they first met, January was a freshman at Brevard College in North Carolina. It was a beautiful campus filled with trees, located near the Blue Ridge Mountains. She had chosen it for its scenic beauty, its history, and the wonderful literature programs it offered. January would only share one year at school with Alexander as he was a senior and preparing to leave the state for his master's degree. It had been an amazing year that started a lifelong attachment to one another.

Brevard College, North Carolina 1995

They officially met one day while January was in the college library. The library had always been one of her most favorite places. She enjoyed hiding from the world among the stacks of whom she considered some of her most trusted friends. Yeats, Emerson, Tennyson, Proust. These were the voices she loved hearing most inside of her head. January was deeply buried in one of those books when a tall, handsome, yet disheveled-looking young man came toward her. He had a cocky grin, glasses, and his hair was a bit long and unkempt. She had put her book down and looked directly at him as he sat down in front of her.

He just stared.

"I'm sorry," she said nervously. "Can I help you?"

Alexander Lane sat down and leaned back in the mildly uncomfortable chair and smiled. "Now that's a loaded question."

January did not like games, and as a new student, she had made the decision to try to focus on her studies and worry about boys later. "I really don't have time for…"

Alexander leaned in. "I think you might be fun. Would you like to come hang out with us one night?"

"Us?"

"Yeah, me and some friends. We are kind of a little social club of sorts."

9

"I have a pretty full schedule already. I don't think I have time for extracurricular clubs, especially of the frat-inspired nature." January was a little bothered, but she couldn't stop looking at him, studying him. He did not have an accent, so he was clearly not from North Carolina. He just seemed so confident and sure of himself.

"My name is Alexander. And it's not that kind of club. Just a group of friends, and we hit some area bars and concerts and such." He looked at her stack of books. "Maybe we can even toss in a boozy poetry reading night just for you."

January smiled, clutching her book of sonnets. "I am a bit too young to have booze. I am seventeen. Graduated early to get here early. Part of my plan."

"Good plan. That means you need to start making new friends now before the only ones you have are all dead writers." Alexander laughed, his hair falling over his stunning green eyes. "Your name is January, right?"

January was embarrassed. "Oh, yes, I am sorry. I am January. January Morgan."

"Hippie parents?"

"In every possible definition of the word. I am lucky my name isn't Rainbow or Star."

"Well, I like your name. I like you. How about you meet me and the group of new friends you will adore on Tuesday at seven? We always meet up at my dorm, Edgars Hall. We can show you the town outside of campus."

January had been reluctant, but so far, he was right; she knew no one. Her roommate was weird and always talking on the phone to her boyfriend in another state and had posters of cats on the wall. Other girls in her dorm had not been very friendly so far, rather giving her the once-over and walking away. January looked up to face Alexander and agreed.

"Wow," he said. "You have amazing eyes. I mean, seriously. What color are they?"

January blushed. "Today, they are gray. Tomorrow, they could be blue. I have mood eyes."

"I didn't know that was a thing, but I dig it. I hope gray means you look forward to seeing me, I mean us, on Tuesday?"

"Okay, I will."

"Good. I will see you then. Oh, I also noticed you are signed up for debate team. I am the captain of the debate team, so I will see you at the first meeting."

"Oh, okay. Yes, I was on the debate team in high school, so I thought I would try it here, too."

"I am sure you'll be great. Nothing like a good down and dirty argument to get the blood pumping. Enjoy your reading, January Morgan." He walked away, leaving her distracted and somewhat breathless. He reminded her of Judd Nelson in *The Breakfast Club* but with a more intellectual flair. She liked smart people and could smell the intelligence on him a mile away.

January tried to return to her reading, but it just wasn't as easy after that.

****

She had experienced a wonderful year with Alexander and his friends. They went to parties, bars, held themed parties in their dorms, and crashed poetry readings on a frequent basis. Long conversations, debate team meetings, long hikes in the mountains, playing quarters in the dorm rooms, Alexander teaching

11

her to play guitar. Alexander had been very fascinated with her, but after a series of off-putting relationships, he mostly enjoyed hanging out with a girl who didn't act needy. January was fiercely independent.

January was the anti-girlfriend. He relished in her feisty words and their intense conversations. Sometimes they would talk for hours at the bar about whatever topic he felt inclined to quiz her on. She always rose to the occasion and fired back. January found Alexander to be amusing but self-absorbed and somewhat condescending. But she also liked a good debate, and for that, he was her man. He was her friend and sometimes her foe and not a day went by without the two of them exchanging a glance, some words, or an alcohol-infused argument. She had dated a few guys briefly, but not without the opinions on each one freely offered by Alex. This did not always sit well with January.

She had caught him staring at her sometimes. Analyzing her like one of his research papers. This usually made January feel judged and, therefore, annoyed. Still she couldn't get enough of him. There had been a drunken kiss in his car one night. She had regretted it the next day and worried it would mess up their friendship. They never talked about it.

Then, there was a moment in the library. Right before the end of the school year, January knew Alexander would be heading out west, so she decided it was time to do something. Anything to make him notice her. Really notice her. She had danced around it long enough. That afternoon, she put on a little lacey black dress, black tights, and heels, took a shot of whiskey, and headed to the library where she knew he would be writing papers.

He was hidden well within the stacks, buried in a paper on some philosopher he needed to finish by the end of the day. January teasingly traced her fingers along the binding of books as she walked past. Breathing in the scent of books always made January happy. It made her feel kind of high to think of what was inside each book and who had read them. She pulled that into herself, along with the tingle of whiskey in her body. Suddenly she felt a bit sexy.

Closing her eyes, January moved her fingers, nails painted a near shade of black, along the books. She skipped along the aisles until a feeling grabbed her and she stopped. The book her finger was on as she opened her eyes would be the one she would choose. Chaucer. It was January's favorite way to read. Randomly. Just not this author.

"Not again," she moaned. "I just read *The Canterbury Tales.*" January shook her head in annoyance. "My system sucks."

"I don't know," a voice called from behind the shelf. "Seems like an adequate way to complete your major to me."

"Ha. Ha," January said sarcastically.

January moved closer to the voice, knowing it was Alexander's.

The voice responded, "And you found Chaucer with your little tactic. Seems insipid. Especially since Chaucer is for little children at bedtime. And it would seem the powers of literature, vis-à-vis, your system, want you to read it again. Nighty night to you, English major." Alex laughed, muffled slightly by whatever book was in front of him.

At this, January felt a burning sensation coursing through her body as it always did before they argued. "Okay. Where the hell are you?"

"Over here, Janny."

As she moved around the tall floor-to-ceiling shelves, she saw Alexander at a table surrounded by books and papers.

"You."

"Yes, January, me." He smirked and looked down at his book.

"And what, pray tell, is the most intellectual beer buddy I have reading? Boring-ass Plato, I presume?"

"No, baby, Nietzsche." He smiled up at her, his green eyes shining. "Want some?"

January took a seat in the empty chair next to Alexander. "I'm full, thanks."

"It's funny. I have never seen you in here. Not since we first met. And I am here a lot." January was trying to flirt, and it wasn't going over so well. Alexander was on to her.

"What's up with you? Why are you wearing a dress? Are you going out tonight?" He sniffed the air. "Have you been drinking? Next to a magnolia tree? You smell like bourbon and flowers. I kind of like it." He laughed. "It's not even lunchtime. Clearly I have been a terrible influence on you."

"Just felt like dressing up a bit and having a little cocktail in my dorm."

"Dressing up and having a drink just so you can come here to read Chaucer? Lucky him." Alexander laughed and put down his pen, looking her over. "I do like that dress, Janny. Really shows off your, um, eyes." His smile was overwhelming now.

"Just what I was going for." January scooted her chair closer to Alexander, looking at him closely. He was different in this place. Not the same as he was when they were out at the bar with friends. She was not looking at him to pass her a light or her beer or share some silly story.

Seeing him surrounded by all those books was enticing. January had always had a thing for intellects. But here, in the familiar house that was her library, suddenly Alexander looked right to her. Really right.

She leaned in to him, removed his glasses, and pushed his book down. "Alexander," she cooed into his ear, and she placed his hand in her lap. Her dress was short, and he felt her skin against his hand. She was wearing thigh-highs. He gasped. "You know you want to kiss me so just do it already."

Alexander moved his hand up her thigh, grabbing it hard, so hard she pulled his head down to her, bringing his mouth to hers. The kiss was slow and deep, and with each tilt of her head, Alexander found his hands lost at what to do. One moved up her leg and the other pulled her into him. He needed more hands. She kissed without inhibition, giving him all of herself in mouth alone. As she moved out of her chair, he placed his hands beneath her, so she would sit on his lap, legs wrapped around him and the chair.

That library chair had no idea what it was in for just moments ago.

"Alexander," she whispered in his ear. "More." She tightened her thighs around his waist. "More of this."

"Janny, where, what…"

"Shhhhh," she murmured. "Just move me on you.

Hold on to my hips while I kiss you."

Alexander did exactly as he was told. This entire scenario was unexpected. She had never made a pass at him before on their Wednesday night bar runs, except for the drunken kiss which he had rationalized was just the booze talking. Where in the world had this come from? Alexander's mind filled with questions, while his chest filled with air he couldn't exhale properly. "Janny, why…oh, God…"

Just as Alexander was growing more and more comfortable with the situation, January retreated. She got up, brushed down her black dress, ran her fingers through her long, blonde hair, and smiled at him. "Looks like my system works after all. I feel full of literary inspiration. Gotta head to class." She turned to walk away and looked over her shoulder once more. "That's the problem with philosophy majors. Always reading about questions. When every answer to life's great questions are already written. In these books. Even Chaucer." She picked up *The Canterbury Tales* and slipped away.

Alexander could barely sit. He certainly would not stand. He could do nothing but stare at the space where January had been. All he could do was breathe in the air. The scent of her perfume mixed with whiskey and the ever-present knowledge that she was just eighteen years old.

Ouch.

January left the library in a fury, forgetting to formally check out her Chaucer and gripping the edition in her hand so tightly her hand hurt. Lighting a Dunhill on the library staircase outside, she tried to get a grip. "What the hell brought that on, Jan?" January knew she would regret what she had done. She just didn't want him to leave without knowing she was into him. "Stupid girl."

She dreaded the next bar night with the guys. If there would even be another one. She had broken her rule. The rule of not messing around with her friends. Her only rule destroyed in a library. It might as well have been a church in January's world. Her sanctuary was tainted and illuminated at the same time. Removing the warm cigarette from her lips, she touched them. She could still feel him. The tingling was still rushing through her body, and her inner thighs felt sore from squeezing them around him.

"Not today. Get to class." And off she went, running to Romantic Poetry class and leaving behind a shocked and somewhat annihilated Alexander. She pulled a flannel shirt from her backpack and pulled it over the black dress.

"I should know better. Chaucer never did me much good anyway. Fucking Chaucer. And what was that? I am horrible at flirting." She put out the cigarette and entered the classroom, more embarrassed than ever.

****

Two weeks went by and she didn't dare face Alexander. Then, on the last day of school, as she was loading up her old yellow Buick to head home for the summer, there he was standing beside her car.

"You were going to leave without saying goodbye to me?" He looked tired, like he hadn't slept in days.

January looked down. "I thought it best."

"Now why would you want to do that?"

"I feel awful about the library. I shouldn't have come on to you like that. We're friends. I messed it up."

17

Tears were stinging her eyes.

Alexander took the boxes from her arms and placed them in the trunk of her car. "Listen, baby, what you did was a surprise. For sure. But it was not an unwelcomed one. I liked it. You are very important to me, Janny."

She looked up into his green eyes, hair in his face as usual. He was wearing a worn T-shirt, a flannel shirt, and jeans hanging low on his hips. Into his arms, she fell. He wrapped his arms around her and pulled her close.

"You feel good to me," she said.

"Oh, Janny. You feel good to me, too. You still have three more years here. You need to carpe diem the shit out of those years. I am moving to Arizona, and I don't want to be a distraction to you. We had some fun this year. I just don't want to be the guy who takes you off your path. Plus, I have my own living to do, and I can't stay here. I would be a distraction to you, and it would delay my plans. Maybe we can find a way to meet up somewhere soon."

January was livid. Her eyes blazed when she looked at him. "Don't speak to me like I'm a child. You never have before. Why now? Don't you want me?"

"Yes. Maybe. Janny, I don't know what I want. I just know I don't want to be in North Carolina anymore. I've been here too long already. It took me five years to finish my undergrad. Let's please not lose touch. I will be back for alumni events. Maybe you can come see me in Arizona."

January was broken. She had put herself out there in a way she had never done before and behaved like a fool. "All right then, friend. We will keep in touch.

Wrong time for us, I guess."

"Maybe it is." Alexander helped January into her car. "All packed up?"

"Yes. I am ready to head home. There's talk of a possible TV news internship waiting for me. I need to get back to Tennessee to make sure no one beats me to it."

This reminded Alexander of the first time he saw her standing in the rain. He smiled. He was worried he was making a mistake by sending her away like this, but he had to move forward, and he didn't want her hanging on to him when he just wasn't ready for another failed relationship. Not that he hadn't enjoyed their interlude. He had. He had enjoyed it so much he had not been able to think or sleep for days. Alexander had been brutalized inside and out by the library experience, but in the end, he approached it academically and practically and knew he needed to keep his cool. As amazing as January Morgan was, he couldn't let a beautiful girl detour his plans. He knew he sounded selfish and egotistical, but he didn't care.

He had no choice.

****

As January drove away, she began to cry. She was angry with herself and angry with Alexander for acting like such an ass. Still, January was not one to wallow. By the time she crossed the border into Tennessee, she'd lit a Dunhill, cranked up the Smashing Pumpkins on the radio, and prepared her mind for a summer away from campus.

Then, Alexander went away to grad school. After some time had passed and smoke had cleared, they kept in touch through letters, email, and snarky instant messages. Eventually, their letters became longer and more about how the real world was slowly replacing the safe confines of university life. Alexander wasn't quite finished with school and had decided to conquer his PhD. January had moved on to her chosen career as a journalist. With each letter, there was always a feeling of unrequitedness. Something that never quite happened between them but always seemed as though it should have.

Their words languished somewhere in the real day-to-day world of their lives and the life they might have had together. Their love was one shared in feelings and dreams with words on paper which hinted at something deeper. Something they had never acted upon.

****

They were married to other people. The letters ebbed and flowed. But they always seemed to happen at the right moment. January would have gone nearly a year without hearing from Alexander, and then one day, she would feel surrounded by thoughts of him. Her body would tingle, and her mind would drift to the "could've been." Then, there on her computer screen would be an email. He always knew when she needed him, even in the smallest of doses. January was a smart woman, but she had no ability to explain how whatever this was between her and Alexander even worked. Somehow, they were always in sync.

Alexander. The intellect. The philosopher. The guitarist. The humanitarian worker. The academic. It was all too much. January didn't just care about him, she needed him. His presence in her life was necessary. She regretted what she had said about cutting off their ties at the hotel. That wasn't fair. But how they would just be friends without the air of their connection just looming in the air above them for the whole world to see seemed equally impossible. And unfair.

January started her car and headed home. Where had she been? Oh, yeah. Lunch with an old friend. That was the story. It was true enough. It was all her husband needed to know. The sun was hot on this Miami summer day. At least 95 degrees and a hundred percent humidity. The sweat dripped down the back of January's neck. The air conditioning in the car could never cool down fast enough.

Zipping past the palm trees and tourists on Collins Avenue, January made good time. Her husband would be home from work in a couple of hours, and she needed some time to regroup, make dinner, and try to get Alexander and his impending move out of her head. She thought back to one of their last encounters as she drove home.

2006: The Bathroom Break

In the summer of 2006, January was newly hired at WSVN in Miami and was loving the new job. She and Zak Tennent had been married for a little over a year, and he was getting his feet wet as a patrol officer for the Miami-Dade Police Department. Part of January's job was to get out into the community and host events, so people would get to know her and be inspired to watch her on the air.

She had been asked to host the grand opening of a brand-new hotel on Miami Beach, a swanky little rehabbed place with plenty of open bars, fancy people, and live swing music. Zak and January had also been given a free night at the hotel which was an exciting bonus. Zak was sipping bourbon at the bar, and January was announcing the owner of the newly updated hotel on a big stage. Two days before, January had received a text from Alexander that he would be in town with his wife on vacation. He mentioned they might be at a Miami Beach bar on the same night Janny would be hosting the party at the hotel. They conspired to ensure the bar he went to with his wife was close enough to the hotel.

The microphone buzzed. "Wow. Let's adjust that audio. Well, thank you all for coming out to the grand opening of the Sunset Breeze. This hotel has been a Miami staple for sixty years but has recently fallen into foreclosure, and let's face it, it had become an eyesore. Now, with the keen architectural eye of Claudio Reyes and his team, we have something to be proud of again! Ladies and gentlemen, Claudio Reyes!" Everyone applauded, and January stepped aside, working her way to the steps to leave the stage.

When she felt her cellphone vibrate inside her purse, her body went numb. He's here, she thought. Somewhere amid the crowd, he's inside. January looked at Zak, who was talking to a couple he seemed to know. He was distracted. It is now or never, she thought.

"Zak," she began, "I need to run to the little girl's room."

"Okay. Do you need the room key?"

Before she even heard him ask, she was walking quickly through the thick crowd. The new hotel was buzzing with people dressed up to see and be seen. It was a red ropes event, and to be on the guest list, you had to be specially invited.

The outdoor pool and patio area of the pool were decorated with disco balls and torches. There were bars everywhere serving drinks to wet any type of wanton whistle. The crowd was tight, and the music was pulsing the crowd as an elegantly dressed January pushed through. Her brow was sweating, and her blue sequined dress felt like the Florida humidity had plastered it to her skin.

She tried to move faster. Picking up her phone, his text read:

I'm outside.

January's heart was beating so fast she could barely breathe. She took a final sip of the bourbon in her hand and tossed the cup, now running through the crowd, passing all the tall women in slinky dresses and men in suits.

She moved slower once she entered the hotel lobby, stopping as the cameras caught sight of her, bulbs flashing her eyes into near blindness.

A man approached. "Hey! You're January Morgan with 7 News…can we get a pic…"

He never finished the sentence. January was about to exit the front door of the new kitschy hotel. The two large bouncers stopped her, and she turned to both and smiled while showing her bracelet, indicating her VIP status. "I'm coming right back in, just need some air."

She could see the long line along the velvet ropes of people begging to get on a list they were never added to. Each had an excuse for why they were somehow forgotten. Lines of media snapped pictures of the long lines, the hotel, the people, the fancy cars, and January because she stood out.

Standing there on the steps of the hotel, her blue dress reflecting the light from the camera flashes, she looked a bit like she had just run a marathon in heels.

Her phone buzzed again as she frantically searched the faces behind the ropes.

To your right.

She turned her head and standing alone and somewhat blocked by a security guard stood Alexander. He was wearing a beat-up, old T-shirt and shorts, and his face was tanned. He looked like he had just gotten off a boat. January later discovered he had done just that.

For a moment, they just stared at one another. Even though they had been talking and writing to each other almost regularly for years, seeing each other in person was strange.

It felt inhibitive. As she walked over to him, the security guard stopped her. "You leaving?"

"No."

Alexander smiled. "It would seem I am not on the list."

"No, I guess you wouldn't be."

"I tend to hate events like this, Janny. Somehow you seem above it all."

"I'm not. I'm in the thick of it. Just another girl in high heels, smiling for the flashing lights. All in the name of a hotel grand opening."

Alexander moved closer to her. He placed his arms around her waist and pulled her close. It was not quite a hug because January remained arched back, so she could face him. The ocean wind was blowing, and the smell of salt and sand filled the space surrounding them, encircling them.

"I forgot how pale your eyes are." Alexander touched her cheek, still holding her waist.

"I don't have more time. I have to go back inside." January was struggling with the feelings bubbling up inside of her.

He brushed her hair out of her eyes. "Let me give you something first."

"Now, Alexander, how can I return with a gift? Who will I say gave it to me? I am supposed to be in the bathroom, by the way."

"So am I. My wife and friends are next door at the other bar. I made them choose that bar out of all the bars along the beach, so I could chance this meeting with you. And give you these." Alexander handed her a gold shoebox.

"Shoes?"

"Not just shoes. Red shoes. Your shoes."

She opened the box and saw the shiny red straps and quickly closed it. "I can't accept this. These are pricey."

"I want you to have them. You always mention how you like red shoes. You have a real shoe addiction, I think. Wear them and think of me." He smiled.

"I already do think of you." She held his hands and looked up at him. He looked more sophisticated than anyone around her, even though he was dressed like a college frat boy. "I can't change my life."

"No, baby. Me neither. But you can wear these shoes."

"All right, Alexander." With that, January, in front of the security guards and a line of, at least, a hundred people, removed her cheap black heels and tossed them in a neighboring trash can. "They are perfect. Thank you."

"I wish I could take you back inside that overpriced hotel and dance with you. In those shoes." Alexander smiled and kissed January's forehead, leaving the spot to burn there.

"Me, too. Rain check? Perhaps another time when we are not faking bathroom trips?" January laughed and hugged Alexander tightly. She wondered if it would be the last time she would get to do that.

"Rain check, then. And they look magnificent on you. Until next time, Janny."

"Until then. Write to me."

They released one another and went their separate ways. As January walked back up the stairs to the hotel doors, she looked behind her. He was already gone. A fake bathroom trip that went far too long. Zak would be worried about her. She ran back inside the hotel and out the back door into the courtyard. Running through the same crowd of plastic, faceless people. The music, now somber, moving her, pushing her forward, back into the arms of the man she married. The man she loved.

****

While next door, in a much quieter atmosphere, Alexander sat at a table surrounded by those he loved and who loved him. He could only think of her. In that sequin dress. Standing on the steps with those red shoes on. The shoes he bought for her when he was supposed to be at a coffee shop writing. He imagined her moving through the crowds of the Miami elite, those red shoes glistening and tapping against the floor. Enveloping a part of her. Since he could have nothing, he was calmed, knowing a piece of her flesh touched something he had given her.

Alexander thought seeing Janny, even for that brief five minutes, would make him feel sated somehow. But even in all his success and in the face of a wife who loved him implicitly, there was a void, a void that could only be filled by January Morgan and her gray eyes. He was not sated. Not completely. As the voices of his friends surrounded him, some congratulated him on his recent publication in *Scientific America*, while others gushed over the humanitarian efforts he was leading in Haiti, he just drifted back to her.

****

January made love to her husband that night. Hungry and fierce. She was angry with herself. She had not anticipated the connection to Alexander would resonate beyond the written word. She had always just looked upon him as her muse. Each letter from him gave her strength and inspiration. Seeing him again electrified her. Bad, bad, bad, she thought. After Zak was asleep, January went into the bathroom and did something she had not done since college. She smoked a cigarette.

The red high heels sat in the corner of the bathroom, somewhat covered by her blue dress. Zak had not even noticed them. She had so many shoes; how could he? She clutched them to her chest as she lay on the cold tile floor and cursed the day she met Alexander Lane.

****

The next morning, January awoke facing a disco ball. It lay on the pillow beside her like an unexpected, mirrored lover. Seeing her own reflection, a hundred times over was frightening to see at best, and she mustered a slight scream.

From the corner, a very hungover Zak laughed hysterically. "I got you a souvenir, honey. Just like you always wanted."

January sighed, feeling the throbbing in her head and the gurgle in her stomach. "Ha. Now how do you expect we sneak this out of the hotel? This was a decoration!" Janny laughed. "Maybe I fake pregnancy?"

"Well, people who remember you in that hot little blue dress will think we had quite a night!"

"Yeah…quite a night." She felt her stomach turn and jumped out of bed and ran past Zak to the bathroom. As she did this, she realized she was naked. Except for the red heels. Her throat went dry as she looked down at her feet, suffocating in the tiny little shoes.

"Holy shit." Zak looked her up and down. And down. Straight down to her heels. "Damn, we did have quite a night. I'm damn good at making love to you," Zak said. He smirked at her as she walked into the bathroom.

Zak's dark hair was tousled, and he had put on a pair of shorts and a T-shirt. This was Zak's "morning after" look. January's morning after look was different on this day. It was one of anxiety and dark circles under the eyes.

She entered the bathroom and shut the door behind her. As the fluorescents flickered, January looked at the small pile of blue sequins on the floor. She sat on the cold tile and leaned against the wall. Then she heard Zak through the door.

"Maybe we made a kid last night. It might be nice to have a little one running around."

January felt even more sick now. She wasn't ready for that, but Zak's enthusiasm compared to her feelings for Alexander made her feel guilty and that was just too much.

"Yeah," she said from behind the bathroom door, "maybe we did."

Zak picked up the bags and handed January the disco ball. "I guess I will just carry it out. I mean, who the hell cares if we stole a disco ball anyway?"

They both laughed and walked right out the door, past the concierge, and to their car. The ride home was silent as Zak thought of what a nice night they had experienced. As her phone vibrated in her purse, she made a conscious decision to ignore it. Sorry,

Alexander, she thought. I just can't. Not now. Not anymore. But it was not over. It never was.

December 2007: On His Way to Haiti

Alexander was in Miami again and had asked to meet January for lunch. She couldn't sleep the night before, and with only hours of time separating the two of them from reuniting, January found herself anxious and chewing on her nails. She wanted so badly to see him and, at the same time, found herself feeling guilty for the wanting. She convinced herself this would be a friendly reunion with a kind hug and words about the old days. There was more, though. There was always more, and she could not fight the feeling inside of her, which she was certain was his own agony about seeing her. She brushed her teeth, and as she stared into the mirror, she could see his face reflecting at her, and the smile hit before the guilt every time. She would wish his image away, but the feeling remained.

His words from the latest letter would roll over and over in her mind, and she could feel those words under her skin. You distract me, he would write. You take claim on my thoughts, he would write. Is it okay that I just spent five minutes thinking about your dimples? he would ask. These words would seep into her and pull at her when she did not want them to. Her dreams of him were so real sometimes she thought he was really with her. One particular dream of them holding each other beside the ocean was the most intense and the most real. This dream would wreck her, and she had it often.

January would wake up in a fit, pulling at her nightgown, as she lay beside her husband. She would feel guilty, but at the same time angry because Alex had gotten into her head again. Against her will. He was like a mirror reflecting her own indiscretions and wanton thoughts. She would breathe heavily as she lay there, sweating on the sheets, knowing Alex was somewhere breathing along with her. But not with her. It was worth questioning at this point—could she love him and her husband, too? Was it possible to love two men? She worked to get her head straight and got up from bed to let the sheets dry. January felt lonely and confused as she watched her husband sleep. She fell asleep on the chair in their bedroom by the window with the moonlight raining down on her from the window. It comforted her, like her grandmother's quilt, but it failed to assuage her overwhelming feeling that Alex was standing right there in the room watching her. How could any of this be real? January closed her eyes and pulled the quilt up high as the moon burned into her, giving its honest assessment of her predicament.

****

The next day was incredibly hot. The steam covered the windows of the bar. It was a hundred degrees, and the air felt like hot, thick steam that would stick to your body the moment you allowed it to hit you in the face. A breeze was blowing, but it was just as hot as the sun. The palm trees swayed, and the salty smell of the ocean filled the humid air. It was suffocating.

January was restless. She sat in her appropriately chosen seat, her back to the wall as she always preferred it, facing the door. There was a large marlin hanging on the wall above her head. It was *that* kind of restaurant. The kind with an ocean theme so over the top it made a person question why they were there in the first place. But January knew it was the right location. No one would suspect her there, as visible as she was. People recognized her all the time now. It was close enough to him to seem like a long business lunch. January was wearing work clothes, a soft gray suit, short skirt, high heels in bright turquoise, and a matching top. She was sure to dress the work part on this day. She had even brought her glasses and some random non-related paperwork to make it look official in case wanton eyes were watching. She was just interviewing a source off the record. She smiled at the thought of this little tale.

The restaurant was mostly empty. It wouldn't be for long. But January arrived early to prepare for seeing him. It had been a year since they had had their few moments outside of the hotel. Prior to that brief interlude, it had been five years. That was when she had accidentally watched him make love to Lilly on a desk in his classroom. The awkwardness of that had somewhat faded. She had never spoken of what she had witnessed. Now he was married to Lilly, and she would take her secret to the grave.

Today they would have an entire lunch together. More if January really wanted to fight for it. He was stopping through Miami on his was to Haiti for missionary work, helping to build irrigation systems. January regretted the restaurant decision. This place was ridiculous. It wasn't supposed to be this kind of place, she thought. In her fantasies, it had always been a dark bar with a nice bluegrass band playing. This was tourist Florida at its finest. Even still, it was something.

And there had been so many years of nothing. Nothing but his glorious letters.

He was late. He texted her. Said he was late. She was tense, and her thighs were tight, as was her chest.

"Wanna try our Mahi tuna rolls?"

"I'm sorry. What?"

The waitress looked unamused. "Our special? Honey, you all right? Need a drink?"

"Oh. Yeah, I guess I will have a water."

"A water. Sounds fine." The waitress started to walk away.

"Wait. No. Please bring me a shot of something."

"A shot of what, honey?" The waitress was smiling now.

"Bourbon. Neat. Top shelf. Not particular about the brand."

"Now, I thought you was more of a bourbon kind of girl. Coming right up." She smiled and walked away.

After a year and a million emails, they were finally going to meet in person for more than just a few minutes. And talk. And eat food together. This was too much to take. That stupid marlin on the wall would witness history. January rolled her eyes. "This moment deserves more than a Floridized Ruby Tuesday's," she mumbled to herself. She checked her face on the camera of her phone. She was sitting facing the sun. Good lighting. He would notice her face more. Had he forgotten her face? Had she forgotten his? What would they talk about?

January took another sip of water. The bourbon arrived, and January took it back before the waitress even laid it on the table. "Well, then. Meetin' an old flame, I suspect."

January stared at her. This woman had feathered hair and smelled of cigarette smoke and yet had the behavioral psychology knowledge of a PhD. "Yeah, how did you know?"

The waitress smiled. "It's my job, honey. To know what people want. And you clearly want this guy to see what a catch you are...or have become."

"Well..." January looked at the name tag. "Barbara, you are a true purveyor of human social behavior. Yes, he is an old friend."

"More than that, my dear. Another bourbon?"

"Oh, no. I just needed to even out. I am, or was, nervous. I feel better now."

"Alrighty then. Just call me if you need me."

Then there he was. Walking through the door, searching for her among the growing crowd. She sank a little. He looked good. Not just good, but exceptionally good. He had a beard now. It was surprisingly sexy. He was dressed in a T-shirt and shorts. Of course, she was overdressed. Her heels were five inches high. They did not match him at all. Then he saw her. Smiling, he walked her way.

The moment he sat down was awkward at first. There were obligatory hellos and questions about how their trips were. Then silence.

January stared into his eyes. It was a pleading sort of stare that made Alexander die a little inside. How could he respond to such a look? He averted his eyes as much as possible. "We haven't even seen each other since the fake bathroom break of 2006." Smiling, she sipped her water.

"Oh, yes. Two bars. Side by side. And I had to pee. For a long time." He laughed. "My wife still thinks I had eaten bad seafood that night."

"My husband thinks I just got lost and was too drunk to remember how to get back to the stage."

"Oh, yes, the stage. You were emceeing some new hotel grand opening runway show or something."

"Something like that."

"We met on the red carpet, but that bodyguard wouldn't let me cross the ropes to get to you."

"He was an ass."

"But then I leaned over the ropes and got to hold you for a second. I had forgotten your eyes were so pale. I had forgotten you smelled like magnolia blossoms."

"And bourbon?"

"Ah, yes, you had a bit of that in you that night." He laughed. "My little Southern girl loves her bourbon."

"Hey, Woodford Reserve sponsored the event. I just ensured the samples didn't go to waste." January laughed, finally feeling comfortable. She crossed her legs under the table as the sweat had begun to build between her legs. Then there was the tightening. That tight, clenching feeling that always appeared when she thought of him. It was stronger than ever now. "So, Alexander, how are you?"

"I'm good. Being a professor at the college is good. Wife is good. Arizona is good. No complaints." His hair was still a bit long and fell into his eyes when he leaned in. He looked like a professor now, and his eyes were deeper with just a few lines beside them. Time had been good to him, though, as he just looked more distinguished now and handsome. "You, my God, Janny, you look amazing."

January blushed. "Good television consultants."

"No, you were always beautiful. Whatever they are telling you is just random humming background noise. There is nothing anyone can say to improve upon you. You radiate light."

January felt her stomach turn. He said things that made her soul ache. "Okay, stop."

He looked directly into her eyes. "For so long, I have waited to have you here in front of me. And here you are."

"I know. Me, too, Alexander. And I don't want to talk about work or spouses or boring daily life stuff. I honestly don't know what to say to you. We say so much in our letters."

Alexander brushed his hair aside and waved the waitress to the table. "I'll take a shot of whatever she had because I know it's your best, and I'll take a water because I know the drink will need to be diluted, and crackers or something, so I don't get hammered and forget to go home to my wife." The waitress gave a quick smile and walked away.

"Ah, yes, the wife."

"Indeed. And how is your husband, January?"

"He is good. Not too keen on me applying for network gigs, but I plan to do it anyway. He has a good job and doesn't want to leave Miami. I don't blame him. But there are many networks now looking for correspondents to be based out of Miami, so it's feasible that I could get a job like that."

"Seems fair enough. You stay in Miami but still get to travel and live your dream."

"Yeah, easy for you say. Hey, again, let's not talk about the spouses."

"Fair enough." Alexander sipped the bourbon that had been placed in front of him. "Wow. Strong."

January cocked her head to one side. "The guy I used to know would not have balked at a little hooch." She leaned in, taking the glass from his hands. "This bourbon took years to age. How you can scoff at it is beyond me. Don't you know what kind of time and care goes into making the perfect barrel of bourbon?"

Alexander took his glass and drank it back fast. "Yum."

"Smart ass."

"It's not that I don't appreciate the process of making booze. I just like to see you get riled up about it."

The waitress brought over two more glasses with the same golden-brown liquid swishing softly side to side, tempting them both. "On the house," she said as she giggled and walked away.

January looked at the drinks. "It would seem Barbara, our server, is an expert in the field of sociology. She wants to see if we drink our drinks and leave together, and I am betting she is usually correct in her assumptions about human behavior."

"Not today." Alexander looked down and moved his drink back a few inches. "I can't."

"Me neither, I am supposed to go back to work. Stories to write, edit, etcetera."

"You look good, Janny. I am proud of you. You really did it."

"Ugh, don't do that. I am a TV reporter; you are a professor...we live our dreams...blah, blah, blah. Alexander, why can't we talk to each other like we write to each other?" January's legs were trembling now.

Alexander began to feel nervous. Suddenly he wanted the second drink. "Janny, I don't know why things are like they are with us. They just are."

"They certainly are." January picked up her glass of bourbon and drank it slowly, letting the warmth roll around in her mouth and eventually fall in a soft, tender way down her throat as bourbon is wont to do. Her stomach welcomed it. Her mind welcomed it. Her inhibitions feasted on it.

She stood up, tall in her five-inch heels and moved to sit beside Alexander on his side of the booth. He initially backed up. He tried to keep his distance. Yet she was there, just inches from him, smelling of magnolia and bourbon. Just as he remembered. She leaned in to him and whispered into his ear, "We are actually in the same room together. We are sitting beside one another. Isn't this a cause for some type of celebration?"

Her voice went through his ear and tingled all the way down his body. He could feel January's words in his toes. He could feel those words in other places, too, but he tried to fight it. January put her hand on his leg. "Alexander…"

He pushed her hand aside. "Baby, we can't."

"Can't what? We are not doing anything. We never actually do anything you and me. We just write letters and feel things miles apart from each other. You think of me when you are with her?"

"Sometimes."

"You think of me in your car? At your desk? When you are teaching a class? You think of me at the goddamn grocery store?"

"Yes, Janny, yes. What am I supposed to do about it? Make love to you? Here at the worst restaurant in Miami? I can't be that guy. We…"

"We, what?" January retreated, removing her hand from his thigh.

"We are more than this."

January knew it to be true. She was letting the liquor take her down old familiar roads. "You're right. I'm being stupid. I am so sorry, Alexander. Are we really supposed to be able to sit at a table and talk about generic life stuff?"

"I guess we can't do that."

"No, I guess we can't. I feel stranded. I don't know how to handle this. Years have gone by. We talk in our way all the time, but I never get to feel you or smell you or hear your voice. I love your words. I need them. I need you." January put her hands over her face and leaned down.

"I need you, too, baby. But the love we have must be censored or something. I don't know what I thought it would be like seeing you again. The last time was brief. We shared maybe five words over a silly rope on a red carpet."

January still held on to that moment. She regarded it as the best fake trip to the bathroom she had ever taken. "I loved that night. That five minutes."

"Me, too, baby. I couldn't do my job for months. My wife thought I was going through some type of depression. We mess each other up, Janny."

January leaned in and kissed Alexander on the cheek. His face caught fire. "I am going to head back to work now. I still have a story to get in before the six." She stood up, tall and gorgeous. Alexander looked up at her in awe. She was a creation that should not have ever made her way into his view. Her hair was still long but far more sculpted now that she was on TV. It was a bit blonder, too. Her eyes, still as gray and pale as ever. She looked like a woman now. The girl was still there, too, but this creature before him was a full-blown woman. She was amazing.

Alexander stood up to walk her out. He wrapped his arm around her tiny waist. It felt good there. "Should we take a photo of ourselves here to show the guys from college that we actually hung out?"

January laughed. "Are you kidding me? No. Not this moment. This belongs to me. I won't share it. I refuse to share you or, at least, the you that belongs to me. No pictures."

Alexander felt the weight of that statement hard. "Okay then. I have plenty from our college days."

"You see, you and I are here." January pointed to an empty space in the air above her head. "We have our own spot in my life. I want to keep us there, away from the rest of the world."

Alexander kissed her forehead. "Okay, baby. Drive safe. I'll be in touch."

January smiled, the familiar burn of tears behind her eyes. "Goodbye again, Alexander."

She drove away. Alexander stood in the parking lot of the worst seafood restaurant in Miami and felt like he had let her go. Again. This was supposed to have been a casual "hello" over a beer. He had hoped the feelings they shared in letters and emails would have slightly evaporated, not made landfall in the real world.

Alexander took a deep breath and tried once again to remove January Morgan from his mind. He failed.

January later received a text from Alexander as he boarded the plane to Haiti.

My beloved J.,

I sat in front of you and I do not even remember what you were wearing. I mean, I think you are beautiful, don't get me wrong. But when I saw you today, I really looked at you, not your dress. Just you. I had you right in front of me, and I know you were wearing something that would have made men blush, but I didn't even look. I just couldn't see past you and your face and the glow you cast upon my soul. I regret not looking at the dress. Several times, I looked away, trying to collect myself, just to feel normal around you, and I just couldn't. I needed more time. Then you moved close to me, and I felt my entire body cave. I wasn't ready. I hadn't collected myself around you. I was melting, and I couldn't look into your beautiful eyes without losing myself entirely. My God, January. I thought we could have a regular lunch as friends, but we can't. The fire is hot and has not even lessened to a smolder.

In other news, the next time I see you, and there will be a next time, I promise to see your dress. I promise to look at your dress and then undress you with my eyes and let you see me doing it.

Always yours and more confused than ever,

A.

January put her phone back inside her bag. She could barely move as his words had numbed her body like anesthesia. All she could think was that she would never put so much effort into choosing a dress ever again.

Phoenix 2010

Alexander had never enjoyed flying, and the trip back to Arizona was a bumpy one. Toss in the fitful dreams he had had about January as he tried to sleep, and it made for a pretty awful flight. He had put a lot of thought into the new job, which would be hard, and the move, and how he and Lilly would get everything together in time for him to start in the fall. It was already July, and they still had a house to sell, and Lilly would have to quit her job at the art museum. She had been curator there for two years, and it was a job she loved immensely. Alexander had told her about the museums in Miami, but art deco was not really her thing, and she had initially balked at the idea. She had said she might return to teaching art, maybe even at the University of Miami, where Alexander would be an associate dean. She had laughed and made a nepotism joke, saying he had to help her get a job because it was his husbandly duty.

Alexander pulled into the driveway just after nine in the morning. It was Sunday, and the time change mixed with a red-eye flight had Alexander feeling worn out and slightly off-balance. He wanted food, and then he wanted sleep. The Phoenix house he shared with his wife of five years was stucco with red Spanish tile roofing. Purple flowers bloomed from the tall cactus near the front door. The place had been a disaster when they bought it two years earlier. A foreclosure. But Alexander had always liked fixing things, and the thought of a cheap project house was perfect. Lilly had not been so supportive, as she did not like the idea of walls being knocked down and rebuilt. "We need something move-in ready!" she had declared. "This place will kill us." In the end, the price was so good she had to cave. "Okay, but I refuse to be without air conditioning even for a second. This is the hottest place on Earth."

Now looking at the beautiful little home with its cobblestone pathway and delicately hung wreath on the rustic, wooden front door, Alexander sighed. It would be hard to leave this place. They had put so much into it. It had been one of their greatest adventures together. He removed the keys from his pocket and went inside.

"Lilly, I'm home!" He put his bag down by the front door, and before he had released the handle, Lilly was practically running down the stairs, a huge smile on her face.

She immediately began kissing him all over his face. "I am so proud of you! I knew you were going to land that job. I just knew it!" She hugged him and pulled him into the kitchen. "I made a celebratory breakfast."

Alexander looked around. The table was filled with eggs, muffins, coffee, and a plate of bacon. He eyeballed the bacon. "Real bacon?"

Lilly smiled. "The realest."

Alexander kissed her again. "Why thank you, honey. And thank you for not making a healthy breakfast for a change. I need grease. That flight was traumatic."

"Oh, I'm sorry. But you are home now, and we can start making plans!" The light filtered in through the kitchen window illuminating Lilly's face. She looked lovely. Her red hair reflected the sun and her brown eyes sparkled. Lilly had always been a beautiful woman, but this morning, she looked especially radiant.

Alexander was already eating the bacon. "I know we have a lot to plan, but I need, at least, a nap first. I am exhausted, honey."

Lilly nodded but clearly was ready to talk now. "Dr. and Mrs. Alexander Lane of Miami, Florida. Kind of sounds nice, huh? Oh, and I have already been in touch with my family in Florida and told them the good news. My sister is over the moon. We will finally be within driving distance of one another. It's so exciting. And don't worry about me finding a job because I have already made a list of some of the museums in Miami, and I spoke with someone at Sotheby's Auction House in Coral Gables. They might be interested in me. Lots of rich people in Miami, and I think I might be able to help sell them some priceless art." Lilly seemed as though she had been awake all night, making plans.

Alexander finished off his coffee and a poppy seed muffin. "Honey, this was really good. Thank you. And the Sotheby's job sounds perfect for you. Why don't you start making some lists and call a realtor agent, so we can get our house on the market as soon as possible."

Alexander was sleepy, so he knew, if he gave Lilly some assignments, she would let him sleep. Lilly always had to have something to do. It was just the way she was wired, and it was one of the things he loved about her. It's what caught his attention when she was his student. She had been twenty-one and he had been thirty-one, working as an adjunct professor while he finished his doctorate. She must have asked a thousand questions in his Greek Humanities class. One thing was certain, Lilly would not let him ignore her. They began dating secretly while she was still his student, and the danger of that was exciting. Lilly wasn't exactly known to be a forward kind of girl, but the whole teacher-student thing was just enough to help her toss some of her inhibitions aside. Alexander was smitten with her. In some ways, Lilly's youthfulness reminded him of January. The sheer innocence of it combined with her idealism made him think of those early days with January on campus. He couldn't help but compare the two. Lilly's love of learning and art amused him, and she was just a good person, always supporting him and working hard to make their home a happy one. Sure, they had had a few ups and downs. Because Lilly was still so young when they met, she still had a few wild oats to sow. Once the other guy was completely out of the picture, they moved forward together. They were married within a year of dating, after an unexpected pregnancy which didn't last.

Alexander kissed Lilly on the forehead and got up from the kitchen table.

"Oh," she said, "how was your lunch with that college buddy? You didn't post a picture or anything, so I wasn't sure if you got to see him."

Alexander felt his stomach tighten. "Oh, we never got to have the lunch. He had work, and I was too busy checking out a few areas where we might be able to find a house."

Lilly beamed. "Oh, yes, and we have to find a new

house!"

He had distracted her. Alexander just didn't have it in him to talk about January. He had never been able to before. He knew he would have to at some point soon, though. He just needed to think of a way to be casual about it. And January was right. They did not need to become friends and have couples' night out. Frankly, he didn't know how he would feel about meeting Janny's husband. What type of conversation would that be? "Honey, I am going to take a nap. I can barely keep my eyes open."

Lilly raised an eyebrow. "Maybe I should come up there and tuck you in?"

Alexander felt a tinge. He needed release. "Maybe you should."

He took Lilly's hand and led her upstairs. She pulled him close to her and kissed him deeply. "I missed you, Alex." Her breath was hot on his cheeks as she took his shirt off and slipped the white sundress she was wearing to the ground. Her skin was pale, like vanilla ice cream. He pushed her down slowly onto their bed and kissed her neck, her shoulders, her breasts. He cupped one in his hand tightly, and she moaned. "Ohhhh." Pulling her panties down, they fell to the floor as he removed his pants. She lay there on their white sheets looking up at him, wanting him. He loved Lilly so very much, and her body was calling to him.

He needed her terribly. Needed it. As he pushed her legs apart to enter her, January's face cut through his mind like a dagger. He found himself thinking of how close she had been to him. That magnolia smell on her skin, her golden skin begging to be seen beneath her top. He tried to shake the thought of her, but even as he pushed himself inside of his wife, the woman he loved and had promised himself to, it was January's body he thought of. It was her voice he heard inside of his head. With each push into Lilly's body, he tried to push January from his mind. His thrusts became stronger, fiercer. Lilly moaned and pulled him deeper into her. Her breasts heaved, and her nipples were so hard they cut against his chest as he moved her further to the top of the bed. January's face again. He opened his eyes to see Lilly. He pushed her harder until he could feel the release building up. Harder. Lilly shrieked, "Alex, honey, slow down." He pushed harder, he pushed until he was delirious with sweat, exhaustion, and tried to free his mind from January's hold on him. Lilly struggled beneath him. "Alex, wait."

Then he came. He came in such a rush his entire body convulsed and convulsed again. As he slipped away into sleep, it was a black dress and the smell of an old library that guided him to unconsciousness. Somewhere in the abyss of his subconscious mind, he had not allowed January to leave that library. He had taken her right there among the stacks. His mind was swirling and his body, weak from travel and sex, was spent.

Lilly slid out of bed slowly, picking up her dress from the floor. Her eyes were still red from the tears. What had happened? It had not felt like her husband had just made love to her. It was like he was in a different place. Now, watching him sleep, she wiped her eyes and decided the stress of everything had just overcome him. She whispered, "I love you, Alex," as she walked out of their bedroom.

Lilly Lane had lists to make. They were moving to Florida, after all.

****

"WSVN reporter January Morgan has the latest on a string of shootings, coming up at six." The news anchor's voice boomed in January's ear piece.

"All right, Janny. We're clear until your live shot."

January was listening to the sounds from the anchor and the producer in the studio. She was covering some drug-related violence in Miami, and three people had been shot at a known drug house early that morning. January was the crime beat reporter, so covering shootings, murders, stand-offs, and just about anything cop-related was her specialty. January spoke into her microphone, "Roger that, Paulina. We are ready to go. I have sound from someone who knew one of the victims and someone who claims to have witnessed the shootings. I've got to be honest with you. They all seem questionable to me."

Paulina responded in January's earpiece. "Yeah, they usually are. Just put them on the air, and let's call it day."

"You got it. Up in five?"

Paulina responded, "Yep. Standby."

January checked her reflection in the camera to make sure her hair was straight. The damn Florida humidity made it virtually impossible to ever look put together. Soon, Paulina was in her ear again, saying, "Okay, you are up in three, two…"

"Good evening. I'm January Morgan, live in the Liberty City neighborhood of Miami, where three people were shot overnight in an apparent drug deal gone bad. The suspect or suspects remain on the loose tonight as police continue to search for answers."

As her package aired, she could hear the soundbites from the idiots she had interviewed playing away. The first soundbite was from the aunt of a victim: "He was such an innocent boy. This never shoulda happened to him!" Wrong. He was a known drug offender with a rap sheet a mile long, had a warrant for his arrest for rape, and was involved in, at least, three other possible homicides.

The next soundbite was from the stereotypical white dude in a wife-beater standing somewhere in a yard nearby: "I just hear like three, no, like ten gunshots, and I knew what was up. This neighborhood has been going downhill for years, yo. I be moving out sometime when I get myself a job."

Pauline in January's ear: "Cue. You are back on cam."

"This is still very much an ongoing investigation, but as you can see, three lives were lost here overnight, wrecking the lives of multiple families and forcing residents to be concerned for their personal safety as the killer remains on the loose. Reporting live from Miami, January Morgan, WSVN News."

January's photographer, Lenny, gave the all clear. "Alrigthy," he said. "Let's be done with this bullshit and get the hell out of gangland."

"I'm with you. I swear, Lenny, if I have to cover one more lame drug deal murder, I might scream. I should be in Bosnia right now or Afghanistan covering actual war. Not this stupid never-ending drug war gang shit. Some days, I just feel so pigeonholed, you know?"

Lenny agreed, "Yeah, twenty years I've been covering Miami crime, and it never changes. Nothing improves regardless of the glossy unified crime reports the police give us showing crime is down. It's never down. Not really." Lenny had a point. He continued, "I don't know how your husband does this day after day."

January knew her husband well, and Zak would never give up on trying to make the world a safer place. He woke up in the morning wanting nothing more than to put bad guys in a jail cell. "Yeah, it's not easy for him. Hell, it's not easy for me either. Sometimes I don't even know if he will be coming home."

"Did he have to respond to this bullshit from last night?"

"No, he is a major crimes detective now but somehow got lucky to not be the guy on call when these murders happened. Trust me when I say he was actually upset by that. Some days, I think he would stay awake twenty-four hours a day just to respond to calls."

"Dedicated man, your hubby."

"Yeah, that he is. Well, good night, Lenny. I am going to put a wrap on this insane workweek and go home to relax a little. I am on call, so take this meaning no disrespect at all, but I really hope I don't see you until next week."

"None taken, Janny. Have a good weekend."

January got into her car and watched as the satellite truck and the crime tape entered her rearview mirror. She needed to see Zak. It had been days since they had had any real time together. Between her job and his new position as detective in major crimes, he was gone almost all the time. Always being called out to some shooting or stabbing. They had been married five years, and he had always been a cop. When they moved to Miami four years earlier, he went to work for the

Miami-Dade Police Department, and he became even more consumed with his job. Zak was from Miami. This had been his home for most of his life and returning to it as a police officer made him extra tense. It was as though he felt like he had to work harder than ever to defend the town he called home. Zackary Tennent had always dreamed of working as a police officer, and it was a crime scene that had brought him to January. She was working in Louisville, Kentucky, straight out of college. While pursuing her master's degree at the University of Louisville, she was also working her first job at the ABC affiliate. Zak had gone through the police academy, after attending college at the University of Louisville. He had wanted to start his career in Florida but, had made such great friends in the Kentucky academy, he decided to stay. January was covering some gang violence on Louisville's more dangerous west side on a particularly rainy and cold spring morning in 2004.

While she was doing early morning live shots, Zak had been sitting in his patrol car to keep the crime scene secured. He noticed January right away. The best word he could think to describe her was stunning, and she was. She stood in front of the camera in such a commanding way. When she moved, the photographer moved with her. This woman was something special. Zak was distracted by her. He found himself seeing her at frequent crime scenes as they both seemed to have the same crazy overnight shift. Finally, he decided to talk to her.

January was speechless. Deputy Zackary Tennent was not only attractive, but he was mind blowing. He was so ruggedly handsome. Dark hair, devilish dark eyes, and olive skin. He was muscular, too. Clearly a man who enjoyed spending time at the gym. When he walked up to her, she played it cool, but inside, she was boiling. "Just checking to see if you have everything you need, ma'am," he had said to her. He had called her "ma'am," which he later regretted.

January responded with a cool smile, "Why no, deputy. What I really need is your sheriff to meet me out here for a live interview for my seven-a.m. hit."

Zak smiled. "I can ask him, but I doubt he will want to come out to talk about another drug crime."

"You then?"

Zak was not allowed to talk to press. "I will call our public information officer because I am just patrol. I don't really know much about what's happening in that house."

"Of course, you do." January felt the heat between them and leaned in. "Patrol deputies usually respond first. What did you see in there when you arrived?"

Zak felt his feet go numb. She smelled like a garden. And her body, it was all he could think about. "Off record. Two dead bodies. A male and a female. Looks like a murder suicide."

"Thank you, deputy…"

"Tennent. Zak Tennent. Hey, keep me off record."

"No problem. Let's pack it up," January shouted to her photog.

"You're leaving?"

"Yeah, we don't cover suicides. Unless it's the governor and his wife in there, I'm finished here." She smiled coyly.

"No, just a couple elderly people. Looks like a planned thing."

"Now, Zak, that's just depressing. Thanks for the information. Now I can get some coffee. Have a good morning!"

As January turned away and began wrapping up her microphone cable, Zak couldn't let her leave.

"Hey, um, so do you want to have coffee with me sometime?" Zak was visibly nervous, despite his obvious physical strength.

January looked up and thought about it for a second. "I usually don't date cops. I'm a cops-beat reporter. It's kind of a conflict of interest."

"Oh. Well, I am getting off work in an hour. How about you come to my apartment and we just…not drink coffee at all."

January was intrigued by his directness. In fact, she loved it. "Address?"

Zak slipped her a piece of paper with his address and phone number. "See you soon, news girl." Zak smiled and walked away.

January was very attracted to Zak, and she had noticed him on other crime scenes. He was always sitting in his squad car looking busy, never making eye contact with her. January also knew cops were known to fancy a reporter from time to time, so she went into this with no formal expectations. All she knew was she liked the way he looked and liked the way he demanded her presence.

Their relationship had started out as a one-night stand, but they just couldn't get enough of each other after that.

January smiled as she thought of those early days with Zak, before they were married. Now he had become so overworked she rarely had time with him alone. She would see him more frequently walking past her on a live shot as he walked under the crime tape. It was safe to say their relationship was going through a bit of a lull. January attributed it to their crazy jobs and wanted to get Zak alone, so they could talk about the future. Kids maybe? She was thirty-two years old. It seemed like kids should be a topic by now. Taking a nice long trip somewhere? Anything that made them focus on each other.

But for now, this was what they had to work with. They lived in a condo, on the nineteenth floor of the Porta Vita building in Aventura. Where January and Zak lived was a beautiful high rise overlooking the water. The place had clocked in at one point two million dollars, but Zak would not be swayed. He loved the building and the security. The view was so beautiful it was nearly ridiculous with water, golf courses, and the city of Miami all in the distance. January made a good living as a reporter, but when Zak's father had passed away from cancer the year before, he was left with a large sum of money. Zak immediately invested in multiple pieces of real estate, including their two-bedroom high-rise apartment. The building had three pools, including one on the roof. Exercise facilities, a media center, and a spa. For January, who grew up rather poor in East Tennessee, this kind of lifestyle was still a bit unbelievable to her. January had even asked if Zak would retire early because of the money, maybe buy a boat, so they could sail on weekends. He responded by asking if she planned to quit her job. The conversation ended there and never resumed, so they continued to work ridiculous hours, even though a million dollars sat in their bank account. They shared stubbornness above all else.

The one thing January had splurged on was a lot of nice shoes and a vintage car. She had bought a 1970 GTO. It was black with red and black leather interior. The car was a true thing of beauty, and every time she started the engine, she felt a wave of pleasure rush down her body straight to that space between her thighs. January's relationship with Layla, as she had named her car, was more than just car ownership. January lusted after that automobile and had dreams of packing up all her stuff and driving Layla as far away as she could take her. Zak liked Layla but was not much of a car guy. He had decided to spend money on a motorcycle. Zak might not have been a car guy, but he was certainly a bike guy.

Once she was home, January greeted the doorman and took the elevator ride to the nineteenth floor. The apartment was empty, with the exception of Decker, who was a fluffy, gray cat and a very old one. He had been eating out of a trash can outside of January's dorm room during her last year at Brevard College. She had taken him in, and they'd been pals ever since.

He meowed at her and then looked at his empty food bowl.

"Sorry, buddy. Long shift. Let me get you something to eat."

As she filled Decker's bowl, she checked her phone to see if Zak had texted her back.

HOME BY 10. HOPEFULLY. LOVE YOU.

It was already seven. January made a salad and poured an extra-large glass of red wine and sat on her balcony, the ocean breeze warm and heavy with salt. She ate alone often these days. And when she wasn't eating alone at home, she was eating in a news truck. She spent more time with Lenny, her photographer, than she did with her own husband. Not that Lenny was bad company, despite his daily cravings for White Castle burgers. January missed Zak. They used to have so much fun together, but when he was promoted to detective in major crimes, suddenly he was out the door before she could even really say goodbye. There were weeks they really did see each other more at a crime scene than at their own apartment. He seemed more depressed and anxiety ridden. The more successful he became, the worse he seemed to handle it.

This damn apartment. It was modern, clean, and lovely but lacking in warmth these days. As January sipped the warm, red shiraz slowly, she heard the familiar sound of her phone buzzing on the table.

The text message was from Alexander.

Hey, baby. Sorry about how we left things. We are planning the move, and I will be in touch soon to let you know when we will be heading to Miami. Guess I should stop calling you baby. We can do this, you and me. We can completely do this. We were friends before we became the other stuff. Let's hold on to that and make a go at being friends again. Please. I beg you.

Yours, A.

Even his text messages were like miniature letters. Sweet and formal.

She responded.

My dearest A., If you think we can be friends, then I am all in. I just cannot imagine my life without you in it. No matter how that might be. We fit. We are friends. Good friends. I can be your friend.

Always yours, J.

57

January deleted the conversation as she had always done before. The only things she kept were the emails and the hard copy letters, and they remained in a lock box hidden beneath a floor board in her closet. She brought her plate inside and refilled the wine glass. She had become far too close to the vino these days. On social media, her reporter friends were asking that she meet them at some swanky new club in the city. She thought about it for a second. She did have a hot little red dress and loved a night of Latin dancing. But then she remembered Zak would be home soon. She needed to talk to him. To be with him.

Three glasses of wine, five hours, and falling asleep on the couch later, Zak walked into their luxe pad. He was rattled.

January sat up on the couch and looked at her watch. It was three in the morning. "Zak, what happened. You never called."

Zak was loosening his necktie and leaning back into the chair directly across from January. "Rough night, honey. I'm sorry. We had two homicides and an armed robbery. I just couldn't get a break."

Zak had dark circles under his eyes. His dark eyes, tanned skin, and short dark hair gave him an ominously handsome look with the moonlight filtering through their huge window overlooking the water. "I just need some rest. I have so much paperwork to do tomorrow." Zak sighed and rubbed his eyes. "How was your day? They have you on the Liberty City murders? That was just drug shit. We've identified a suspect, but he is being a bit uncooperative. Either way, I should have something new for you on it by tomorrow."

"But, Zak, I don't even work tomorrow. I don't

care about the story." January got up from the couch and let the blanket fall to the floor. She was still wearing her skirt and a camisole. "I just missed you so very much." She walked over to the chair and straddled her legs around Zak's lap. "Don't you want to fool around a little?" She lifted his broad, strong hand and placed it on her chest. "Don't you want to touch me?" She leaned in and kissed him slow and deep. He smelled a little like cigarette smoke. Must've stopped by a bar after work.

Oh, well, he was home now. He throbbed beneath her, and she pushed herself further down onto him, unzipping his pants. "Make love to me, Zachary. I need you," she whispered into his ear and nibbled on his earlobe and his lower lip, something he had always liked.

Zak breathed in deeply and pushed his hips further up as January removed his pants. "I'll do anything you want me to, Zak. Just tell me."

He looked into her eyes and placed his hand on her cheek. "I'm a lucky man, January. You are so unbelievably hot." He removed his shirt and the gun holster underneath, laying his handgun on the coffee table. He pulled her down onto his throbbing heat and pushed himself deep within her. She moved slowly on top of him in the chair, the moonlight cascading in through their window. January's skin glowed with the light and the sweat of their lovemaking. Zak lifted her up, and she wrapped her legs around his waist. He laid her down on their bed and moved into her hard, her hands digging into the muscles of his back. He was broad shouldered, and January felt so small beneath him. His mouth moved over her breasts, sucking and biting. He pinned her arms to the bed, and he ravished her body mercilessly. "Oh, Janny…I need to…"

"It's okay. You can." January knew he needed it this way. Sometimes he was gentle, but then there were the other times. Times like tonight when he was stressed.

He flipped her over and spanked her. Softly at first. Then a bit harder. He did this several times until she felt the pain searing all the way down her thigh. Then he flipped her back over, pinning her arms over her head again and lifted her hips up to take him inside of her again. This time harder than before and without slowing down for what seemed like a long time. January was beginning to feel numb between her legs, but then the numbness became warmth. The harder he pushed, the stronger the warmth became until it filled her whole body, wrecking her. She lay there, shaking from pleasure. Zak kissed her breasts and rolled over onto his back, covered in sweat. "I needed that."

"I know you did. Me, too."

Zak stood up, his magnificent body shimmering in the soft moonlight. He was strong, his muscles well-defined. January wrapped in their white sheets and fell into a deep sleep, the aching between her legs not quite sated, and the pain on her backside deepening as she drifted.

He would be gone again when she woke up. She knew this but was grateful even for the night they had shared. They were so rare anymore, and the intimacy of them was fading.

****

The next morning, January woke up to the bright sun hitting her in the face. She jumped out of bed, still naked from the previous night's lovemaking, and closed the curtains. Her body was sore. There were bruises on her arms where he had held her down, bruises on her inner thighs, and she dared not even look at the marks on her ass. January had never been opposed to wild, even painful sex, but lately Zak had taken it up a notch and was more aggressive than usual. He liked tying her up, blindfolding her, and he especially loved sneaking in and taking her when she was sleeping. Sometimes that was a bit terrifying, but Zak said that only added to the rush. Bottom line, January knew police officers held a lot inside of them. Zak was no different. He didn't talk about his work much in detail, and he had to get the intensity he built up out somehow. Usually it was at the gym. Sometimes at the gun range. Other times, it was using her. He had been more open with her in the past when he first started working patrol. The days wore him down, and eventually major crimes came calling, giving him the challenge he had been waiting for. He had always wanted to be a detective, just like his father had been. When his father died, Zak retreated. His mother had died when Zak was in middle school, so he basically raised himself because his cop father was never home. Zak always seemed like he was trying to beat something. Trying to win. Losing his father was a terrible blow, and ever since, he had committed himself so deeply to his job that it had become almost an obsession. Interrogating suspects was his specialty. He loved getting them to crack open, spill their guts, and give him what he needed to charge them. If they were not so cooperative, Zak was not opposed to "shaking them around" as he had phrased it. As a reporter, January knew that wasn't ethical, but they had to keep their opinions separate when it came to work. It was already such a conflict that she covered stories involving him as the lead detective.

January crawled back into bed. It was her day off, and she thought about spending it on the beach with a good book. Her phone buzzed on the nightstand.

Good morning. See, I didn't call you "baby." I'm already improving. It's four am here right now, and I can't sleep. My mind is swirling with moving plans and thoughts of you. You in that damn red dress. Next time, meet me wearing a potato sack or mom jeans.

Your friend who no longer calls you "baby," A.

January laughed and held her phone to her chest. He really needed to stop texting her. Where was his wife? Sleeping beside him while he clicked away on his phone?

January responded. *To the man who no longer calls me "baby." It is with great regret that I shall no longer be addressed by you in such a way, but it is also quite improper for a man to speak to a married woman using such intimate familiars. I'm sorry you cannot sleep. I, on the other hand, am off to the beach. Sometime soon, you will also have that option, as Miami has some lovely beaches.*

Not your baby, J.

January deleted the texts. He always made her smile with his wit. Sometimes it was as though they could keep a conversation going nonstop all night in an almost 1930s patter-speak kind of way. She lived for his words. When the days and months passed when they shared no correspondence, it was tough for January. It had happened that way multiple times during the fifteen years since that day they parted on campus. They would write and talk for several months and then nothing for several months. Then, as though they both suddenly couldn't take it any longer, they would resume their communication. Their letters were not sexual in nature, flirtatious yes, but mostly just casual talk. Always with a thick fog hanging over it filled with unrequitedness. Unrequited everything. January and Alexander absolutely had to be in each other's lives. They had established that from the beginning. And when they tried not to be, they both began to feel the same black hole reopen. January had been feeling it a lot lately. She thought it had to do with Zak's depression over his dad and working too much. She needed attention from him and wasn't getting it. But it was more than that. Even when Zak was worshipping January on a daily basis, she still needed a little bit of whatever it was Alexander did for her. January had always described Alexander as her muse. And he called her his muse.

Muse. It was the right word. They inspired one another. Fed each other ideas and feelings of self-confidence and joy. After January would have a particularly fabulous conversation with Alexander over the phone, usually while she was out on a liveshot somewhere, she would then go on the air and do an even more amazing job than usual. She just felt fueled. Once Alexander got into her head, he got into her soul. She just felt him moving around there, stirring up her creativity, her ability to write and produce solid news for her viewers. Alexander had said she did the same for him. So that was how they referred to each other. Muses.

January rationalized that any artist or writer needed a muse; therefore, she must keep Alexander in her life.

For the sake of sanity and for her creativity.

In the shower, January quickly realized the bruises were far too many for a bikini at the beach. She decided to meet up with friends for shopping on Lincoln Road. There was a pair of high heels she felt she deserved. If sex was going to be so irregular in her marriage, that did not mean spending money on shoes had to be.

Waving farewell to the doorman, January went outside to give Layla a spin over to her favorite shopping district. Layla's plush leather felt great against her aching rear. January patted the dashboard in appreciation. "Thank you, Layla." With that, she revved the engine and took off to spend some money.

August 2010: Phoenix

Alexander had been lucky. They sold the house within two weeks of placing it on the market. They had even made a healthy profit on the place. Considering how much work they had put into it, he was glad for that. Lilly cried as they packed their boxes. "I remember when we painted this room," she had said. "I remember when that light fixture came crashing down in the dining room." There was a similar story for every room she entered, and each one was coming out of her in a sob.

As Alexander was packing up his office, he found his box of letters from January. Careful to make sure Lilly was still packing another room, he sat down at his desk and opened the box. The smell of magnolia hit him in the face. The oil on her skin as she wrote the letters, he thought. Christ.

He found one dated October 1999.

My dearest A.,

I graduate in just three months. This campus has not been the same without you, although, had you stayed here, it might not have allowed me to graduate Magna Cum Laude. Distraction that you are. Feel free to congratulate me in person if we are ever lucky enough to see each other in person again.

I see, from your previous letter, you are enjoying Phoenix and have purchased a boat. I also noticed several beautiful women on the boat with you. I should be jealous, but instead I will simply say, I am glad you are living your dream. Speaking of which, you are really moving to Tanzania? I would ask why, but that would be silly. You are moving there because you are you and you search for things in the damnedest of places.

Your next letter to me had better have a Tanzanian postmark, or I will be most disappointed. Oh, I got a cat. He's a pain in the ass, but he tolerates me. Also, I am preparing to move to Louisville where I have been offered a job at the ABC affiliate. I will be working on my master's degree there, too.

Stay tuned. Your baby is finally going to be on TV.

Always yours,

J.

There were so many more. Hundreds. Many of them written but most had been emails he printed just to keep and reread whenever the mood struck him. He kept his letters in a locked box hidden in a drawer in his bookcase. Her handwriting was beautiful. She had taken several classes on calligraphy, "for fun" she had said, and as a result, her writing looked like something from a historical archive. I guess it kind of is, he thought. He quickly folded the letter and placed it back in the box.

He had moved to Tanzania for a little over a year. Partly for research, as he was starting his PhD, and mostly just to get away and clear his head. He did some missionary work while he was there and lived on the cheap. Internet cafés had just started to become a thing, and he remembered spending hours in one Tanzanian café, drinking coffee after coffee, emailing January. He had made a decision when he was there. Once he returned to the states, he would go to her. He would go see her and figure out what the future might hold for them.

May 2004: Louisville

With Tanzania now only visible through the window of the plane, Alexander was flying home. He had a layover in Atlanta but then planned a connecting flight to Louisville. He had not told January he was coming, as he wanted to surprise her. They had emailed each other almost every day during his sabbatical. Each email had become more intense, and there had even been a few late-night phone calls. Some of them were riddled with sexual overtones. He couldn't take it anymore. He had to have her. He had to make love to her to know she belonged to him. Alexander was ready to take their love outside of words on paper and take her into his arms. He'd been a fool for having waited this long.

He arrived in Louisville late in the afternoon and checked into a bed and breakfast in Old Louisville. A beautiful part of the city made up entirely of Victorian homes. He booked reservations at a romantic restaurant suggested by the sweet elderly couple who ran the inn, and he had his room filled with magnolia blossoms and jasmine, along with an expensive bottle of champagne.

Alexander felt ready.

He texted her.

Wanna hang out?

No response.

He waited. Maybe she was at work. He turned on

the news. She was there, wearing a navy pea coat, her long blonde hair falling around her shoulders. She held the microphone with authority and walked around pointing at a mobile home that had suffered storm damage. His heart filled with pride to finally see her doing what she had worked so hard to do. Her gray eyes sparkled, and she took up the whole screen. It was almost difficult to look at her that way. On a television screen. Much of their relationship, or whatever it was, had been in writing. Now he could see her. Not in a flat picture, but a moving image in front of him, living out her dream. He heard her say, "Reporting in Bardstown, January Morgan, News 11."

Alexander smiled. She was magnificent. He was ready.

This time he was ready.

He texted her again.

Me again. Baby, I need to see you. I am here. In Louisville. I am at the Tucker House B&B. Please come see me. Let's have a drink and catch up. In person for a change.

No response.

Alexander was getting worried. He always heard back from her right away. He ordered room service and cancelled the restaurant reservations. Maybe she just needed time to get back or had more work to do. He opened the champagne and took a swig. Then another.

Time passed. It was now nine pm. He called her.

No answer.

Finished off the champagne.

Finally, a text appeared on his phone.

I cannot believe you are here. Of all the times, it cannot be now. It just can't. Alexander, I have met someone. I wanted to tell you. It's serious. I still want to see you. I just worry about what I would do.

Alexander was a little drunk and a lot hurt. He was also angry. How could she not have told him? He always told her about his sexual exploits, his temporary girlfriends. She had even joked with him about hers. But never had she mentioned this guy. The champagne and two hotel-sized bottles of Kentucky bourbon soon had him swimming. He had come all this way. For her. Always writing to her. Always thinking about her. He decided he had two choices here. He could let her come over and prove to her the other guy was not the one because he was, or he could tell her "good luck and good night." She would both appreciate and be angered by the Edward R. Murrow reference.

He texted her.

Just get over here. No reason we shouldn't still have a drink.

She responded.

I can't, Alexander. If I do, I'll do something I'll regret. My feelings are too strong to resist you. I'm so sorry. Don't let this forsake our friendship. You mean the world to me.

He hurled his phone against the wall and sank down into the big feather bed where he quickly passed out until the next morning.

As soon as he awoke, he packed up his few belongings, tossed the flowers in the trash, and caught the next flight to California to start his first teaching job as an adjunct professor at San Diego University while he finished his PhD.

January and Alexander did not correspond after that for nearly a year.

Phoenix, August 2010: Moving Day

The truck was loaded up, and two years of memories had been carefully removed and packed away inside a giant moving truck. The Lanes were officially moving to Miami. Alexander stood in front of the house, truck keys in hand, and took a deep breath.

Lilly held his hand and kissed his cheek. "We are ready for this, Alex. Let's go. We've said our goodbyes; we've done all we can do here. It's time to move forward." Lilly, with her tender optimism, was a supportive voice to Alexander. He was nervous about the new job and the move. He was nervous about living so close to January. There was more to be afraid of, too. Alexander just wasn't ready to face it yet.

Lilly hopped inside the truck. "Let's hit the road, baby!"

Baby.

"Let's do it!" Alexander started the engine, and the two of them prepared for the cross-country drive to Florida. The state where Alexander had been born and vowed never to return to again. Yet, the job was too good to pass up. Lilly wanted to be closer to her sister, who had moved there a few years earlier. Plus, Alexander was anxious. He needed a change.

He needed to be closer to *her.*

Alexander quivered in the seat.

"How can you be cold?" Lilly laughed. "It's a

hundred and five degrees here."

"Oh, just a chill. Let's blow this popsicle stand!" Alexander was on the road now, their destiny distorted by his unrequited love and an unknown future.

Miami: Liberty City Neighborhood 2 A.M.

The shootings began just after midnight, and Detective Zackary Tennant had been dispatched after confirmation of, at least, four dead. The gang violence was at an all-time high. The Latin Kings had waged war against a few smaller gangs not affiliated with such a large crime organization for messing around with their dope sales. The vice narcotics team was out there, the ATF, DEA, forensics, members of SWAT, and major crimes, including Zak.

The crime scene tape was set up in multiple areas with a perimeter marked off around, at least, four different houses. Three known gang members sat shirtless with their hands cuffed behind their backs on the curbside. Their heads hanging down, crown tattoos marking their membership in the Latin Kings decorating their bodies.

Zak arrived in his unmarked white Impala and walked underneath the tape to his speak with his lieutenant. "Hello, sir. What are we working?"

Lieutenant John Gray was a thirty-year veteran of the force, most of his time in major crimes. "Well, Zak, just another night in paradise. Four dead. Gunshot wounds to the head, execution-style. All victims are rival gang members, not with the Kings, and they are all juveniles. Sounds like some kids thought they could play tough gang members and mess around with the real gang's drug business. Bad, bad decision."

Zak surveyed the area. Lots of patrol cars, sad little houses with beat-up cars parked on the lawn, and a few hookers standing around to watch the chaos. "Okay, who am I talking to?"

The lieutenant pointed to the men shackled on the ground. "You might need a translator. They are not speaking English, even though they can."

"I can give it a shot." Zak loosened his tie and walked over to the curbside where the three arrestees sat, refusing to make eye contact with anyone.

"Good evening, gentlemen."

No response from them.

"Let's try this again. Look up at me when I'm talking to you."

One of them spat on the ground. "*Hijo de puta blanca.*"

"Ah, that was a not a very nice thing to say to the man that might be able to let you little pissers go tonight if you just answer a few questions."

One of the three, a bald one with a sugar skull tattooed on his head looked directly into Zak's eyes and said, "Fuck you, pig."

"Well, since this is the path you have chosen to walk down, I think it's important for you to know we have taken Queen Maria, Luiz, and a few others into custody where we are, let's say, getting a lot of information. Oh, the other ones…your children. The state has them all. Congrats, you are now not fathers! Don't really hear that much. Usually it's the opposite, but I am sure, in your case, the kids probably had shitty lives anyway. They will fare much better in the foster system. As for Queen Maria, she is fully dethroned. I can assure you of that. Probably being fucked from behind by our agency's janitor right now in the interrogation room for all I know. And Luiz, well, he's a talkative little asshole. Gave up the names of several of your meth suppliers, and DEA is visiting them right now. Granted, these little brats you killed should never have messed with an actual gang like the Latin Kings. You probably should have found a better way to handle them than just flat out murder."

One of the guys spoke up, "Fuckers deserved it. Lying to us and trying to take our business."

The one with the skull on his head kicked him. "Shut up, Raul."

Zak leaned down and looked at them all in the face, his dark eyes flaming from the adrenaline. "I need one thing and one thing only from you, and perhaps some of the evidence becomes, shall we say, a bit circumstantial and perhaps the witness statements become a bit unreliable, you follow?"

They made no movement.

"Okay, I'm going to assume that was a fucking affirmative. You, skull drawn on your skull guy."

"My name is Gabriel."

"Of course, it is. Okay, so here is what I need, and perhaps you can maintain your legion of punks and your reputation as the dark angel. I want the address of where Queen Maria has been spending her weekends."

Gabriel laughed. "Fuck that. I don't know shit about where Queenie goes."

"Yes, you do, Gabe, *mi amigo*. You see I know you do because we have some guys on the inside, won't tell you who because I like you being all freaked out all the time, not knowing who the snitch might be. But my guy tells me you and Queen Maria are a bit of an item, and she has taken you with her on these little adventures. Address. I want it now, and with Queenie out of the picture, you might stand a chance of advancement. No address and you get to be some Nazi's fuck-toy on the inside. Racially, they discriminate, but when it comes to assholes, the sky is the limit. C'mon, Gabe, you and me, let's take a little walk. Or in your case, a short hop over to that patrol car. Let's chat."

Gabriel, with Zak's help, stood up from the curb. He whispered an address into Zak's ear. "Better fuckin' take care of me, cop."

"I will. You might have to spend tonight in the jail, but by tomorrow, you'll be out. Your two buddies over there, well, they're fucked."

Gunshots ripped through the air, and everyone went down to the ground. Women were screaming and crying, and members of the SWAT team jumped out of their armored vehicle and busted into the house where the sounds came from. A woman ran outside holding a child covered in blood. "*Mi bebe*! *Mi bebe*! Antonio! Oh, God! Oh, no!" She fell to her knees, and deputies stepped in to help her and the obviously deceased toddler in her arms. Gabriel looked up at Zak and shook his head. "Best be getting to that house soon, detective. Looks like hits are being demanded left and right out here tonight. That bitch over there and her kid, they were helping move meth for those little fuckers that had to be put down. Latin Kings won't stop til' we have gotten rid of people who fuck with our business, yo."

Zak walked over to his vehicle and sat down in the seat to make some notes in his computer. He typed up the verbatim required to ensure Gabriel Santoza, a captain among his gang ranks, would get to walk away with a minor drug possession charge while the other nitwits served time for murder. Gabriel might not have pulled the trigger, but he gave the order. But that was how these games had to be played. You kick a few to the inside while leaving one out to become your information man. Gabriel was a gangbanger, but he was no idiot, and he certainly would not forget Zak let him out of this. Zak passed the address along to DEA and ATF, as he believed it was not only a human trafficking location but also where the top-tiered Miami Latin Kings conducted business. All kinds of dirty business with major cartels.

Detective Zackary Tennant, after three more hours at the scene, headed back to the office to fill out paperwork for another three hours. The sun was up, and he was on his eighth cup of coffee. He also realized he had, once again, failed to call his wife.

As he tried to dial her number from his desk phone, he noticed his hand was shaking and the image of a bloody baby and a screaming mother, who would also end up dying at the scene, shrouded his mind.

He put the phone back down on the receiver and sighed. Sometimes even forming words had become tough for Zak. Especially the simple, casual words. Every day, it became more challenging to feel normal.

****

January had waited all night on a call or a text from Zak. She was well aware of what was happening with the shootings, and she was worried about his safety. Out of pure concern, she had texted his lieutenant, who confirmed Zak was okay and should have returned to the office for follow-up paperwork, so she had tried his desk phone, to no avail. Sometimes, being the wife of a police officer was so stressful and infuriating it made January question how police officers maintained marriages at all. Many of them didn't.

Sitting at her own desk and prepping a story for the day, January flipped through stacks of documents about a cold case. She had received a tip from the victim's family members that there might be a break in the twenty-year-old case of their daughter who had gone missing back in 1990. She was a teenage girl who had been riding her bike home from school and never made it home. Now, with DNA evidence, the family believed police might have a suspect who was already serving time for a child sex abuse case. January had developed a good relationship with the family over the years, trying to help keep their story out there, so it didn't disappear like their daughter had. Today, if this was confirmed, she would break a major story.

"Hey, Janny, you've got a call on line one," Rob from the assignment desk shouted to her from across the newsroom bullpen.

"Thanks, Rob," she said. After picking up the phone, she said, "This is January Morgan."

Long pause. Then, someone took a deep breath. "Good morning." It was Zak and he sounded exhausted.

"Zak, dear God, why have you not even texted me? I was so worried about you. Where are you?"

Zak cleared his throat. "I'm still at work. Looks like I will be here for awhile. Looking like a twenty-four-hour day, at least. I'm sorry, Janny. Last night was…it was just a rough night is all."

"Zak, I heard about the mother and baby. I cannot imagine how seeing that must be messing with your mind. Please talk to me or talk to the department's therapist. You can't just bury that stuff in your head."

"Janny, I love you, but I can handle myself. I don't need a fuckin' shrink. What I need is a good workout, a stiff drink, and a long nap. I love you. I will call you when I am heading home."

January felt defeated. When he got like this, there wasn't much she could do or say that wouldn't exacerbate the situation. "I love you, too, sweetheart. I have a big story today, so I am not sure when I'll be home. Probably after the eleven o'clock news tonight. I might have a lead on the Sullivan cold case. Sounds like DNA might have helped ID a guy who is currently in the Dade County jail."

"That's great news. Do you need any help from me?"

"No," January explained, "I have a strong in with the Florida Department of Law Enforcement DNA unit. And I have the family, and soon I will have the name of the guy in jail. I might pay him a visit."

Zak didn't like the sound of that. "Honey, I like your aggressive approach, but it's not always the best idea for a reporter to go in asking questions before police have even had the chance to question the guy about his possible involvement in Danielle Sullivan's disappearance. Let the law work it."

"The law has had twenty years. I have until the five o'clock news. I love you, and I will see you tonight. Get some rest, Zak."

"Bye, babe."

January hung up the phone and got to work. First, she called the Sullivan family to set up her interviews with them. Danielle Sullivan had been thirteen years old when she went missing. Her parents still lived in Miami, once stating they refused to leave in case Danny ever returned home to them. They didn't have any other children, and anytime January had visited them for stories, it was always a depressing experience. They had never changed Danielle's bedroom, for instance. For twenty years, it had remained just as she'd left it. January hated seeing that room. It made her stomach turn. Still, this could be the break the Sullivans had waited so long to get. It was obvious, by now, their daughter was most likely dead, but they needed to know how she had died and where her body had been taken. This family deserved closure, and they deserved to look the man who had taken their baby away in the eyes.

Today, January hoped to look him in the eyes herself. This could be the story that would put her on the map. She had been feeling stagnate lately, like all she did was cover the day-to-day crime. Nothing ever stood out. She needed to stand out, if she wanted to make it to a network.

Her cell phone buzzed. A text from Alexander. Her body lit up.

J., You and me. We need to have a beer when I finally make it into town. Long-ass drive and now somewhere in big-ass Texas at some less than appropriate roadside motel. How is your day going? Entertain me for a moment.

A.

January did not have time to entertain him right now. Her photographer was standing by the backdoor, ready to head to the Sullivans' house. Plus, she had just received the name of the suspect from her DNA analyst source. She had to move fast on this before someone else sniffed out the story.

A.,

No time to be your entertainment right now. On a big story. Could be very, very big. I will leave you with this, however. I'm wearing the lapis necklace you sent to me from Tanzania today. It's my news-gathering good luck charm. Drive safe and enjoy your nefarious little motel. Show your wife what those motels are all about. Everyone needs a little kink now and then.

Somebody's baby,

J.

His name was Randall Marshall. He had just been popped on a lewd and lascivious and a sex battery on a ten-year-old girl. He had been sitting in the Dade County jail for only two weeks. A DNA swab had been taken because of the little girl and entered the CODIS, the FBI's Combined DNA Index System. According to the analyst, Marshall's DNA made another hit, and that was a match to a piece of clothing belonging to Danielle Sullivan. That piece of clothing, a part of blue shorts, had been found along Alligator Alley about two weeks after her disappearance. Some DNA evidence was collected from the shorts and like thousands of similar cases, that evidence was banked away in a vault surrounded by other unsolved cases. Little Danielle Sullivan, the last remaining piece of her sitting in a box in a dark room. Unopened for nearly twenty years.

Until now.

January called a friend over at the Dade County jail while Lenny drove them to the Sullivan house. "Hey, Pedro! How are you? It's January, over at WSVN."

Pedro was a sergeant at the jail and had known Zak and January for years. They went to bars together, along with Pedro's wife, and always had a great time. "Hey, Janny! Long time no see. We need to get the squad together for a night out soon."

"I know. We both could use a night out. That's for sure. Hey, Pedro. You have an inmate by the name of Randall Marshall, fifty-four years old. In on an aggravated sex batt on a kid. I want to request an interview with him. For today. At around two pm. And, Pedro, I need you to convince him to say yes. It's imperative he talk to me."

"Wow, Janny. That's a mighty big request. You and Zak will owe me a beer or two."

"You got it. Just make sure he agrees and it is in writing. I cannot stress enough how much we need him to say yes. I just need five minutes with the guy." January was nervous. This was the most important piece to her story. It was one thing to have the Sullivan family claiming a suspect had been identified, but it was something altogether better to have the suspect admit it, even before the police released it.

January and Lenny continued their commute to the Sullivans' home. They lived in Coral Gables, about thirty minutes outside of the city. They're house was a classic Florida ranch-style home, made from cement block and stucco, painted a pale salmon color. Julia Sullivan was a retired teacher, and her husband Michael Sullivan was a contractor. Despite the pain of the past twenty years, they had stayed together and continued to try to have relatively normal lives. Michael had once told January, it was the basic mundane activities of the day, like checking off a never-ending to-do list, that helped make the days easier to bare.

January knocked on the door and was greeted by

Julia, a fifty-year-old woman with brownish-gray hair. She was a little heavy and looked much older than she was. Her eyes were sunk deeply into her face, and she wore glasses. "Come in, Janny. We are so happy to see you! How have you been? How's Zak?"

"Oh, thank you, Julia. We are both good. Zak is working hard all the time, and so am I. But things are good."

"Any plans for a little one in the near future?" Julia smiled. Photos of her daughter were all over the house. Baby pictures, toddler pictures, Danielle's first birthday, and the photo that circulated through the entire country after she went missing, a beautiful photo of Danielle sitting on her blue bicycle, her long dark hair loose on her shoulders, green eyes sparkling. The photo had been taken just days before her disappearance. She was riding that bike when she went missing. January imagined Julia must have looked like that when she was a teenage girl. Bright-eyed, beautiful, full of promise. January had interviewed so many grieving parents in her career, and it never got easier. Even twenty years after their children had passed.

Julia motioned for January and Lenny to have a seat on the couch. "Michael will be here in a minute. He has been outside building a new kitchen table. Our old one finally went kaput. He did keep a piece of the wood where Danielle had written her name in marker. He built that into the new table. Quite talented, my husband." The pain in Julia's eyes was obvious. "So the police haven't called us yet, but we have a private investigator who has worked with us over the years. He's the one who told us a DNA hit was made."

January looked up, jarred from looking at the many photos of Danielle which surrounded them. Everywhere she turned, Danielle was staring right at her. "Yes, Julia, this is a bit unorthodox what we are doing, but I have great faith in my source at CODIS. I also have a name. His name is Randall Marshall, fifty-four years old. In jail on a sexual battery on a ten-year-old girl. He has a history of, and, Julia, forgive me, I just want to give you all the information here, he has a history of pedophilia and has been arrested multiple times for aggravated assault, lewd and lascivious behavior, drugs, you name it. He lived in Coral Gables at the time Danielle disappeared, but he was just staying with family members. He had recently been divorced and needed a place to stay, so his parents let him stay with them. Their house was on Juniper Drive."

Julia took a deep breath and wiped the tears from her eyes. Michael was standing by the door and walked over to sit beside his wife. He was a tall man with a thick beard. Kind, green eyes. He spoke to January, "Juniper Drive is just two blocks from here."

"Yes. The parents have since passed away, and the house belongs to a new family now, not related to the Marshalls. I am interviewing Randall Marshall today at three. I also plan to seek out his ex-wife and find out more about their marital problems. But listen, after I interview him, depending on what he says, I want to show you the raw interview before I put him on the air. You should see it first, unedited. Are you comfortable with this?"

Michael stood up and paced around the room. "I don't know, Janny. Maybe we should just wait on the police to do their due diligence with this guy. That's what they do. They get people to talk."

January interjected, "So do I, Michael. And I am a lot less intimidating than a police officer. He thinks I am coming to talk to him about this latest crime. He has no idea I will be there about your daughter. He'll never see me comin' until it's too late. If he's our guy, and DNA says so, I can get him to crack."

Lenny nodded his head. "That's what she does best, Michael. She gets people to spill their guts. They tell her anything. It's the craziest shit I have ever seen, and I've been a photog for thirty years. Even the slimiest assholes trust her."

January gave a partial smile to Lenny. He had her back.

"We all want the same thing, here," January said. "A confession. Just give me a chance to get it. First, I would like to interview you about the possible DNA match on a suspect, but we won't name the guy. Just your reactions after all these years, and what you hope it means for your family. Closure? Justice? You've done this enough to know the drill. And hey, I care about you both, and I care about this case. It shouldn't be cold any longer."

Michael sat beside his wife and put an arm around her shoulder. "Okay, let's do this."

Lenny hit the record button and the red light came on.

Dade County Jail 2:45 P.M.

When January arrived at the jail, it was just before three. She was worried Pedro had not been able to convince Randall Marshall to talk, but when she checked in with her press credentials at the front desk, Mary, the receptionist, winked at her.

That was a good sign. Mary smiled and handed January an identification badge. "Head through the double doors and Sgt. Pedro Leon will take you to meet with Inmate Marshall."

January thanked Mary and breathed a sigh of relief as Lenny checked in his equipment through the metal detectors. The hard part was getting in. Now she would have to work extra hard to get the confession. Her phone was buzzing. It was Zak. She hit ignore. No time for his apologies now.

Pedro greeted January and Lenny at the doors. "Okay, Janny. You owe me. He was not going to talk, so I had to have a couple of correctional officers threaten to send him back to general population if he didn't. He's in isolation right now, and if he went to general pop, well, let's just say he'd be beaten to a pulp and wouldn't be much good to anyone for an interview."

January followed Pedro down the long hall to a small room set up with cameras and two-way mirrors. The jail was older, having had its heyday in the mid-seventies, so wood paneling and green floor tiles decorated the space. The smell was something between bleach and urine. The sound of clicking heels along the tiles and Lenny's bag of audio equipment dragging behind them filled the hallway.

"That room up ahead," Pedro motioned. The door had glass windows and the back of a man's head could be seen through the door. His hair was dark, like it had been dyed coal black just recently. Perhaps he had been disguising himself.

Pedro opened the door, and two other deputies stood inside, watching from the corners. "They have to stay, Janny. I will be just over there. He pointed to the mirror."

"Thank you, Sergeant. I can take it from here. I appreciate your help."

Her phone buzzed again. Zak texted: *"Don't do this interview. It could mess up the investigation. I am begging you."*

She turned off her phone and sat down in front of Randall Marshall. She smiled and held out her hand. "Good afternoon, Mr. Marshall. I am January Morgan with WSVN TV. Thank you for meeting with me."

His eyes were as dark as his hair. If he wasn't a child killer, he certainly looked like one. His black hair was greasy and hung down in uneven layers on his shoulders. His face was pockmarked and had cuts from a recent shave. He eyeballed her up and down. "I'd shake your hand, Ms. Morgan, but they have me pretty well tied down here." He showed his shackled hands, shackled to his feet. His voice was quite soft, and he was well-spoken. A contrast from his appearance. His inmate clothing was the standard brown of a new arrestee.

"I am going to have Lenny, my photographer, record our interview. My goal here is let you tell your side of the story about your arrest and allow you to say anything else you feel is weighing on you."

"I wasn't given much of a choice on doing this interview, and I would rather not. But here I am, and here I will have to stay for a long time. Sexual battery on a kid carries a lengthy sentence."

"Yes, sir, it does."

Randall Marshall laughed and looked up at the deputies. "She called me 'sir.' Do you believe this?"

January shuffled in her seat. "Well, you still deserve my respect. You have not been proven guilty in a court of law yet."

"Well, ain't that the truth. I didn't hurt that little kid. She was playing in my yard, and I just tried to get her to leave. When she refused, I picked her up and carried her to the sidewalk and demanded she return home because she was trespassing."

January pulled out a copy of the arrest affidavit. "It says here, you pulled her into your garage, after you found her petting your dog in the yard, and digitally penetrated her. She struggled and got away after scratching your face with her nails."

Randall touched his cheek, clearly marked with three nearly healed scratches. "She did that to me when I picked her up to make her leave."

January took a deep breath. It was time to soften him. "Yeah, I guess I can see that. I did some checking on the girl, and she was known for wandering into people's yards." One of the deputies standing behind Randall raised an eyebrow. "Yeah, she was a problem child with her parents, too. They had even taken her out of school for behaving badly in class every day, so I actually don't completely doubt your story." January was lying, of course. The victim was an A student, a cheerleader, Girl Scout, and her parents adored her. This man was a monster and his eyes betrayed him as he nodded his head in agreement with January's lies.

"Well, now that sounds about right. My lawyer needs to know this shit, maybe get my charges lowered or something."

"He is considering it after I told him this morning." Another lie. January didn't even know the poor public defender who had been assigned to this lowlife.

Randall Marshall leaned back in his chair and cocked his head. "Why do you care about this case? Doesn't seem high-brow enough for a pretty little thing like you to be reporting on. Unless you like naughty types like myself." He licked his lips and looked at January's chest. A deputy moved forward, but January shook her head.

She leaned in to the evil sitting before her and smiled. "I do have something else I want to ask you. It's kind of a big thing."

Randall leaned in, too.

A deputy shouted, "Away from her, inmate."

Randall backed up. "I got a big thing for you right here, honey."

"I bet you do, Randall. What about Danielle Sullivan? Did you have a big thing for her, too?"

His eyes widened. He licked his lips. He clenched his hands. They began to sweat. January could smell him more strongly because he was sweating a lot now.

"I don't know who the fuck you're talking about,

honey."

"Oh, come on, Randall. She was thirteen, very pretty. Hot day in 1990. She was riding a blue bicycle right by your momma's house. You'd watched her for a few days take the same route. You wanted her, so you took her."

"I never heard that name in my life."

"Oh, Randall. Don't lie to me, darling. My little birdie in a special office downtown told me a special secret that even the detectives don't know yet. Your DNA, you know, those little disgusting pieces of you left behind on the little girl from last week? Well, it appears some of those disgusting little pieces are a match on Danielle's clothing. Something kept in a vault for twenty years. The short of it, your DNA is now linked to a girl who has been missing since 1990. A girl who lived two blocks from you. A girl you did things to. Terrible things, I would suspect."

Randall Marshall averted his eyes from January and stared out the tiny, square window. "I want my lawyer here now."

"He will be here soon enough. In fact, I know you are feeling a little hard just remembering her. Aren't you?" A deputy stepped forward again, but January waved him back. "How did she feel to you, Randall? Soft, young, malleable? Do you remember how she smelled? You are sweating right now just thinking about it. How did it feel? That's what I want to know. How did it feel to take a girl and make her yours?"

Randall slammed his shackled hands on the table. "Shut up, bitch! Shut up!"

"You liked it. You liked hurting her. You liked *owning* her."

Randall's face was red, and the deputies quickly restrained him as he lunged at January. Lenny kept rolling as he had been instructed. "Get me away from her. Get me the fuck away from her."

January wouldn't let up. "Did you fuck her? How did you kill her? Did you cut her up? Did you do it slowly over a period of several days or strangle her while you raped her? Did you regret you killed her so fast?"

He was kicking, and the deputies were going for their Tasers when he shouted, "I never cut her. I would never have cut her. I loved her."

The deputies carted him out of the room. January sat back in the chair and took a deep breath. Her heart was beating so hard; her chest ached. She looked up at Lenny and smiled. "Got it?"

Lenny wiped his brow with his baseball cap. "Damn straight."

The door busted open and there stood Zak.

"Zak, what are you doing here?" January was stunned. He had never just shown up like this when she was on a shoot before.

"Don't ever turn your phone off when I am trying to call you. That guy could've hurt you."

"He didn't. In fact, he confessed."

"Everything you got is not official. He did not confess to a detective."

"Oh, but he said it to me, a reporter, on record and on camera. Zak, don't fight me on this. I don't want to have to start citing the First Amendment to you this afternoon. Not to mention, I have a job to do, and you didn't call me all night while you worked!"

Lenny left the room with the camera equipment.

He did not want to see these two go at it.

"Listen, this is police business. You know that. Don't try to be Little Miss Detective. You are a reporter, not a fucking cop."

"I am also your wife, not some person you are interrogating. Spare me the lecture, Zak. I have to get back to work."

January was livid. She tried to walk past Zak, but he grabbed her shoulders and looked into her eyes. "I don't understand why you never listen to me."

"I don't understand why you don't want to spend time with me or talk anymore. I guess we don't understand a lot about each other lately. I love you, Zak, but I have to go."

January left the building and turned in her press visitor badge at the front desk. She was upset with Zak for ambushing her like that. Had he busted in seconds earlier, she could've lost the soundbite of a lifetime. She headed out to the news truck to begin editing her video.

By eleven that night, January would have the exclusive on a twenty-year-old cold case. Her source at the DNA lab wanted to remain anonymous, but she was able to get a detective on the case to meet her outside by the news truck to look at her video on the monitors in the back of the truck. It was Detective Frank Williams. He was the fifth detective in a series to be handed the cold case. As detectives left the agency or were promoted, the case just kept getting passed along. Detective Williams worked with Zak but was not particularly fond of him. There was some bad blood there, but Janny did not dare ask why. The important thing was he didn't hold any of it against her.

After he watched her interview, he immediately called his contacts at CODIS. In a matter of minutes, he received confirmation—the DNA was a match.

"So what do you want out of all this, January?" He was young, only thirty or so, and quite handsome. He smiled, revealing a mouthful of exceptionally white teeth. His hair was blond, streaked from the sun, and his tan was unmistakably Miami. "I know you want something."

"I want exclusivity on the story. I want to be there when you tell the family. I want to be there when you formally charge him. I want all of it. I also want to be able to use my interview with him on air. After your approval, of course. I also want to put this on the air tonight by eleven."

January smiled coyly, noticing how Frank was looking at her. He seemed to fancy her a little, which she felt slightly embarrassed about. However, after her little tiff with Zak, it was nice to be ogled a bit.

"Fine. I'll give you what you want. Let me get the fax from CODIS, and I will meet you at the Sullivans' house. Afterward, I will add the charges to Mr. Marshall's already lengthy list. Then, I will take him into a room and make him tell me where he dumped her body. I might not be as easy on him as you were, though." That smile again.

January was blushing. "I did what I had to do. Sometimes foul things just fly out of my mouth if it means getting someone to talk."

"Should've been a cop."

January laughed. "Not in a million years. I was made for TV trucks and live shots. Thank you, detective."

"Frank."

"Thank you, Frank. See you at the Sullivans' house."

"Yes, you will. Nice work in there."

"Oh, and, Frank?"

"Yes, January?"

"I want to be there when the body is exhumed."

"Is that all, January?"

"Yep, that ought to do it."

"You reporters, always demanding things. I could say no, you know."

She hopped out of news truck and stood facing Frank. "But you won't. You'll help me because I am going to make you famous. You and me, baby, we are going places after this."

Frank laughed. "You can have the fame, Janny. I just want to solve the fuckin' case."

Lenny and January headed back to the Sullivans' with their video evidence of Randall Marshall's near-confession. In an unmarked squad car behind them, Frank followed. While en route, Frank had confirmed with the DNA analysts that there had indeed been a match with Marshall's DNA found on the piece of Danielle's clothing. It was a good match, too, which made the case even stronger. Toss in what he had said on camera about "loving her," and it did not look good for Randall Marshall. Based on that statement alone, it made it sound like he was a classic pedophile who had spent some time watching her, stalking her while he planned to rip her out of this world. Danielle's body had never been found, but Frank knew in his heart and based on his training that Marshall had either asphyxiated or strangled her. Detective Franklin

Williams was about to break a case that no one had been able to do in twenty years. Granted, it helped that Marshall had made a big mistake with his recent victim by leaving a bit of himself behind, but either way, this was his case. His win. His conviction. He smiled as he followed the reporter who had helped him finally make a name for himself. A reporter of all people!

When they arrived at the Sullivans' house, Michael and Julia were sitting on the front porch, waiting. Frank exited his vehicle, and January practically bounded out of the news truck and walked toward the couple, the look of hope in their eyes.

Julia stood up, her eyes filling with tears, and she hugged January. "He admitted it, didn't he?"

January was careful with her words as Detective Williams would need to address the law enforcement questions. "I can only say he acknowledged he knew her. And he said...he said..." January couldn't go on. The look on Julia's face was too much to bare. This family had suffered unimaginable pain for so long.

Frank stepped in. "Hello, Mr. and Mrs. Sullivan. I am Detective Frank Williams, the detective on your daughter's case. Mr. Marshall became physically defensive when questioned about Danielle by reporter Morgan, and while he did not say he took her, he admitted to loving her. I know that is hard to hear, but what it says is he coveted your daughter in some way and had affections toward her." January held on to Julia's hand and sat down on the bench beside her. Michael Sullivan stood on the porch, stone-faced.

Frank continued, "What we do have, without a doubt, is strong DNA evidence tying Mr. Marshall to your daughter. This is irrefutable. What January could get in her interview will make a good start as we break him down in further questioning, but no matter what he says at this point, the DNA is our key to putting him away. We just need to be careful about showing him our cards this soon. We want to know where he took your daughter, what happened to her, and we will need him to be cooperative to make that happen."

Michael stepped forward. "Detective, you say you got this guy dead to rights with DNA, so why can't he be charged right now and then asked where he took her later?"

Frank understood Michael's concern. "I do plan to charge him. But I am not going to do that until tomorrow after meeting with the state attorney and getting some good alone time with the piece of shit in a tiny room. Excuse my language, Mrs. Sullivan."

Michael shook his head. "Okay, sir. Do what you gotta do, but I want to know where he took our baby. I want to know what he did to her." Tears filled Michael's eyes as Julia stood up to embrace him.

Frank felt the weight of their agony. "The good news is we have made progress. The first break in this case in a long time. I'm going to get this guy prosecuted to the fullest extent, and I promise you, I will find your daughter or, at the very least, find out what happened to her." Frank looked so sincere and forceful. January was impressed with his demeanor and how he handled the Sullivans.

January motioned for Lenny to come over. "Okay, guys. This is what we talked about. I need to ask you a few questions."

They nodded and sat beside each other on the porch bench, hands clasped together. "We're ready,"

Julia said, her voice shaking.

January pulled up a chair on the patio in front of them and positioned herself for the interview. Frank stepped aside but remained within earshot of January's questions. "Today, you have learned some very disturbing information. Tell me, after twenty years, how do you process finally getting *the call*, that ever-important phone call when someone tells you they might know what happened to your daughter?" January had to build it up slowly.

Julia spoke first. "When I heard there might be a DNA match with a man currently incarcerated, I felt my knees buckle. I fell to the ground and stared blankly at the wall. I didn't cry, not at first. I just looked at one of Danielle's pictures and said out loud, 'I think we are going to find you now.'"

Michael wrapped his arms around his wife and began to speak. "All we have ever wanted is to know what happened to our daughter. We know she is most likely no longer on this earth and in heaven. We know this, and yet, every day for twenty years, we have still held out hope that she would walk through that door. Home from school, like she should have back then. No parent should have to endure this kind of pain. No parent should ever live with the unknown. I think it would be better if we just knew. If we knew, we could bury her properly. Say our goodbyes properly. Finally know for sure that door is not ever going to open."

January continued, "You never changed her bedroom."

Julia's tears were flowing heavily now. "No. We just couldn't. The police went through it a bunch of times in the beginning, but I put everything back the way she had it."

"Will you go in there now? If the police have caught the man who took your little girl, will you be able to go back into that room?"

Michael sighed. "Not me." He looked at Julia. "I'm sorry, honey. I just can't."

Julia nodded her head and placed her hand on her husband's shoulder. "I just want to set her free. If going inside that room helps me feel like that happens, then it seems like I should consider it."

January crossed her legs, leaning in to Julia. "The DNA match is strong. The suspect is already in custody on a child molestation charge. His name is Randall Marshall. He lived just two blocks away from you at the time of your daughter's disappearance. He was never questioned before by police. What do you want to say to him now?"

Michael looked directly into Lenny's camera, his voice low and stern. "If you are the man who took my daughter, I want you to confess it. I want you to tell me what you did to our baby. Where did you take her? We just want to give her a proper funeral. Please. You stole everything from us. At least, give us the chance to bury our little girl."

January stood up and moved off the porch to the front yard, microphone in hand to record her on-camera stand up.

"The case is still under investigation as the detective works to obtain more information, but my sources at CODIS tell me the DNA found on an article of Danielle Sullivan's clothing is an exact match to fifty-four-year-old Randall Marshall. Marshall is currently in the Dade County jail on a sexual battery charge of a ten-year-old Miami girl. He has a history of criminal charges, ranging from petty theft to fraud to possession of child pornography. While charges involving the Sullivan case have not been filed against Marshall just yet, sources at the state attorney's office tell me it's only a matter of time. A matter of time that took nearly twenty years to accomplish to finally make a break in one of Miami's most notable cold cases. Reporting in Coral Gables, January Morgan, WSVN News 7."

Lenny gave the all-clear. Frank walked up to January, looking a bit peeved. "You have sources at the state attorney's office?"

January blushed. "Oh, yeah, I have a source there, too. They are expecting your call as they are fully ready to help you move forward with the charge. Once that happens, get your full confession, find out what he did with Danielle's body, and I will interview you. Making you the most visible detective in the country. Even if it's just for a few days." January smiled and touched Frank on the shoulder. "I know I move fast. It's how I work. But I have known the Sullivan family for a while, and I'm like you. I want justice."

Frank smirked. "You want fame."

"No. I want justice. Don't mistake my aggressive reporting for a need to get to the top. This is my job."

Frank let the Sullivans know he would be coming inside for more questions, and they nodded as they walked inside. "You are a frustrating woman. Kind of maddening, really." He then laughed as he smiled flirtatiously at January.

"I have that effect on people. Until tomorrow, detective. Tonight, I will put this on the evening news."

She handed him his copy of the interviews. "Maybe you will stay up and watch my report?"

"I'm not much of a TV guy. Maybe I will make an exception. For you." He walked back up the stairs and went into the house.

Lenny looked at January and shook his head. "You've got issues, Janny. Either way, let's get back to the studio and make some fuckin' history."

January was ready to do just that. By this time tomorrow, her story would be national, and she hoped, more than anything else, that sleazebag Randall Marshall would just tell Frank where he had hidden that poor girl's body.

January called Zak to tell him about her success and ask him to watch her report. He answered, his voice sounding rushed. "Detective Tennent."

"Hey, honey! I did it. I got the interviews with the Sullivans, and Frank is helping me with my story. It looks like he's going to break the case, and I am going to have the exclusive. I can't believe it!"

"Janny, you just walked away from me over at the jail. That was so disrespectful. I told you to hold off because I wanted to help you get this story the right way. You are too eager, and you're trying to use law enforcement for your own advancement."

January was stunned. "Zak, this story means the world to me. The Sullivans mean the world to me. I wanted to help them. That's what I'm doing."

"You should've let us do our job first. What if this guy turns out not to be the killer or CODIS fucked up the DNA results? You are in too much of a hurry to win, and you're not looking at the big picture."

"Zak, my sources are solid. Frank has even spoken

with…"

"And I don't want you using Frank as one of your pawns. He works in my unit. It's just too…familiar."

"I am sorry you feel this way, Zak. I thought you would be proud of me. You know how much my job means to me." January felt like she was talking to a stranger. "I'm your wife, not just some reporter you can pass off that code of silence bullshit to."

"Then you need to remember to act like my wife and respect my career. Your mistakes could ruin me and my place here."

January hung up the phone, reapplied her lipstick, and headed into the studio. No matter how hard she tried, she just felt like she failed when it came to men. Even when she tried to test the waters with Alex in person, it had been a disaster.

Phoenix 2005

By 2005, January had been married to Zak for a few months, and it had been wonderful. They just worked well together. To the average person, they were the picture of perfection, a beautiful news reporter married to a handsome cop she had met on a story. Something wasn't right, though, and immediately into their marriage, Zak became more possessive of Janny. He had issues with her being on television and said it made him worry for her safety. He was always concerned about safety, but January just blamed that on him being a police officer. Otherwise, they had a lot of fun together. They couldn't get enough of each other, and she loved his strength and loyalty to his career, and she made him laugh.

January still had her emails and texts from Alexander to keep her company on the lonely nights when Zak's job kept him out late or when her job sent her out of town for days at a time. They just talked about life and the old days and about each other. They were friends and their conversations were friendly. January felt like they had reached a good point after so much time had passed since their last correspondence. After she had so terribly ditched him in Louisville. She felt badly about that but had been forced to make a difficult choice. She rarely discussed her marriage, but Alexander knew she was married. They just enjoyed each other's wit and presence in each other's lives, even though far away. The air would always be thick between them, laden with something bigger than they could ever talk about, especially now that Janny was married.

She enjoyed reading emails about Alexander's teaching work and how he was now taking frequent mission trips to help educate children in various countries. Then, one day, her news director asked to send her to their sister station in Phoenix to go through anchor-training with a news anchor there, who was known for being especially good with transitioning reporters to the desk. She was thrilled with the prospect of a trip, and the fact that her boss wanted her to learn how to anchor meant a possible promotion in her future. And then, there was the location. Alexander's home. Where he lived and worked. Where she could see him. In person. She had not seen him since college. She could've seen him when he visited Louisville that time, but she didn't. She had been so scared of what might happen. The pain of her decision still burned fresh. January loved Alexander and had wanted to be with him. Until she met Zak. Zak was ready to commit to her. Alex had never seemed to want to move forward with anything more than being pen pals. Alexander always danced around the idea of them being together, but he just never made a move on her. His letters were one thing. They filled her heart and made the pit of her stomach tense with joy, desire, and longing. But never had he tried to make her his in the flesh. Zak wanted her flesh immediately, and January had been tired of waiting. She was not a patient person by nature, and she had come to accept Alex was a wayward soul, a beautiful soul, but one that would never stop for her.

When she told Zak about the trip, he responded as January feared. "I can go with you," he said. "We can make a vacation of it."

"Zak, it's training. I will be working ten to twelve hour days and will only be there for three days. Let me go out there and prove myself. When I get back, my boss will let me anchor the desk. This could mean more money for us and maybe moving out of our dinky little apartment. Maybe even a bigger television market. Don't you want to get to Miami someday?" She had kissed him and smiled. "Aren't you proud of me?"

"I am proud of you every day. You are an amazing reporter and an amazing wife, but Phoenix? Why so far?"

"That's where our station's ownership company is based. It is just where I have to do this. It's the way it works, and it is an honor to have been chosen. I'll be back by next Tuesday night, and we can have dinner."

Zak grabbed her waist and pulled her close. He was wearing his uniform and smelled like sandalwood. He was wearing the cologne she had bought for him. "I love you, Janny. Be safe and call me the moment you land. Then call me from the hotel, so we can say naughty things to each other over the phone." He laughed and bit her lower lip as he kissed her.

Zak headed to his shift, and January began packing. She texted Alexander.

A.,

Coming to Phoenix for training. Coffee? Whiskey? Anything?

J.

Alexander responded quickly.

Yes, a thousand times yes. Are you coming alone or is this a family trip?

A.

Just me. We're friends, right?

J.

Yes, of course, we are. Good friends.

A.

Then we can absolutely have a friendly moment together. Just because I am married does not mean we can't have a drink. Be there tonight.

J.

January was going into this with maturity and grace, or at least, that's what she told herself. She would just have a drink with her old friend. What was the harm in that? Inside, she was gushing. She could not wait to see him. Her hands were shaking as she packed her bags. She was nervous. It had been nine years since they were face to face. In the same room. What if what they shared in their letters was just that and that alone? Something for the written word but not for real life. Either way, she had to go. It was for work. Alexander would just be a little side dish. A long awaited, much anticipated side dish. Seeing him in person would be good. Maybe it would close the door on all that longing. Simplify things.

January had two martinis on the plane ride from Louisville to Phoenix. It helped take the edge off flying, which she did not enjoy, and helped with the nervousness she was feeling over seeing Alexander. Once she arrived, she took a taxi to her hotel and freshened up in her room. The time change was throwing her off a bit, and she was slightly exhausted. Still, she made sure she looked her best.

Her hair was loose, hanging on her shoulders, and wavy from plane travel. She decided on a peach-colored dress and taupe high heels. A little gloss and a dab of magnolia oil on her neck. "It'll have to be enough." She was twenty-seven now and felt like she still looked mostly the same since college. Only a little taller, thanks to the heels.

She grabbed her bag and headed to the Arizona State University natural sciences department where Alexander would be teaching a class. She had mentioned meeting for drinks after but thought it might be fun to sit in on his class if she got there in time.

She arrived by taxi at five, and the class would be starting in just fifteen minutes. The campus was huge, and the natural sciences building was equally intimidating with its large white buildings and blue and red Spanish tile roofing. It was a gorgeous day, sunny and low eighties. Way hotter than Louisville, though. After tipping the cab driver, January stood and faced the grand entrance to the science building. He was in there. Her Alexander. Her dear friend. The man whose words kept her floating high above the rest of the world. The pull inside January's stomach was growing ever stronger, pulling her into the building. The closer she was to him, the more the ache inside her grew. That ache, the same as it was in college. The same one she woke up in the middle of the night feeling sometimes. Alexander was here. She was here, too.

She fluffed her hair and waltzed into the building, feeling beautiful and confident. After all, she wasn't that silly little girl in the library anymore. She was a television reporter. She was married to a police officer. She was all grown up and a force to be reckoned with.

There was no reason for her to feel nervous over seeing an old friend. Yet, she felt vaguely nauseous.

There was a large staircase leading up to the fourth floor where Dr. Lane would be teaching his students. Not eyeballing an elevator meant January would have to hike up the steps in her five-inch heels. Adding a little more gloss to her lips as she made the incline, she spotted the classroom. It was a large one, with auditorium-style seating. Should make it easy to go unnoticed, she thought. Except for how she was dressed and not having a backpack or a laptop. The door squeaked as she opened it slowly. The class was assembling, and students were still milling about and talking.

There, on the floor, he stood. While he looked the same, his hair still a bit long and his face golden, his round glasses low on his well-defined nose, but his manner was much changed. He held himself like a teacher. He commanded the room and spoke to the students who approached him with a knowing gaze. Soon, everyone was taking their seats, and January found one in the very back top row in the darkest corner she could locate. A student sitting next to her eyeballed her curiously as he clearly had not noticed her in this course before. She smiled at him and he blushed. I can command a room, too, she thought.

Alexander, or Dr. Lane as he was known, spoke intelligently about biology and in this class focused his lecture on the value of natural resources. He was wearing jeans, which hung low on his waist and a blue T-shirt. The jeans were worn, and he easily would've been mistaken as a student had he not been standing in front of the room. January assumed his bosses had complained about his choice of attire as any professor of a major university should not be dressed so casually. Even still, January liked it. Seeing him brought back so many feelings for her, and those feelings were extremely uncomfortable to be having in the presence of a room filled with strangers. She crossed her legs and sank down lower into her seat. The student sitting next to her looked down at her legs and then tried to avert his eyes back to his professor. January, unable to avoid a challenge, had to mess with the poor young man.

"Excuse me," she said in a whisper.

"Me?" he asked with a confused and embarrassed look on his face. He must have been around twenty-one or twenty-two, but he had the response of a fifteen-year-old boy as his voice slightly cracked.

"Yes, you. I am actually auditing this class, and I was wondering what you thought of Dr. Lane?"

"Oh, Alex? He's great, I mean, he does a really good job, ma'am."

"You just called me 'ma'am.' Wow. I mean, I am not that much older than you, but you called me 'ma'am.'"

"I'm sorry. I didn't mean offense."

"I am just messing with you. I plan to meet with Professor Lane after this course. Does he usually remain in the room for a bit or head straight out?"

"He sticks around for questions." He sniggered. "And for other stuff."

"What other stuff do you mean?"

"Oh, nothing, sorry I said that. I need to pay attention; his tests are hard."

"Sorry. No problem. Thank you." January smiled at the student, and he blushed again and, this time, leaned a bit away from her.

January smiled and took out her phone to text Alexander while she sat in his class.

I can see you.

Alexander was pointing to a mathematical equation on his board and touched his pocket as it vibrated. Ignoring it, he continued his lecture.

She texted him again.

You really should wear a tie or something. This casual outfit business cannot possibly be acceptable to your provost.

Again, he touched his pocket and kept talking. January loved higher education as much as the next person, but this class was dullsville. She sent one more text.

Okay, I tried to listen to you talk about math and science and worms and I am now completely bored out of my mind. I still want to have drinks. I will wait in the hallway for you.

January made as little fuss as she could and slid out the door unnoticed. She found a chair in the hallway and planted herself there with her purse and her phone. Surely, he would check his text messages and then meet her outside the classroom.

Surely.

****

The class was over by now, and January continued to wait. Finally, she decided to walk back inside the classroom to see if he was still in there. No point in waiting anymore, she thought. The room was slightly darkened and seemingly empty, except for the two figures on the ground floor of the classroom by the podium and blackboard. They hadn't noticed her, so she remained in the shadows while the two figures moved into one another in the soft darkness of the classroom. Because it was an auditorium style room, January was looking down onto the pair who had begun kissing and embracing in such a way that January officially felt like she was violating some type of law. They moved together in sync, and he pulled her head back and kissed her deeply. January could then make out the male figure was clearly Alexander, and he was not only kissing this young woman in his arms but pummeling her with his tongue. He had pulled her legs around him and laid her out on his desk. He seemed oblivious to anything around them as he unbuttoned her blouse and lay his lips upon her breasts which seemed firm and perfect. Her hair seemed slightly red, but the fading light made it tough to know for sure. January thought of running out the door, but she couldn't move. She was stuck there, standing by the darkened door in a corner, as though her feet were glued in cement. All she could do was watch and feel her soul fall to her feet as she stood there numb from what she was witnessing. Of course, he had someone. Of course, he did! Why would she think he didn't? She was married; he might even be married, too, for all she knew. They just didn't talk about that stuff in their letters.

And yet as much as every part of her mind told her to leave and her heart sank inside her chest begging her to look away, she just couldn't avoid seeing the two of them together.

Something about the way he was pushing himself into her and had lifted her skirt high above her hips was too familiar. It was what January had wanted so badly in the library that day back before school let out for the summer. He was making love to another woman, and now January knew she was not nor ever would be his. Not really. They had words. Words on paper. Words in texts. Words on a blinking screen but nothing like the scene unfolding before her. The young girl moaned. He was pleasing her so much she writhed and moved on the desk, kissing him, grabbing his beautiful, unkempt hair, pulling his hips deeper into her. "Oh, Alex, don't stop."

January couldn't bare it anymore, as she heard Alexander's breathing increase and then slow down, she could feel her own inner thighs tighten. Her panties dampened from watching him make love to another woman. A seemingly beautiful, younger woman. She took a deep breath as she watched them embrace and kiss while the mystery girl remained on top of the desk. She slipped out of the room and left the building as quickly as her high heels would take her. Once she reached the street, she called the taxi service and waited there to have someone take her back to the hotel. It was clear she should not be meeting him as they had originally planned.

She returned to hotel. She had training all week and a future to plan for. This had been a ridiculous idea. She was jealous, and she couldn't explain why the very thought of him loving on someone else, worshipping someone else just dug at the very pit of her soul and made her feel pain. Actual physical pain.

In her room, she opened the mini-bar and drank the first three drinks she found. Vodka, rum, something darker, maybe another kind of rum. She drank them all and laid them in the middle of her hotel bed and cried. Zak had texted to ensure she arrived safely, and she confirmed, telling him how much she missed him and how she felt it had been silly to leave. He told her it was for the good for her career, but she just felt stupid. Because at the end of the day, she had wanted to see Alexander. Just to have a drink, just to be friends, just to somehow find a way for them to be normal together. Get past the haze of whatever it was that held them together and find common ground. But no. Not now. She couldn't shake the image of him with that girl from her mind.

Her phone buzzed.

J.,

Are we still meeting? I had hoped to see you even if just for coffee. Did you stop by class? I looked for you.

A.

January sobbed into her pillow, tiny bottles of empty depression surrounded her. There was no reason she should be behaving this way. She was a married woman and had no reason to feel jealous over whomever her friend was screwing. Yet, she did care, and it filled her body with so much anger and jealousy she almost couldn't believe she was capable of those feelings.

The vodka was the first to kick in, always beating out its rum-based brethren.

She picked up her phone.

I am at the US Grant. Room 617. I want to see you, but it might be best if we take a rain check. I have too much going on this week, and I don't want to get in the way of your work.

J.

He responded quickly.

Okay. Janny, I got your other messages. You must

have seen me with Lilly or heard about her or something. I am not sure. Either way, you must know, this does not change us. Who we are. What we are and what we do for each other. I mean, you are married, and we still find a place for each other in our lives. Lilly does not remove you from my life. Please reconsider. Friends, right?

January closed her phone and buried her face in a pillow and sobbed. She cried for a man she thought she knew, she cried because he never told her, and she cried for her own marriage because what kind of marriage did she have if watching a man make love to another woman made her so jealous she could barely think straight? She had reached a new all-time low.

****

When January Morgan woke up the next morning, head aching from the liquor, she decided it was time to focus on her career and learn to be the best damn news anchor she could be. That was what brought her here after all.

Not him.

January did not return anymore texts or emails from Alexander for the remainder of her trip. She did, however, work extra hard to call Zak as often as possible and made every effort to be the best wife she could possibly be. January made a promise to herself to be better at what she had committed herself to being, and that was Zak's wife and a good journalist.

The Neon Roadside Motel, Outside Houston
3 A.M. August 2010

Alexander shot up in bed with a start. Sweat
dripping down his face, his chest, hell, his entire side of
the bed was soaked. His wife slept beside him,
undisturbed as she could sleep through a tornado. He
swung his legs over the side of the bed and felt his
boxer shorts sticking to him. He was trembling.

Walking into the bathroom, he turned on the lights,
which flickered blue for several seconds before
blinding him with a fluorescent eye-searing pain. He
washed his face in the sink and looked into the mirror.
His eyes were bloodshot. His hair, a bit longer than
usual, touched the top of his shoulders. He pushed it out
of his face and wiped his face with his towel. His
cheekbones were high and had deep shadows beneath
them because of the poor lighting. He couldn't tell if it
was just the shitty motel or if he was coming down with
something. He thought about taking a shower but didn't
want to wake up Lilly. He sat on the edge of the tub and
suddenly felt January all around him. Calling to him.
He became tense, and the trembling got worse. The
door of the bathroom started to squeak open. "Lilly, I'm
okay, just needed to use the bathroom."

It wasn't Lilly who walked in. It was January. She
was wearing a white slip which looked painted onto her
body. It was sheer, and he could see all of her through

the fabric. He started to talk, and she put her finger to his lips. "Shhhhh." She got down on her knees in front of him, her breasts heaving beneath the slip. Her pink nipples hard and protruding against the clinging fabric. He looked down at her as she rubbed her hands and nails all over his inner thighs. She began kissing his thighs and moved her mouth closer to his length. He felt like he was going to explode. He grabbed a handful of her long hair and moaned as her lips, painted the deepest red, moved around him, moving him in and out of her mouth until he thought he might die. Then she stopped and stood up, facing him. He pulled her body close and kissed her stomach and ran his hands across her breasts.

"Stay with me, Janny. Get lost with me. Let's get lost. Please, Janny. I should've touched you in the past. I want to touch you now. Please let me touch you."

As Alexander sat on the edge of the bathtub with January standing in front of him, she lifted his hand and placed it between her legs. Warm and wet and welcoming him into her. She moaned slightly as he moved his hand over the parts of her that had always been forbidden before. He could feel she was about to come.

He did come, in his sleep, rattling the motel room bed.

When he woke up just before the sun came up, his wife still sleeping beside him, he realized the dream had been so intense he really had soaked the bed.

He quickly retreated to the shower.

He needed a cigarette. He hadn't smoked a cigarette since college. But right now, he needed one. He tossed on a T-shirt and shorts, and sure enough, out on the balcony, even at five in the morning, there stood a guy smoking. The only benefit of roadside motels.

"Can I bum one of those?"

The man smiled. "Absolutely. Girlfriend trouble?"

"Not exactly. Just a really bad dream."

The man laughed. "Sometimes the bad ones are the best ones."

Alexander inhaled the smoke deeply and tried to shake the images of January's mouth between his legs out of his mind. How could he travel under these circumstances? It's like the closer he was getting to her, the worse it was becoming to keep her in the little box in his mind where she had fit so well for all these years. Now she was all over the place.

The cigarette was good. The smoke slipped from his mouth, and he imagined it was her he was exhaling. Whatever it took to get his head right. Perhaps this move was a terrible idea, after all.

Miami

January was relishing in the praise she was receiving for her coverage of the Sullivan cold case, and Zak was being commended for his work in busting up a major drug king pin and human trafficking ring. They were, by all accounts, on top of the world.

"We need to celebrate!" January kissed Zak's neck as they lay in bed beside each other for the first time in weeks. "Maybe we could start right now." She started kissing his chest and put her legs around him, so she was sitting on his lap. "Come on, Zak. Celebrate with me. Maybe we could fool around and then go have lunch somewhere on Bayshore."

Zak smiled, his face tanned and handsome. He did not look tired for the first time in weeks, and January knew he was finally getting a moment to think about other cases again and maybe even her. "You are so goddamn sexy, Janny."

He flipped her around so that he was on top of her and pulled her lace nighty down to reveal her breasts. He ran his mouth over both, biting softly until she moaned. She raised her hips to meet his and could feel how hard he was. "I know things haven't been great with us, Janny. But we can move forward now. You've had your big story, and I've had my big case. Maybe it's time you step away from TV for awhile. Take a break. It's not like we need the money."

January sat up, pushing Zak off her. "Leave TV now? Are you out of your mind? This story is getting me noticed, Zak. I might land a better job because of this. This is only the beginning. No, I am only going to work harder now, more than ever. I don't do what I do for money anyway."

Zak shrugged. He pushed her back down onto the bed. "Fine, but we aren't moving away from here. I have a shot at lieutenant because of my busts. I need that promotion." He leaned down over her. "Open your legs."

January wasn't feeling quite as amorous as before, but she couldn't deny she needed him. It had been weeks since they'd made love.

"I said, open your legs." He pushed her legs apart. "You like it when I'm a little rough with you, don't you?"

January was breathing heavy, the space between her legs wet, and wanting him. "Yes, I do like it." She moaned. "Oh, Zak, I need you inside of me."

"Not yet." He flipped her, over onto her stomach. She could feel cold metal being moved slowly along her back. "Give me your wrists."

She moved her arms behind her back, and he put his handcuffs on her, a little too tightly. "Now you won't get away from me when I touch you."

January couldn't move, her heart was beating, and she could feel the sweat dripping down between her breasts. He lifted her nightgown up from behind. "Your ass is so firm, so creamy white. I'm going to kiss you down there." He lifted her up, so she was on her knees, her face in the pillow, her hands cuffed behind her back. "You are going to let me do whatever I want to you." He ran his tongue all over her sex, moving it in and out rapidly and then slowly bringing her closer to ecstasy each time and then pulling away. "You taste so good, baby, like honey." He pushed his finger inside of her, forcing her to shout out, and then he moved them slowly into her, rubbing her clit with his thumb.

"Oh, Zak, I need it…"

He took his hand and spanked her hard on her right butt cheek. It hurt and January was not expecting it. She screamed.

"You need to be spanked. You don't listen to me at all. You need to remember you are the wife. *My* wife." He spanked her again, harder than before. Her knees bucked, and she fell flat onto the bed, on her stomach. "No," he said sternly, "back up with you. Don't be so weak." He pulled her back up, her wrists rubbing raw from the handcuffs. Then he removed his shorts and kissed the place on her behind that he had hurt. "My poor little girl. Now I am going to fuck you. I am going to fuck you hard, so you remember to listen to me, so you remember you belong to me."

He pushed himself inside her with such force that January's knees bucked again. He pulled her back up and sat her on his lap with her facing the wall away from him. He moved her up and down on him, pulling her back with the handcuffs and pulling her back by her hair. Zak was being so aggressive with her. He had never taken her like this before. He unlocked the cuffs and turned her around, so her back was on the bed. Leaning over her, he pushed her legs apart which were numb, and entered her again.

"Janny, I'm going to make you come so hard you get your head out of the clouds and remember who I am and what I can do to you."

He pushed her and pushed her to the brink. Her aching wrists, he pinned behind her head as he continued to fill her up with every part of himself. When January climaxed, she felt the waves of pleasure hit her strongly, repeatedly, until she felt she might go unconscious. "Oh, God…"

Zak began biting her nipples as she came. "I want you to say my name."

"Zak, oh, Zak, I…I…oh, God, Zak." January was breathing so hard she was practically panting. He kissed her long and slow, moving his tongue inside her mouth and then back onto her breasts. Another wave a pleasure took her, making her whole body shake.

"I am not done with you yet." Zak got up from the bed while January lay there, trembling, her nipples red and her wrists bruised. He opened the closet and took out a whip. "You need to be spanked some more, Janny. You need to be spanked until you learn to obey your husband."

His body was glistening with sweat, his broad chest, muscular and beautiful, was on top of her once more.

January was spent and wanted to fight him. "No, Zak, can we stop…"

"Are you fucking kidding me? We've gone weeks without time together, and I plan to make this time memorable."

Weak from everything she had enjoyed and endured, she couldn't fight him. He picked her up and wrapped her legs around his waist. Pushing her against the bedroom wall, he pushed himself into her again. She was becoming sore, but he just went faster and harder into her. She moaned loudly, begging Zak to slow down, but this only spurred him on to damage her more. "You don't get to waltz around here looking so fuckable all the time. I've seen other men looking at you. I know that worthless-ass Frank at work wants to fuck you. But he can't fuck you. You're mine." He pushed her into the wall and held her up as he pushed into her over and over again. Then he took her back to the bed, laying her down on her stomach, her already red behind there for his viewing. "I like seeing you like this. Helpless." He took the whip and ran it over her thighs and between her legs against her swollen sex, and then he smacked her behind with it. Lightly at first, and then harder. He did this several times before January screamed for him to stop.

"No, Zak, no more. I can't handle it anymore."

He rubbed her behind lightly with his hand, massaging both sides. "Oh, baby, I needed that. I needed it so much."

January rolled over onto her side and pulled a blanket over herself. Zak lay down behind her and put his arms around her. "You needed it, too. Didn't you, my love?"

January was speechless. She had felt such intense ecstasy, and then he just wouldn't stop which had been overwhelming to her. "Yes, Zak, I needed you."

Zak took a deep breath and kissed the back of January's head. "I've just been so pent up, you know. My job, it's just too much sometimes. And then seeing that fucker Frank eyeballing you like that. I just couldn't handle it."

"It's okay, Zak. And you don't have to worry about Frank. He is just a friend and barely even that. He's your coworker. I love you. You are my husband."

"Damn right, I am. You lay there and rest up a bit. I'm going to get in a long run and take a shower. When I get back, I am going to need you again."

He kissed January on her back and patted her rear. "You are so good. So very good."

January lay there as she heard Zak leave the apartment. She was so happy they had finally been able to be alone together, but this was not quite what she had expected. It seemed like Zak was liking his lovemaking to be more violent these days. Not that she minded the occasional aggressive version of him, but that was all she seemed to get lately. Each time was like this now. The sweetness of their intimacy seemed to have evaporated.

January did not feel loved by Zak as she once had but rather owned by him and used by him when he needed release. There was no talk about children or taking trips or making plans. There was only work. He used to look at her lovingly, and now he looked right past her. Even when he was inside of her, it was like he was somewhere else.

January retreated to the bathroom to take a hot bath after Zak left for his run. She took a glass of whiskey in there with her. As she lay in the warm, soapy water of her large claw foot tub, her mind wandered to Alexander. With each sip of the warming, medicinal whiskey, she could feel him getting closer to her. He had said they were arriving in Miami sometime tomorrow.

She checked her phone.

J.,

Closer to you. Closer to the unknown. Closer to

trying to be your friend. Just your friend. Only your friend. Forever your friend. I just need two days. Two days should do it. The first day to grow accustomed to seeing your face and talking to you in person. The second day to feel the fog of our long, unrequited emotional affair lifted so that we may exist as normal adults with nothing to hide.

Closer to you. Always aching the closer to you I get. I might need another day to deal with that, too. You have been haunting my dreams and I feel heady.

Yours,

A.

January sank deeper into the water, letting the warm suds envelope her aching body. Her wrists, red and bruised from the handcuffs, were stinging from the soap. She finished the whiskey and closed her eyes. Heady, she thought. She made him feel heady. His words clung to her mind and filled her heart as she felt the tears fall down her cheeks. Soon, Zak would return, and she knew he would want more of her in the way he had just had her. Or worse, he would not want her at all. She knew one thing was for certain, he would not be giving her what she really needed right now which was to feel loved, comforted. January began thinking it was time to have a talk with Zak about their future. The first few years had been wonderful and fun. They had been a team, but since his father had died and since he had moved to major crimes, he had simply not been the same man.

Arrival

Lilly was beyond excited to get to Miami. The drive had been a long one with far too many stops at far too many shady little motels and gas stations. There had been a fun night in Louisiana along the way but driving with a hangover the day after on very little sleep had set them back a whole day. "The apartment is supposed to be just down this street. Wow! Coral Gables is so pretty! And super close to campus for you. Even closer to Sotheby's. This area is going to be perfect!" Lilly was practically hanging her head out the moving truck window. "Smell that sea air!"

Alexander was glad to see her so happy, and she was right. Coral Gables was a nice area. They would have to eventually find a house here, but for now, they had found a nice little apartment to rent. He knew what she was thinking, big house on the water and plenty of children. They had been pregnant once. Right before he married her. It was part of what pushed them along into the whole marriage thing. He had been with her for just a few months, and they were all over each other. All the time, even in his classrooms and his office. The whole student-teacher thing was officially out of hand, but he cared for her. He loved her optimistic nature and her love of life. He always thought he would have eventually married her anyway. But three months into their whirlwind romance, she discovered she was pregnant.

Alexander was initially freaked out. He had not planned on children and had barely even thought of marriage. He was focused on his job and was, quite frankly, just messing around. Lilly was not his only student affair, but she was the one he liked best. Then, there she was, standing in his apartment, holding a stick with two blue lines on it. She had been crying and was concerned about not finishing school, her career plans being destroyed, and then there was even a mention of not keeping the kid. Alexander had fought that idea immediately. "No, Lilly, I love you. We fit, you and me. We will love this little person," he had said. His voice filled with fear. He did care for her, and he truly believed he could be a good father. His own father had been a good one to him. "I'll teach him to play guitar and how to write a solid dissertation," Alexander had said as he held her. Lilly had laughed and cried at the same time, but in the end, they both agreed they could raise the baby and be happy together. They already were happy together. He had her move out of her dorm and into his apartment, and they were engaged within a month. They got married when she was about four months along, so she wasn't even showing yet, but they had already found out they were having a boy.

Alexander was over the moon. Something that had been so terrifying suddenly became the most wonderful thing he had ever imagined doing. They spent time together, planning their future and thinking of names for the little one. His world had fallen into place, unexpectedly but beautifully.

Until one night, just before she had reached twenty-eight weeks, she woke up in pain, and the bed was bloody. Lilly was heartbroken and barely spoke for weeks. Alexander took a semester off work, and they tried to survive the nightmare together. It was singularly the worst thing Alexander had ever endured, and it was far worse for Lilly. After they lost their baby, he had committed himself even more to her, promising himself to be a good husband and to give their marriage every chance it deserved with or without a child. Secretly, Lilly was so devastated she thought about leaving Alexander and leaving school. It had all been too much too fast and she felt broken. Alexander had refused to give up on her and promised her a wonderful life, despite their strange and difficult start.

Now they were here, in a beautiful new city with all the possibility of trying new things and maybe even making that family they had almost once had. Pulling the truck into the parking lot of the apartment building was a relief. Alexander turned off the truck ignition and leaned over to kiss his beautiful Lilly. "I love you, ya know. We're going to love Florida."

"I love you, too." She smiled, her golden eyes shining against her copper hair. "I am ready to get out of this truck and start unpacking. But first, let's disconnect our car from this giant heap of a truck and go find a beach bar."

"Best idea I have heard all day."

The apartment was basic. A two-bedroom empty box fortunately on the bottom floor. "Only temporary," Lilly said. "Until we find the right place on the water for your boat."

"Ah, yeah, my boat. I do miss having her around."

"Well, soon you will have both women in your life!" Lilly laughed as she carried a box into the apartment.

Yeah, both women, Alexander thought. While Lilly was unpacking, he sent a quick text to the dean of the university to confirm he had arrived. And he sent a text to January.

J,

I hope this day is treating you well. We are here, in Coral Gables. Settling in. Maybe next week we can have coffee?

A.

January responded.

A.,

Welcome to your new home. I just left Coral Gables after landing a pretty amazing story. I did the follow up with a family of a murdered child today. Watch me tonight on the news, if you get bored.

J.

Alexander had not really thought about it before, but he would be able to watch January on television every day now. The strangeness of that would add another element to this already strange situation. But it doesn't have to be strange, he thought. We are going to make this work as friends. As he unloaded a few more boxes with his wife, he took her into his arms and held her close. "I love you so very much. A new start and maybe we can revisit the idea of a family?"

Lilly's face fell. "Too soon for that talk. Let's focus on getting settled first." It was clear she still was not finished dealing with the pain, but Alexander hoped their new life here would help her heal. Lilly picked up another box and smiled at Alexander. "Don't think I'm not up to it. I just need to get settled in my new job and make sure we have a better place to live. I love you, too, honey, and I do want a family with you. Let's just unpack a little and grab that beer first."

"Fair enough. I don't mean to push. I just want you to be happy."

"You make me very happy." Lilly wrapped her arms around her husband and pulled him close. "We should swing by campus, so you can check out your new digs as well. Plus, I called my sister, and she invited us over for a barbecue tomorrow at her house."

Alexander's head was swimming. There was far too much to do and a new job to start next week. He took a deep breath and picked up a box.

****

That night, as Alexander and Lilly sat on their couch watching the TV, which was situated on top of a milk crate temporarily, the evening news came on.

Lily sighed. "No news. It's so filled with evil. I would rather watch nothing at all."

"I want to catch a few minutes of it, if I can. I need to get to know the community, and what better way than to watch the local news?"

"Oh, I don't know, living in the community seems a better way to me. The news is selective and does not represent an entire city with its coverage. In fact, I think journalism is so biased these days. It's basically pointless."

"Wow, Lilly, I had no idea you hated journalism so much."

She pointed to the screen as the news anchors opened the show with what they called "breaking news."

"This is not journalism. And they use the phrase 'breaking news' for things that do not even fit that phrase. Let's go to bed. I am beat."

The male news anchor continued, "Tonight at eleven, we continue our follow up on the ever-evolving cold case of a missing Coral Gables girl, Danielle Sullivan, who disappeared near her home twenty years ago. Our own crime beat reporter January Morgan had the exclusive when DNA evidence tied a current Dade County inmate to an item of Danielle's clothing found a few days after she went missing. Now, we have new information, and we go live to News 7's January Morgan with the latest reporting from the Dade County jail. January?"

January stood in front of the jail, a bright light illuminating her from the darkness. She was wearing a black suit, and her hair was loose on her shoulders. Her face was serious and her eyes intense as she began her report.

"Thank you, Alan. Yes, breaking news tonight in the Sullivan cold case. I first reported to you that suspect Randall Marshall, already in custody for an alleged sexual assault on a child, submitted his DNA for review. That DNA not only matched the victim he is now in jail for allegedly attacking, but it hit on something else, too. A pair of blue pants that belonged to thirteen-year-old Danielle Sullivan, who disappeared while riding her bike home from school back in 1990. Tonight, I have here with me Detective Frank Williams with the latest break in the case."

Frank entered the shot and stood beside January. He looked nervous and kept his eyes on her. "Detective Williams, this is your case. What can you tell us about suspect Randall Marshall, the DNA match, and what the suspect has revealed to you?"

She held the microphone out in front of Frank, who pulled a little at his necktie. "Well, January, Mr. Marshall was not cooperative at first, but as you reported earlier, he made some damaging statements when you interviewed him. Today, he revealed to me and two other detectives the details of that tragic day, telling us that he not only kidnapped Danielle Sullivan, but sexually assaulted her, and eventually strangled her to death. He has given a full confession and has also revealed where he allegedly took Danielle's body."

"Can you comment further on that at this time?"

"No, we are still working on that particular piece of information and working closely with the Sullivan family, as you can imagine this is a very tough time for them."

"Yes, it certainly is. Thank you, detective."

When January was back on camera alone and looking right into the lens, Alexander felt like she was looking at him for a moment, which was jarring, as she continued her story.

"Tomorrow, I will have an exclusive ride-along with the Miami Dade Police forensics unit and Detective Williams as the search for Danielle's body begins. For now, Randall Marshall has officially been charged with kidnapping, but until the body is located, a homicide charge cannot be added. Reporting live downtown, January Morgan, WSVN 7 News."

Alexander leaned back into the couch. January had been right. This was a big story. He was proud of her. She had really grown as a reporter and had the chops now to really tell the hard stories.

Lilly yawned. "Sad story. Now I get to go to bed depressed."

Alexander was still staring at the screen.

"Hello," Lilly said. "Earth to husband."

"Oh, sorry, yeah, that is quite the story." He turned off the television and looked over at Lilly. "I used to know her."

"Know who?" Lilly was curious.

"That news reporter. We went to college together. Just for a couple semesters, but I remember her."

"Small world, huh?"

"Yeah, it is."

They both got up from the couch and headed to their bedroom, their mattress on the floor because Alexander had not put the bed together just yet. Somehow mentioning he knew January made him feel better. At least, that was out there. That was something. A step forward in diminishing the secret of her.

As he lay in bed that night, the moonlight filtering through the cheap apartment blinds, he thought of January standing there in front of the camera. That look in her eyes as she spoke to the camera but, at the same time, speaking to every unseen individual person watching her. So many sets of eyeballs on her. It overwhelmed Alexander to think about how she could do that job so effortlessly. It was like she was just talking to a group of close friends. She came across in a way that made you *want* to watch her. Alexander did, in fact, want to watch her. As he drifted to sleep, his body aching from the move, January's face clouded his subconscious while Lilly's arms were around him.

University of Miami

It was singularly one of the hottest days of the summer so far. Even though the heat was not as bad as Arizona, the humidity was so beyond awful; it made it tough to breathe. After a long morning of trying to find a suitable suit to wear and the coffee, both of which were packed in boxes marked "miscellaneous," Alexander was lucky he found anything he needed to make it to his first day of school. He had paperwork to fill out in human resources, a bunch of school safety videos to endure, and he was supposed to meet with the dean. As associate dean of the university, Alexander would be working with this man daily, so he hoped the chemistry they seemed to have in the interview was not just a fluke.

The campus was still mostly empty as students had not yet moved back for fall semester, but there were a lot of faculty members already there, setting up their offices and preparing for the craziness that would soon descend. Alexander pulled into a parking spot in an area made for faculty and quickly ran a brush through his tousled hair. Adjusting his glasses and dusting off his soft gray suit jacket, he felt as ready as he would ever be. He had forgotten a tie but hoped that would not be a point of contention. Every university was different, but generally, high-level staff were expected to dress well. He grabbed his brown leather bag, stuffed some paperwork inside of it, and headed to the main administration building.

A young woman sitting behind a desk in the lobby greeted him with a smile. She appeared to be a graduate student. "Why, hello, sir. Can I help you?" She was blushing.

Alexander smiled at her, sensing her embarrassment. "Yes, I am Alexander Lane. Here to meet with Dean Walters. I am the new associate dean. I guess you could say today is my first day of school."

She giggled and blushed even more. "Okay, I will let his secretary know you are here, Dr. Lane."

"Alex."

She laughed again. "There is no way in hell I am calling the new associate dean by his first name. But thanks. Have a seat, and Ms. Harris will be out to get you soon."

The young woman slid down a bit in her chair and returned to reading her book. Advanced physics. Impressive.

Alexander sat down and waited, checking to make sure he had all the documents they had asked him to bring in. He checked his phone, too. A good luck text from Lilly blinked from the screen. She was going to be interviewing at Sotheby's today, so this was a big day for her, too. He responded to her with "*Knock 'em dead, babe.*"

Everything about this was nerve-wracking. New job, new city, tiny apartment, wife looking for a new job, and of course, January on his TV. Alexander was overwhelmed by the changes but optimistic it would all work out in the end. January and Alexander had always been each other's muses, giving the other inspiration to get through the not-so-creative times. Alexander really believed they would find a way to evolve their relationship and become better friends. Had it been in the cards for them to be anything but friends, that would have happened already, and seeing as it had not, it was perfectly fine to imagine a life with her as a friend. He loved her. There was no question about that, but he did not know if qualifying it as romantic love was even accurate anymore. It was a deep love that filled his soul and made his mind churn in ways he didn't know it was even capable of. They simply inspired one another to be more creative people. The connection between them was indescribable, but it was not intended to be romantic. Alexander wished a psychology professor was sitting beside him right now, so he could hear his or her take on the matter.

He imagined the shrink would laugh him out of the room. Denial, they would say. Alexander just needed to bury himself in his work and make sure Lilly was happy here. He had great hopes for her at Sotheby's. While she had never worked at an auction house before, her knowledge of art and antiquities was unmatched by most people in the profession. She had been an amazing curator, and she would, no doubt, be wonderful with antiques.

A gray-haired woman wearing a tan pantsuit entered the lobby. Alexander stood up to shake her hand.

"I am Elsa Harris, Dean Walters's executive assistant. It's nice to meet you, Dr. Lane."

"You as well, ma'am. I am looking forward to getting started."

"Well, we have a pretty full day planned for you,

starting with human resources. I know that will not be the highlight of the day, of course." She laughed. "But the dean would like to take you to lunch when you are finished with your paperwork."

"Sounds great. Thank you."

"First, I will take you to your office, so you can get acquainted with your space, and then we will head over to HR."

Through two large wooden doors and down a long hallway, Alexander passed room after room, some of which had a person sitting behind a desk furiously typing away at their computers. A few of the unfamiliar faces looked up and eyed him suspiciously. "This is our faculty area, so most of these offices are administrative and some are professors," Elsa pointed out as they walked. "Your office is right here, across from the dean's." The door was also dark wood and had been recently stained as the smell was still quite strong. "We just repainted it, so I apologize for the smell, but we wanted it to look nice for you, Dr. Lane."

He stepped inside and looked around. The office was huge.

"I'll give you a few minutes and come back to get you to take you over to HR. I will bring coffee with me. How do you take yours?"

"Ah, oh, just black. Thank you."

Alexander walked into the office and gasped. "Holy shit."

The room was quite large and filled with molding and high-walled wainscoting all in a deep mahogany. The paint was a soft shade of cream, and the curtains were orange and green, the school colors. His desk was a large wooden spectacle of a thing right next to a big window overlooking the campus. His name plate was already there, gleaming at him like a new penny. "Dr. Alexander Lane, Associate Dean. Nice."

Half of the office was set up like a small living room with a couch and a couple chairs, and there was still plenty of space for bookshelves and a round conference table, which would easily hold six people. "Now *this* is an office." Alexander walked over to his chair and sat down. It was real leather, and it felt good on his aching back. He logged in to his campus desktop, and his schedule came up on the screen.

A slight knock at his door. "Umm, Dr. Lane. It's Sally from the front desk. Elsa said you needed coffee?"

"Why yes, Sally. Thank you." She walked the cup of steaming coffee over to him and placed it on his desk. "I appreciate it."

"No problem. Nice office, doc."

"It is, isn't it? So, advanced physics?"

"I'm sorry?"

"Your textbook. Out in the lobby?"

"Oh, yeah. I am getting a master's in physics and aeronautics. I plan to work for NASA."

"Damn. You have a solid plan."

"I do."

"Well, good luck, Sally. I hope to see you around campus."

She blushed again. "Yeah, I'm sure you will. I work here most days in between classes. Good luck in HR. That woman can be a bit of a pain, just so you know."

"Thanks for the heads up." Alexander smiled, raising his eyebrow over his glasses. He knew he was getting to her and tried not to enjoy it. But he did. She left the office and closed the door. "Still got it, Lane."

Dr. Alexander Lane stood up, coffee in hand, and stared outside his oversized window, overlooking the campus quad. He was beginning to wonder why he even doubted making this decision, even for a second.

He belonged here.

****

January was sitting at her desk, making notes for her next story. Soon, she would be meeting the forensics team to search for Danielle's body. This was a big day, and no other station had the access she had. In fact, they had all been left in the dust, scrambling to get sound bites from the police department long after her story had aired. The Sullivans weren't talking to any other press, so she had them exclusively, too. At this point, it was safe to say January was winning. Her boss had noticed and had been by to congratulate her several times. Their ratings were spiking. She was being asked to fill in on the anchor desk, which had not happened in a long time. Her star was rising in a way it had not before. "'Bout fucking time," she muttered to herself. January was feeling amped up today, and she was ready to take this story to its bitter end.

Another reporter, Carl Chambers, walked up to her desk. "Hey there, girl of the moment." Carl's teeth sparkled, and his bright fuchsia tie was blinding.

"Hey, Carl, how are you today?" January kept typing her notes and barely looked up.

"Some of the other reporters and I are planning to hit a bar tonight and blow off some steam after the eleven. You in?"

January could use a night out and nodded. "Yes, I

am definitely in. What's the place called?"

"It's a little pub called Flannery McNasty." He couldn't contain his laughter. "I mean, with a name like that we have to go, right?"

January smiled. "Yeah, I should think so. I will meet you all there after my live shot."

Carl put his hand on January's shoulder. "Good. It will be nice to hang out with you outside of this place." He sauntered back over to his desk in the bull pen. January's shoulder tingled. She was not a fan of people touching her like that, but Carl was a bit of a touchy person. So many of his stories contained a shot of him hugging a victim or leaning in for an empathetic arm on the shoulder. It worked for Carl, but January thought it was ridiculous. She, by nature, was not a hugger.

The news room was buzzing today, with multiple reporters running around with scripts in hand, typing scripts on their computers, and getting an assignment from the assignment desk. Lots of news to cover between the drug shootings, the same ones her husband had been investigating, a few local political races, and just the regular daily beat stuff. But it was January's story, if a body was found, that would be the lead. The damn lead, she thought. Smiling to herself, she printed out her notes, grabbed her bag, her earpiece, and the giant energy drink on her desk.

"Get that body!" Carl shouted from the bull pen.

"Geez, Carl!" January shouted as she headed for the door. "See you at the pub later, everyone!"

Lenny was outside loading up the live truck. "You surely brought a change of clothes, right?" He looked her up and down.

"Of course, I did! I packed jeans, a Channel 7 T-shirt, and hiking boots. Trust me, I do not plan to miss a second of this." January had planned to change from her skirt and top in the news truck, depending on where they ended up going. They still had no idea where Randall Marshall had said he dumped the body.

She took her seat in the truck and reapplied her makeup using the scratched-up mirror in the glove box. This mirror had been used by a hundred different reporters over the years. Her phone started buzzing.

"Hello?"

"Hey, Janny." It was Zak, and he didn't sound good. "I'm having a bit of a tough day." His voice sounded slurred.

"Are you drunk?"

"Maybe just a little."

"Where are you?"

"With some of the guys. We hit a bar."

"It's only two o'clock. A bit early, don't you think?"

"Don't judge me, Janny. I was up all night working that fuckin' drug case. I needed a release. And since you are nowhere to be found…"

"Zak, I'm working today. I will be home after the news tonight. Is anyone with you?"

"You mean Frank? Hey, Frank," he shouted into the noisy abyss behind him, "You wanna talk to my wife?"

There was a banging sound, like the phone dropped. "Hey, January. It's Frank. I'll make sure he gets home okay. I have to head out to meet forensics in a few. See you out there?"

"Yeah, we are already on our way. Frank, thank you. I am so sorry about this."

"He's just had a rough case. It happens to us all."

Zak took his phone back, his words jumbled together from the alcohol. "Yeah, see, baby. Frankie has it all under control. Janny, did you like our little party the other day? I could use some more of that."

"Zak, I love you, but you need to get it together. Please. Let Frank take you home, so you can rest. I will see you tonight. It'll be okay."

"Fuck that. Nothing is okay. Hey, honey, come over here."

"Zak, are you at a strip club?"

"Yeah, but it's not a good one. I have yet to get an offer for one goddamn lap dance." January could hear Frank in the background, trying to help Zak out of the bar.

"Go home, Zak. Just go home. I love you."

"She loves me, Frank! The hot piece of ass reporter loves me!"

"Zak, I am your wife. Remember that."

"Oh, I know you're my wife. You can show me tonight."

Then the phone went dead.

January sat in the passenger seat of the news truck as Lenny pretended to focus on the road. "You okay, Ace?"

"No, not so much, Lenny. Zak is going through a bit of a rough patch. I don't know how to help him."

"Cops have a hard job, Janny. I can only imagine how they cope with what they see and deal with every day. I'm sure he just needs to sleep it off."

"Yeah, that'll be a start."

January wiped the tears from her eyes and fixed her makeup. I've got a story to cover, she thought. Things were not well with Zak, and she didn't know what to do to help him. She decided to talk to him tomorrow about maybe looking at counseling. Maybe they could both go. She loved her husband, but his downward spiral was getting worse. It would affect his job soon if it hadn't already. She was grateful to Frank for helping Zak get home. What a mess.

January received a text message from her friend Nancy in forensics. *Be at Marshall's old address in Coral Gables as soon as possible. The place he lived when Danielle went missing.*

"All right, Lenny, we got our location. Head to the scumbag's old house, the one he shared with his mother when Danielle was taken."

"On it."

That whole street had been searched by cadaver dogs for weeks after she went missing. All the streets in that area had been searched, and nothing was ever found. A new family had moved into the house fifteen years earlier. What did they think could be there? Maybe some evidence? January could feel her stomach turn to knots just thinking about it.

When they arrived at the small home on the corner of Hibiscus Street, yellow crime scene tape had already been put up all around the house. The home was a typical Florida one-story block house, painted a shade of pale blue. The flowers were well kept, and the lawn had been recently mowed. At least, four marked cruisers were parked along the street and two unmarked. Multiple neighbors, including the people who owned the home now, were standing in the middle of the street, arms folded, shaking their heads in confusion. The forensics tent appeared to be set up in the backyard, and Nancy walked around the house when she saw the news truck.

"Hey," Nancy said, sounding rushed, "I can't take you back until the detective gets here, but we are investigating in the backyard."

January stepped out of the truck and looked around. Soon other media would get tipped off to all the activity, and she would lose her exclusive. It was only a matter of time before news helicopters would be circling overhead. "Where are the Sullivans?"

"We have them staying at their home with a deputy there to make sure they are left alone while we conduct our investigation."

"I thought this street had been checked back in 1990." January was confused.

"It was. But we didn't use cadaver dogs back then. Plus, Randall Marshall claims he, well, I can't say, Janny. Wait for Frank." She was wearing her all-black forensic uniform which could not have been comfortable in this heat.

"Okay, Lenny, let's get out the camera and get ready to roll. I think I see Frank's car approaching up ahead. Also, let's get tuned in with the satellite truck, so we can feed back everything as quickly as possible. We should be ready for a live cut-in. I won't let another station steal this from us."

January fixed her hair in the truck's side mirror and checked her teeth for lipstick. "As good as it's going to get in this humidity," she mumbled.

Frank got out of his car and approached January, dark sunglasses shrouding the expression behind them. "So," she asked, "how is he?"

Frank wiped the sweat from his forehead with a

cloth he pulled from a pocket. "Janny, you need to get him some help. If he doesn't get his shit together, it's going to start affecting his work. More so than it already is. As it stands, our captain is eyeballing him and his behavior. There have been complaints. He used to be nice to me, but now he just comes in, hangs out at his desk, and won't speak to anyone. He's slipping."

"I will see if he is willing to meet with a therapist or something. I don't know what else to do."

Frank looked at January's arm, noticing a slight bruise. "He do that to you?"

"Frank, no, I'm fine. Like you said, he's having a rough time. I will get him some help."

"So help me, Janny, if he's hurting you!"

"Frank, I got this. Thank you for your help today. Now I need you to get me behind that house."

"All right. Let's go." He stomped off ahead, leaving January to walk quickly in her heels. Lenny was following with his camera, and the mast was up on the truck. They would be able to go live in a moment's notice if needed.

"So, Frank," January began as she followed him through the lawn, "why are we here?"

"Randall Marshall said he buried her here."

"But you guys checked this area. I read about it in the case file."

"He waited. He kept her alive in a different location for three weeks before he finally killed her. He said he then brought her here and buried her beneath the back porch. After we had called off the neighborhood search. He called it 'bringing her home,' the sick bastard."

"Three weeks?"

"Yes, he claims he held her at an old warehouse about ten miles from here. I already have techs out there looking for evidence. He said he fed her, but eventually she tried to escape, and that was when he strangled her. He claims to have put her body in a blanket and buried her here one night when his mom was working the night shift at her factory job."

"Shit."

"Yes, shit indeed. Let's go see what they've found, shall we?"

"Okay, Lenny, let's start recording." January's heart was beating ferociously in her chest.

"Hey, what's she doing back here?" a uniformed deputy asked as Frank led January under the yellow tape.

"She has exclusivity on this story and aided in Randall Marshall's confession. She's also been asked by the family to act as their liaison. Kind of like a victim's advocate."

"Fine, but she needs to be careful what she shows."

"I will, sir."

Frank walked inside the white tent to get an idea of what was happening while January and Lenny waited outside, the eyes of angry, distrusting officers upon them.

January was nervous. She had never been this close to a crime scene before. Her phone buzzed. It was Zak calling. She hit ignore. No time for this right now. Just no time. She hoped he would just sleep it off.

Frank reemerged from the tent, sweat pouring down his tanned cheeks. "Okay, Janny, we have found pieces of a blanket and human remains. Consistent with Marshall's confession. I can't let you get video of that, but I can let you shoot the exteriors of the tent, police activity, and I have been given permission to give you a soundbite on what we have found. The body is still not identified as being her. The bones need to be sent to the medical examiner's office, but so far, it's all matching up with his statements."

Lenny collected a few shots while Frank wiped off his face in preparation for an on-camera interview.

"Thank you, Frank."

"You deserve this. You've worked this story for a long time and kept it in the spotlight, even when no one cared."

"You deserve this, too. Prepare for the networks to be calling you by tonight."

"I am not doing any formal interviews with anyone else until the Sullivans know what we have found."

"Good call. Thank you again. You have helped my career in a way you cannot imagine. I finally feel like I did something good as a reporter and have helped find justice for a family. This means the world to me."

Frank smiled and took off his sunglasses. "Anytime, news girl."

"All right, Lenny, are we ready for the live?"

Lenny was on the phone with their producer back at the station. "Yep, up in two minutes."

She faced the camera, keeping Frank to her side, and adjusted her necklace, the one Alexander had bought for her so many years before. In her earpiece, she could hear the anchor in the studio: "We go live now to January Morgan in Coral Gables with a shocking discovery on Hibiscus Street, just one street over from where Danielle Sullivan went missing twenty years before. January, what can you tell us?"

January straightened herself and looked into the lens. "We are live at the former home of suspect Randall Marshall. He lived here with his mother during the time of Danielle Sullivan's disappearance. In an interview with police, he confessed to burying her body here behind the house, several weeks after her disappearance. You can see the forensics tent behind me. This is a very active scene right now, as human remains have been discovered. Those remains have not been confirmed to be Danielle's, but a medical examiner will soon make that determination. Detective Frank Williams, who is the lead detective on the case, joins me now with more. Detective, what can you tell us about the investigation so far?"

Frank stepped into the shot beside January. "Randall Marshall has been very forthcoming, and so far, his statements have been supported. He told us we would find something here and we did. Now, what happened in the alleged three weeks after he kidnapped her is what we need to know. We also want to confirm what we found today is indeed Danielle Sullivan's body. Still a lot of work ahead of us, but for the first time in a long time, we are making progress toward a formal first-degree murder charge."

"Detective, thank you for your time." January faced the camera again for her outcue. "So that is the latest breaking news from Coral Gables, as police have found what appear to be human remains at the former home of suspect Randall Marshall. I will continue to follow this story and bring the newest information, first, as soon as it becomes available. In Coral Gables, January Morgan, WSVN 7 News."

"And you're clear," Lenny said. "Good work, news

girl." He laughed as he flipped his baseball cap around backwards.

Nancy and another woman walked out of the tent, carrying a small body bag on a stretcher. Nancy shook her head at January, her eyes red from crying.

"All right, Frank. Thank you. I am going back to the studio for the late show."

Frank looked concerned. "Then home to Zak, right?"

"Of course. He needs me right now. I just hope he's been resting. Maybe I can convince him to take a few days off."

"Good luck with that. His drug case is now full-fledged human trafficking. He is not going to want to let that one go. It stretches all the way to the cartels."

"Lovely. Well, I will do the best I can. He's my husband. I love him, and he just needs a little extra care right now. We all do sometimes."

Frank glanced at her arm again. "Yeah, as long as that caring doesn't come with pain."

"Frank. Stop."

He shook his head. "Okay, Janny. Good luck." He walked back inside the tent.

January and Lenny drove back to the studio for her in-studio story. She would package everything from the day together and get to intro it from the set with the anchors. A rare thing set aside for very special stories. She was excited about the chance to be back on the set. It had been awhile since she was an anchor. She sometimes missed the chair.

As she sat in the green room, sipping iced coffee and refreshing her makeup, her phone buzzed. Zak texted her. *You coming home soon?*

January sighed. *Yes, after the 11. I have one more live hit and then I am done. Are you doing any better?*

I guess. I'm sorry about today. It's been a tough week for me.

Yeah, for me, too. We can work on this together, Zak. Just let me help you.

We can talk later. I'm going back to sleep now. Terrible headache.

I should say so. All right, I'll be home later. I love you.

No response.

"Great, just great." January felt defeated. She needed a break from all of this. He was so negative all the time and not loving toward her at all. She decided to text Alexander.

A,

How was your first day at school?

J.

J.,

Quite amazing. How was your hunt for a body?

A.

Also amazing. When can we have some coffee? I am feeling a bit overwhelmed and could use your friendship right now. I need conversation with someone who doesn't use the words "dead body" or "drug pimp" in a typical day.

Please.

J.

J.,

I will try my hardest to give you the conversation you so desperately require. Still a bit too soon. Trying to get settled in, you know? Will you be gracing my television again tonight?

A.

Yes. Tune in and watch me. I need all the viewers I can get. Big break today. Big.

You amaze me, Janny. Seeing you on television is still a bit strange for me, but I'll take it, until I can have the real thing in front of me again. At an acceptable distance, of course.

Of course. I'll be waiting. Goodnight, Alexander.

Goodnight, library girl. Go make some news.

January deleted her messages. At least, he was here now. She didn't have to feel the weight of his arrival constantly because now he was here and they could be friends. She needed a friend right now. Between work and Zak, she really needed a friend. January often wondered why things worked the way they did with her and Alexander. She wondered if there were other couples out there like them, not together, yet always united in mind and soul. January would call for Alex in her quiet moments alone, speaking his name within her head, and a message would appear from him blinking on her computer screen. An answer to her call. That first breath after waking from a coma. One thing January was certain of—this thing they shared was permanent. It wasn't going away. It wasn't changing. Their connection was far too deep and engrained somewhere within their souls to be taken from them. More importantly, they could not deny it, even if they wanted to. God knows they had tried several times. January had even tried to fight it. When she was angry with Alex after seeing him with Lilly for the first time, she thought for sure that would make it easier never to communicate with him again. She had been in a happy marriage. Even that had not been enough. Sometimes she thought Alex could literally stab her in the heart, and she would still feel joy because the last thing she would see on earth would be his green eyes. January wasn't a fool. She knew how that would sound if she said it out loud to someone. Yet, she felt it. She simply could never let him go. Even if he was not hers to have. Another fitful night of sleep awaited her. It always did when she felt the ache.

She was drifting when Carl, as though on cue, stepped into the green room. "Hey, news breaker, you still joining us for drinkies after?"

January had forgotten. "Oh, yeah, sorry, Carl, long day."

"Oh, come one, Janny. You never come out with us. Just one beer. You deserve a night to celebrate your success! Your story is being picked up by the networks already. One beer!"

January smiled. "What networks?"

"Uh, all of them. Where the fuck have you been? Have you not checked your messages with the assignment desk or your email?" Carl looked appalled.

"No, I guess I haven't. Been a crazy day."

"One. Beer."

"Okay, okay, just one drink. Then I have to get home to Zak."

"Ah, yes, the handsome cop husband. Some of the reporters think that's how you landed this story. Nepotism and all."

January went red in the face. "No way. He didn't even want me on the story. I don't need his help."

"Hey, no biggie, we all love you and the important thing is you got the story. We do what we have to."

"But I didn't…"

"See you after the show at McNasty's! Ha! Love the name. Should be a blast." Carl walked out and January sighed. She had dealt with accusations of her husband feeding her stories for years. It always made her mad, but she was used to it.

January turned to face the mirror. She added a little concealer beneath her eyes because she was looking tired. After adjusting her hair and adding a bit of gloss to her lips, she stood up and straightened her blue dress. She wanted to make sure her eyes popped on camera tonight. A consultant had once told her to wear blue because it would emphasize her eyes. Another consultant had once told her to dye her hair red, so she usually took their advice with a big grain of salt.

"Here goes nothin'."

January headed out into the brightly lit studio and sat next to the anchors for the three shot. "Hey, Walt and Marsha."

Walt smirked. "Well, it's nice to see they let you in here finally."

Prick, January thought. Then, she said, "Well, yes, every now and then, they let the alley cats come in to mess around with the house cats." She turned to face the camera and teleprompter.

As she heard the producer count down in her ear, all she could think about were the two devastated parents who were sitting in their living room right now with Frank and a preacher, being told their daughter's body had finally been found. She thought of them and remembered why she did this for a living. Because stories needed to be told.

"And cue, Janny."

The red light came on, and January introduced her

story. The rest zipped by in televised glory. Relief washed over her with the hot studio lighting as she relayed the days' events.

****

The bar was loud and crowded, and when January arrived, she could barely move through the crowd to find the table where her co-workers were sitting. She looked at her phone; no text or call from Zak. She would stay for one drink and then text him that she was on her way home, running late from work.

"Hey, Janny! Over here!" It was Sally McVey, another reporter from the station. She was a tall, gorgeous woman with long, dark hair and eyes. Her mother was Puerto Rican, and her father was Italian. What they produced was a true beauty. She was also a beautiful person inside, and January liked her a lot. They had both landed in Miami around the same time and become fast friends. January sat down beside Sally. Carl was at the table, so was a new producer named Paul, and another reporter named Carrie Carlisle. Carrie was fairly new to the team, having just moved to Miami from Des Moines. It must have been quite the culture shock for her because she had been partying almost every night after work since she had moved here. She already had two empty wine glasses in front of her as she tossed back her third.

Sally leaned in so January could hear her better, "So you have had quite the week! I am so proud of you!"

"Thanks, Sal. I think the story still has quite a bit more to go, but the most important parts are out there. I feel bad for the Sullivans, but at least, they are going to know finally what happened to their daughter."

Sally lifted her mug of beer. "Uh…I would like to propose a toast to our little media star, January Morgan, for breaking a huge story this week, just in time for a ratings month, I might add, and giving us all a little renewed faith in the power of being aggressive with our sources. To Janny!"

Everyone held up their drinks and echoed the statement. "To Janny!" Carrie spilled a little wine as she clinked glasses.

"Aw, that's sweet, guys. Thank you. But let's talk about something else." January sipped her beer slowly, trying to enjoy every drop. After the day she had experienced, she felt like something stronger would be more appropriate, but she still had to drive back home to Zak. The crowd buzzed around her, and the words people exchanged just seemed to fade into the air. January kept thinking about Zak and his state of mind. She was worried about him and needed to convince him to talk to her. He had been so closed off lately.

Carrie was whispering something into Carl's ear. He seemed quite pleased with whatever she was saying. Clearly, they would be hooking up later.

"You doing okay?" Sally asked.

"Yeah, this story has just had me running all over the place. Add in some issues with Zak and I am a little overwhelmed."

Sally turned her seat around to face January, her dark eyes wide. "What issues? You guys seem perfect together!"

January sighed. "Things with us had been good, great even until last year, until his father died, until he became a homicide detective, and suddenly I became shut out a little. He won't talk to me about what he's

153

feeling. Instead he's being aggressive and somewhat mean. In a nutshell, all is not well."

"He's hurting you?"

"Nothing like that. I mean, sexually he's been a little more into the pain than the intimacy, if you know what I mean. But you know I'm not exactly a prude." January stifled a laugh.

Sally's face was pale. "A little bondage here and there is one thing, but if he's using you as some type of rage medicine, that's something else."

"He's just so angry, and I can't get to the heart of it. He hates me reporting the news, doesn't want me to cover crime stories because he thinks I'm stepping on his turf. That used to be something he loved about us! We would see each other at a crime scene, and it would be kind of sweet, you know, even under the circumstances. I'm so wrapped up in him; I just want him to come out of whatever the hell this is. Oh, and he's drinking. Alone. In strip clubs. That was today's big slap in the face while I was at the forensics scene. Sal, I don't know what to do." January felt tears stinging her eyes. She looked down, so the others wouldn't notice.

Sally took on a defiant tone and raised an eyebrow. "You listen to me, January Morgan. You are a strong, independent woman and a damn good reporter. You do not deserve to be treated this way, especially by the man who promised to love and cherish you."

"I think maybe marriage counseling?"

"Darlin', you are thirty-two years old. Young, vibrant, and beautiful. Don't let him forget who he married. He needs help, yes. But he needs an ultimatum. He needs to know you won't stand for this shit. What about children? Wasn't that a thing with you guys for awhile?"

"Well, yeah. We talked about having a baby, and he was so adamant we do it right away. Then his dad passed, and our work became crazy, and we talked about it again earlier this year, and I explained I needed a little more time. Mainly because of work and how his mood had been so off-putting. I want things to feel right. They might have felt right last year but now, a kid? That is the very last thing on my mind." January tossed back the last of her beer.

"Going home?"

"Yeah, I gotta get home to him. We need to talk about all of this."

Sally nodded. "Agreed. But you also need to check your voicemail. Carl said the networks were calling."

Carl gave a thumbs-up from across the table.

"They just want copies of my video and my sources, I'm sure, so they can repackage it on the network level."

Sally rolled her eyes. "Honey, you really have no idea why they are calling you? You've gotten their attention. Seriously. Call your agent first thing tomorrow morning. I'd bet all the single people in this bar, a job offer is coming. That's how this shit works, Janny. You know that."

January gave Sally a hug and waved goodbye to Carl and Carrie, who was now nibbling his ear. Paul gave a friendly wave as well.

****

It was a long drive home. All January could think was how much she wished she could talk to Alexander. "Stupid idea," she muttered as she pulled into the parking garage at her condo building. January knew she was just seeking someone who made her feel inspired and important when her husband had become so good at doing the exact opposite.

When she turned on the lamp by the front door, Zak was sitting on the couch, a glass of whiskey in his hand. He was wearing boxers and a SWAT T-shirt. His eyes were bloodshot. "I thought you would be coming right home."

"I just made one stop to see Sally for a few minutes. But I'm here now." January took off her heels and walked over to sit down beside him. "Zak, honey, talk to me."

"Just going through a rough patch, I guess. You were really with Sally?"

"Yes, Zak. Don't you trust me?"

"I don't know what I think anymore. About anything."

"What am I supposed to make of a statement like that?"

"January, I did some rifling around the apartment today and found a few letters from some guy named Alexander. Are you fucking someone else?"

"Zak, no, absolutely not! Alexander is an old, dear friend. I've known him since I was seventeen."

"They looked like pretty old letters." Zak picked them up from the coffee table and tossed them back down. It looked like just a few, and they were hand-written. Definitely from a long time ago. January's heart was beating fast. Her Alexander was out there to be seen. Her secret friend. "Why do you still even have old letters from some old boyfriend?"

"I'm a packrat, Zak. You know that. Why were you

digging through my stuff? Last I checked, it was you sauced out of your mind at a strip club."

Zak stood up and drank down the last of his whiskey. "I had a rough night, I told you."

"So that makes it okay for you to let naked women dance on top of you? And get so hammered your friend has to bring you home? You scared me today, Zak."

"I'll be fine." He walked over to January's bag by the front door. "If I pick up your phone right now, am I going to find calls from this Alexander guy? Or Frank?"

January felt sick. She didn't want to lie, but at the same time, she feared his reaction. She knew her phone was clean and decided it was best not to tell Zak her old friend from college still communicated with her. And now lived in the same city. "You know what, Zak, go through my phone. Do what you must. But I can't live like this anymore. I want my husband back because I don't like this suspicious, angry person who is never here and hangs out in skanky bars. That is not the man I married." January handed her phone to Zak. "Here it is. Call all the numbers, read all the texts, do whatever the hell makes you feel better about yourself."

Zak refused to take the phone. "Forget it. I'm sorry, Janny. I just can't handle the idea of you with another guy."

"I am not with anyone but you. And right now, I am wondering why I am even here. Good night, Zak. I'm going to bed."

"Janny, wait. I'm sorry I've been such an ass. Can we maybe have dinner tomorrow? A normal date, so we can work on things?"

"Yes, Zak. Yes. That's what I want. I don't want to

fight with you, and I know your job is hard, but you can't take it out on me. Not emotionally and not like the other day. You went a bit too far."

"I know. I didn't mean to hurt you. Sometimes I get carried away."

"Never like that. That was a new level, even for you, and it scared me. I will see you in the morning." January, still clutching her phone, got in bed. She wished she could talk to Alexander about all of this. At the same time, they had never really talked about their marriages on a personal level. That had always been kind of an unspoken rule between them. Either way, as she cried herself to sleep, it was Alexander's words she craved. Anything to help her feel like herself again.

****

Alexander was still learning his way around campus but already felt comfortable with the surroundings. It was only his second day, but the people he had met were polite and accommodating. He was referred to as "sir" a lot, which was somewhat strange to him. Being in a position of power also meant lots of head nods from staff members, ensuring they acknowledged him as he walked by or that they stopped to introduce themselves. Some of them would talk on and on about their plans for the upcoming semester, wanting to impress him with their proactive ideas.

He was also happy because Lilly had done exceptionally well in her interview with Sotheby's and expected an offer for the job any day now. In the meantime, she was organizing their apartment, trying to make it look a little bit like a home.

He was trying not to call January. Trying not to think about her. He had watched her news story the night before and continued to be amazed at her skills. He had no idea she was this good. He had assumed she was but had never had the privilege of seeing her in action. He flipped his phone around in his hand as he walked through the quad. The air was humid. It was, at least, ninety degrees outside. He held his suit jacket over his arm with his briefcase as he headed back to the comforts of an air-conditioned office.

Then there she was.

Standing in front of him.

"Hello, Dr. Lane."

"Janny? What are you doing here?" He was flabbergasted.

"I actually have a story here today. My photographer is getting video of the new drama and arts building that's under construction. It's just a short video piece but a welcome break from the missing girl. I'll be heading over to the medical examiner's office next for the official confirmation the body is Danielle's. I thought I might try to say hello." She smiled and tilted her head. "Got a minute or two for me?"

Alexander walked up to her, careful not to get questionably close. "For you? I have more than a minute or two. Walk with me. I will show you my new digs." Alexander watched January carefully as she walked beside him. He always had a hard time averting his eyes from her skin. It was also still very difficult to breath around her without that magnolia scent sending his mind into a blur. She flipped her long hair back, and he noticed a bruise on her arm.

"January, I don't mean to pry, but what happened to your arm?"

"Oh, nothing. I just bruise easily. Probably got it at

the gym." Got to start wearing long sleeves until this thing heals, she thought.

"Okay, be careful please. My office is in this building," Alexander pointed to a large brick building with a white spire.

"Swanky. They give you a nice office?"

"It's too nice for me. I feel very small inside of it."

"Nothing is too nice for you. You deserve this job."

"I watched your piece last night. You looked nice on the set. I even told Lilly we used to know each other."

"Used to?" January laughed. "I told my husband the same thing."

"It would seem we cannot make enough progress on bringing the spouses into our little world."

"Alexander." January stopped and faced him, her blue eyes more vivid than usual. "I don't want them in our world. I need to keep this for myself. Please? I thought we could try the whole 'let's all meet the spouses and be pals' thing, but I just can't. I can't do it." She looked like she might cry.

"Janny, of course, whatever you want. I am your friend. Are you all right?"

"No. No, I'm not all right. Things with me and Zak are not good right now, and my job is really pulling at me. I just, I don't know, Alexander. I am just so glad you are here." Her eyes were pleading and held such a world of depth, Alexander could barely stand to look into them. He didn't want to make a public scene, but he wanted to hold her so badly. She kept walking. "I'm sorry about that. Let's go see that big office of yours."

"Janny, I don't want you to be hurting. How can I help?"

"I need your words, Alexander. Just don't stop feeding them to me. Your words have always sustained me."

As they walked down the hall to his office, he almost touched her hand but pulled away to point out which door was his. "That's it right there at the end on the right."

They entered the office, and January texted her photographer to let him know where to find her once he had finished getting the video. Alexander closed the door and turned to face January. "You will always have my words. You will always have me in the best way I can be there for you. Don't worry, baby. Everything will be okay."

January's heart was beating, and she could feel him all around her. They were alone in a room, and all she could think about was moving in closer to him, falling into him. It was suffocating. "I know it will. Thank you, Alexander." She wiped the tears from her eyes and looked around. "Nice office, Dr. Lane."

There was a knock at the door. Alexander looked at January again and put his hand on her cheek.

January moved over to the couch and sat down while Alexander opened the door. Lenny stood there with his camera in hand.

"Hey, I'm Lenny Gould."

Alexander shook his hand. "Nice to meet you. I am Dr. Lane, the new associate dean here. How was your video? Did they give you everything you need for your story?"

"Yes, they did. Janny, are you ready to head over to the M.E.'s office?"

January stood up and straightened her white skirt.

"Yes, Lenny, thank you. And it was a pleasure to meet you, Dr. Lane. Thank you for accommodating us today. Welcome to Miami."

Alexander gave a smirk, trying to stifle a laugh. "Why thank you, ma'am. I look forward to seeing the story tonight. If you ever need anything, please don't hesitate to call. I am very pro-media. We have a lot of great stories to tell here."

"Pro-media, huh?" January beamed. "Good to know. Take care, Dr. Lane."

"You, too, Ms. Morgan." He closed his door as Lenny and January headed out to the parking lot.

Lenny was quiet until they got into the news truck. "Hey, Janny. What was up with the professor dude in there?"

"What do you mean?"

"I mean, that guy was into you. Like in a serious kind of way."

"You're funny."

"I am also a guy, and you could cut the tension in there with a knife. Heavy vibes, man. Heavy." Lenny shook his head as they headed to the medical examiner's office downtown. "I don't know how you didn't pick up on that. You are usually pretty good at reading people."

"And you can sometimes read too much." January laughed uncomfortably. "Frank just sent me the text. Body is confirmed to be Danielle Sullivan. Time to get the formal statement on camera and then get the Sullivan family's reaction."

"Sounds good. Whatever will we cover once this story has lost steam?"

"I guess back to drug murders and college campus

expansions."

"Yeah, I know a certain college dean who would love to have you back in his office."

"Associate dean," January corrected and grinned.

Somehow, she felt better. Just seeing him had made her feel better.

She only worked through the six o'clock show tonight, and January was determined to have a nice evening with her husband. Everything was going to be okay. Alexander had said so. She just needed to get Zak to refocus on their relationship a little bit. Somehow, they would work through all of this.

****

Zak was in turmoil. He was hungover from the day before and worried about his marriage. On top of it all, his chief had called him in on his day off to "discuss things." He sat at his desk tapping his fingers on the table, just waiting on the chief to call him into the office. Frank was packing up his bag to head out.

"Hey, Frank, I never got the chance to thank you for taking me home the other day. That was damn cool of you, man."

Frank shook his head. "No worries. Glad to be there. I know this job can be tough on the head. Hang in there."

"Heading to a call?"

"No, I am actually meeting January at the medical examiner's office. Body is the kid's, so the story just got a little bigger, if that's even possible. I am beginning to dislike being on the news every night."

"Well, you spend enough time around Janny, and you will be on television all the time. She's hard to say no to."

"Yeah, well, she's done a good job. I usually don't like dealing with reporters, but that wife of yours is a rarity."

Zak nodded. "Yeah. Yeah, she is. I need to behave myself. She's pretty upset with me right now."

"Just talk to her, Zak. Cop wives have a hard time. I know this all too well. It destroyed my marriage. Don't let this job destroy yours." Frank patted Zak on the back. "Good luck with the chief. I'm sure it's nothing to be stressed about."

"I sure hope not."

Frank left and Zak continued to stress. He checked his phone.

How about we meet at that romantic little Italian place tonight at 7? I love you, honey. Please have a better day.

He texted January back that he would be there. She was far too patient with him. The chief's secretary walked over. "You can head in now, detective."

Zak took a deep breath and walked into Chief Ellison's office. The chief was a large man and had only been the acting chief for two years but, during that time, had been tough on drug crimes and very adamant about being in front of the media every time he got the chance. He was not just an experienced politician but had been a police officer for thirty years. He was sitting behind his desk when Zak walked in, his dark hair slicked back neatly.

"Detective Tennent! Thank you for coming in on your off day. Have a seat."

"Thank you, sir." Zak sat down and watched as Chief Ellison opened a large file on his desk and began shuffling through some papers.

"I have been following your Liberty City stuff. Good work with those Latin Kings. You've made sixteen arrests, secured us three confidential informants who are high up on the Kings' list of crowns, and now you have traced them to cartel-connected human trafficking rings. Impressive work, detective. Very impressive."

"I appreciate the vote of confidence. This has been a very intense case, and it just seems to keep getting bigger. Our C.I.s are providing useful information almost every day."

The chief leaned back in his seat and looked at Zak, his eyes intense and not revealing a single element of what was happening inside of his head. "Okay. I've got something else for you. Something kind of big."

"Yes? I am at your service, sir."

"We want the trafficking ring. We want everyone associated with it. That includes anyone we can nab connected to the cartel. I am thinking about putting you as lead on this task force. It would mean some deep undercover work and possibly traveling to Mexico. I want Florida to know Chief Ellison is not just arresting drug dealers but the pimps and the kidnappers, too. This whole thing is connected, and human trafficking is becoming a bigger problem than drugs around here lately. They have access to boats and can get the girls out of here and bring them in more easily. I will be pairing you up with vice narcotics on this. Detective, do you think you can do this?"

Zak was stunned. He had been expecting to get reprimanded for his little side trips to the titty bars while on shift. "Of course, chief. I'm your man."

"Now I know you've been having some personal

issues, but you need to work those out. Talk to your wife, but you cannot tell her about Mexico, and there will be other things you cannot tell her. Not just because she is a reporter but because it will be classified. This will be a big case for you, and you need to prepare for it and prepare your wife for it once the task force is assembled and we have our action plan in place."

"Yes, sir. I will. Thank you again for the opportunity. I won't let this agency down." Zak shook the chief's hand.

"I know you will do good work. I knew your father, Zak. You were born to be a cop."

Zak swallowed his emotions. He missed his father dearly. "That means a lot to me, chief."

"You can go now, Zak. Go home to your wife. Enjoy a day off for a change. Soon, you won't have any more."

Zak nodded and walked out of the chief's office. He was not expecting this and was worried about what January would say. She was already worried about him just on the daily beat stuff. Undercover was something altogether different. And far more dangerous.

****

Alexander was still reeling from his visit with January when Lilly showed up to his office with lunch for the two of them just minutes after Janny had left.

"I think I saw that news reporter you know out in the parking lot," she said flatly. "Why would she be here?"

Alexander shook his head. "Not sure but I heard the theater arts building was having a media walk-through today of the new auditorium."

"Hmm. I brought you some sushi from this little place down the street. I thought we might have a little office picnic, maybe make out a little on your big office couch and then celebrate my job offer from Sotheby's!" Her face lit up as she clapped her hands.

"You got the job? That's fantastic news, Lilly! We will celebrate indeed, and I like your plans for my office couch." Alexander opened his box of sushi and started eating. "I think we are going to be very happy here."

"I am so excited about Sotheby's. The auction items are amazing, and I will get the chance to really hobnob with some of Miami's most elite. Could lead to a curator or docent gig down the road at a museum." Lilly's shorts had yellow paint spots on them. She had been painting the living room all morning.

"You know you didn't have to paint. We won't be living there long enough to need paint. We can start house shopping in six months or so."

"I need some cheerful colors. All that white is making me feel like I'm living in a hospital."

"Well, we don't want that now, do we?" Alexander leaned in and kissed Lilly on the cheek. "You look pretty covered in paint. I have a full day ahead of me, but I am so glad you stopped by to see me for lunch."

"Why does it smell like flowers in here? You have a candle or something?" Lilly sniffed the air. She is smelling January, he thought. Lilly continued as she shook her head, "I met the dean. He thought I was a student." Lilly's face was solemn.

"I married a beautiful, young woman. He's just jealous."

"I am twenty-six, not sixteen." Lilly sighed.

"Just be proud to be young and vibrant. Most of the women around here are dinosaurs. You will be a nice splash of youth to the cocktail parties."

Lilly laughed. She had always worried about the age difference and the way their relationship had started out since it had been a bit controversial, too. Now, they didn't have all that baggage to contend with. They could actually be baggage-free, normal married people here. She liked the idea of that. A clean slate felt good.

"Okay, Associate Dean Lane. I will let you get back to it. Maybe we can have that couch make-out session another time." She kissed him long and hard on the mouth and left his office to return to the apartment.

Alexander was glad to see her happy. They had dealt with so much in Arizona. A fresh start for them might have been the best thing they could have ever decided to do.

He sent her a text telling her he loved her and returned to his work. As he turned on his computer to begin writing up his strategic plan for the coming year, he smelled the magnolia blossom oil again. He decided he should probably get a candle, after all, or he might never get work done.

January was everywhere. All the time. He could feel her inside of him, even at that moment. She had been hurting. It had been all he could do to keep from holding her in his office. He just wanted to take her pain away, whatever that pain was.

****

January typed furiously on her script, so she would make the slot for the six. She finally had all the interviews and Frank on camera confirming the body was Danielle Sullivan. Her agent had called four times during the day, but January had been too busy to take the calls. She just wanted to get the story on the air in time and meet Zak for dinner.

The producer was getting nervous. "You have that script for the anchors yet, Janny?"

"Yeah, it's on the printer. Lenny just finished editing the package, and I am heading over to the newsroom camera for my live intro. We are going to make it by the skin of our damn teeth." January put on her green jacket and hooked up the newsroom wireless microphone to her jacket. She looked into the camera and adjusted her earpiece. Within seconds, she could hear the anchors cussing about having just gotten their intro script for her story. Assholes, she thought.

Commercial ended. "Good evening and thank you for joining us for the evening news. Breaking tonight, the body confirmed to be that of the missing girl Danielle Sullivan. We go live to the newsroom where our own January Morgan just returned from the medical examiner's office with the latest information. January, what do we know tonight?"

Lenny pointed to January to let her know she was on camera. "Well, we have learned the body is indeed that of Danielle Sullivan. What we still do not know is how she died and when. Detectives with Miami Dade continue to investigate and say suspect Randall Marshall is being cooperative as the charges against him continue to mount. As for the Sullivan family, they are both devastated and relieved. I spoke with Danielle's parents today, and they say they are ready to plan the funeral for their little girl. Twenty years after she disappeared from that quiet Coral Gables street."

Lenny motioned to the monitor. "Our package is

up. Outcue in two minutes."

January stood there facing the camera until she heard the story they had put together wrap up in her ear. Lenny pointed to her, and the red light came back on. "So, as you can see, a lot of new information today and a sad end to a twenty-year cold case. Finally, some closure for the Sullivans and a murder charge for Randall Marshall. News 7 will continue to follow this story. For now, January Morgan live in the newsroom. Back to you in the studio."

January removed the mic and the earpiece as she stepped down from the newsroom live shot platform. "All right, Lenny, great stuff today. I need to haul ass out of here and meet my husband for dinner at Toccianos."

"Enjoy your evening, Janny. Drink, eat, and work shit out with Zak. You guys both just need a break. I'll see you when I see you." He smiled and turned his Boston Red Sox hat around backwards. Then he took the camera off the tripod.

"Thanks, Lenny. Good night."

January grabbed her bag and headed out to her car. This dinner was important. She texted Zak to let him know she was on her way. He replied, letting her know he already had a table in the back for them and had ordered wine. Perfect. He had kept his word. January was smiling as she thought about him. He was acting like his old self, and she was so relieved.

On her way to the restaurant, January called Gabriella, her agent. "Gabby, I am so sorry, but this story has me running around like crazy. Is everything okay?"

Gabriella shouted in Spanish and then slowed

down and took a deep breath. Her Spanish accent was strong, and she was clearly frustrated. "How do you not call me? I have been fielding calls for you, January. I have three networks vying for your attention. One of the offers is damn good. Wanna hear it?"

January couldn't believe what she was hearing. "Well, yes, of course, I want to hear it!"

"CBS News. They need a correspondent. It's the job you have always wanted, Janny."

"Correspondent? Corresponding from where?"

"It's overseas, embedded with the troops in Afghanistan. It's a serious gig, and you would be there for awhile, filing nightly reports live from the war zone. January, this job is an amazing offer. Good money, an apartment in New York once you return, of course, and then a promotion, depending on your work overseas to daily reporting on crime. The contract is solid, and I want you to consider it. It's your dream, Janny."

January was speechless.

"Hello? Hello? Janny, are you there?"

"Um, yes, but Gabby, I am married. I can't leave Zak like that."

"It wouldn't be forever. Like six months at the most. Honey, it is a small price to pay for a network job. I need an answer by tomorrow. They have already been hounding me for days. They want you in New York for a meet and greet, but the job offer is already on the table."

"Okay, I am on my way to meet Zak for dinner. I will talk it over with him and call you first thing tomorrow morning."

"Don't forget. These network types don't like to play around. They've been watching your work on the missing kid case, and they like what they've seen. I told them that was only an ounce of your talent. Honey, this is the job offer of a lifetime."

"I know, Gabby. Thank you for everything. I'll let you know tomorrow. Promise."

"I'll be waiting!"

January ended the call and pulled in to the restaurant parking lot. Her hands were damp from sweat. The job offer of a lifetime. She worried about Zak's opinion, but mainly she wanted to have dinner with him first and have a regular, adult conversation. No drama or accusations.

Zak was seated at a white linen-draped table in the back corner, his gorgeous face illuminated by a candle. He was wearing a blue shirt and tie and looked genuinely happy for the first time in weeks. January walked over, and he stood up to pull out her chair. He kissed her hair. "I've missed you."

January sat down and looked at him curiously. "I've missed you, too. I am just wondering which version of you I am sitting with right now."

His eyes showed guilt. "Not the asshole version. He's gone. Janny, I am so very sorry. For everything. I've been a jerk."

"Yes, you have. I'm not perfect either. Let's just move on. I love you."

He put his hand on hers. "I love you, too, my beautiful angel. I am proud of you. I watched your story. It was really good." He poured her a glass of wine.

"Thank you. It has been a tough one, but I did it." January did not sip; instead she took a large gulp of wine. It was red and warm and made her feel infinitely better. The waiter brought her a menu. "I'll have the angel hair pasta with basil and tomatoes."

Zak ordered the lasagna. They sipped their wine and chatted about the story January had been covering, and it felt normal. Zak said, "I knew the killer had to be a sex offender; they usually are, and they are usually local. I don't know how they missed that guy back then."

"Randall Marshall didn't have a criminal record in 1990. He was just a divorcé, living with his mom. I don't know. I am just glad the Sullivans can have some peace now." January sipped more wine as the warm, garlic bread was brought to the table. She was starving and immediately started eating a large piece.

"Geez, honey, did you even eat today?" Zak laughed.

"Not really, just coffee and some beef jerky in the news truck."

"Babe, that's not food. You should just eat all this bread. You're too thin as it is." He put his hand on her knee and squeezed.

Once their food arrived, they both sat in silence and ate for a few minutes. January was trying to figure out how to tell Zak about the job offer. Just when she thought she was ready to say something, Zak wiped his mouth and tossed back the last of his wine. "Okay, honey, I have something kind of big to tell you."

January was taken aback. "You do?"

"Yes. It is very important that you listen to me and understand the impact of this and what we will have to do. What I will have to do. What you will have to do."

Already, January was feeling nervous. "What are you talking about, Zak? You're scaring me."

"I have been offered an important job, a promotion of sorts. It's a deep undercover gig. I cannot go into much detail except to say I will be working undercover and traveling a little. For your protection, you will need to leave television. I cannot have you being such a public figure during this operation. It's a big one, and the consequences could be dire for both of us. It wouldn't be for long. We have plenty of money, so there's no worry there. This is a huge case and a big opportunity for me, for us." He poured another glass of wine for both of them.

January sat in her chair and felt her legs go numb. She drank back the new glass of wine. She tried to form words, but they wouldn't come out of her mouth.

"Well," Zak said, sounding worried, "what do you think? I told you this was big news. The chief met with me personally today. He offered me the position as head of the taskforce. I will be working with the FBI and ICE. This operation is going to be history making!" He was so excited he could barely contain himself. "It's the quitting your job thing, right? Or the danger I could be in? Say something, Janny!"

January took a deep breath and placed her hands on the table to keep them from shaking. "Zak, I love you, and I am so very proud of you. You deserve to lead an operation like this, and you will do well. I am terrified, yes. Extremely. I don't even know exactly what you'll be doing, but it sounds highly dangerous. Suicidal, even."

Zak touched her hand. "Honey, I can do this. I will be working with the best of the best, and I will be safe. I will catch the bad guys and come home to you."

January felt the tears behind her eyes and tried to

fight them back. "I know you will, sweetheart. You always catch the bad guys. Sometimes you don't come home to me after. I am proud of you even when you don't come home because I know that means you just had to go dark for a while to cope with what you've seen or had to do. But, Zak, even with all of that and all we have been through together these last five years, I cannot quit my job."

"Janny, you have to. It's not safe for you to be on TV while I am working undercover. I can't let you be at risk. You don't seem to understand how serious this is. This is not just me wanting a stay-at-home wife."

"I know that. But you see, I, too, have been offered a job with the *CBS Evening News* as a correspondent. I just got the call on my way here tonight. Zak, I really want to take the job. It's my dream job. It's all I have been working for."

Zak just stared at her from across the table. The look of enthusiasm drained from his face and was replaced with confusion and disappointment. "No, Janny."

"No?"

"No, you cannot take the job. I have already accepted this mission, and it's too important. I cannot go back and tell my chief I've changed my mind. No. You will have to say no."

"Zak, I love you so very much, but I just can't do that. My job will be overseas. Isn't it feasible I could work overseas and you do your work here? I'd be safe and out of the way. We could make this work. It would just be challenging for a while until your operation is completed, and then we can settle in New York, once I return from Afghanistan."

"You sound crazy right now. Afghanistan? Are you out of your mind? There is no way you are going into that war zone! And New York? This is our home, Janny. This is where we live, where I work. I don't want to live in New York, and I don't want you anywhere near gunfire and fucking bombs." Zak cupped his hands over his face. "This is unbelievable. No, Janny. No." He tossed some cash on the table and walked out of the restaurant.

January sat there alone and finished her wine. How had it come to this? There had been a time when they had been happy and had a future. Now January didn't know what to do and could not imagine their future together. It was disappearing right in front of her. Just like he had in the middle of what was possibly the most important conversation they had ever had.

Poof.

****

January went home and fully expected Zak to not be there, given his penchant for exotic dance venues these days and bars. But there he was, lying in their bed. "You left me alone in a restaurant, Zak."

"I couldn't sit there and listen to you any longer."

"Listen to me? Listen to me tell you my fabulous news about being offered a network job? I couldn't listen to you tell me I must quit my career and tell me you are going off to some secret operation where drug dealers are going to think you are one of them. The whole conversation is fucked up, I guess."

"January, this is our marriage, our life. Can you not see what's happening here?"

"I see you are not willing to compromise or work with me at all. I want this job, Zak. It means something to me."

"Don't I mean more to you than some job?"

"You mean everything to me. But you can't expect me to cancel my life while you take off to God knows where and leave me alone to worry like a little puppy. I'm not that kind of girl, Zak. You know that."

Zak stood up and put his arms around January and held her close. "Please. Please don't take that job. It's too dangerous. I love you."

January was indignant. "I love you, too, but I want this job. Please support my decision. We will figure it out. Together."

That night, they didn't speak any more about the job offer, the task force, or the fact that they were at an impasse. They made love, though. It was slow and loving, as it had once been. January sobbed as she took him into her, knowing it might well be for the last time. He kissed her mouth and her arms as he lost himself inside of her. His warmth fell from her thighs after he fell asleep, leaving her alone in the dark with the fear that her marriage was over.

Lilly Lane

Lilly Anne Lane was insecure. She had always felt that way, especially around Alexander's colleagues. They were older, and even though she was a highly intelligent woman, they always regarded her as his arm candy and did not seem to be as curious about her profession or interests. At her first day at Sotheby's, she was committed to improving her self-worth. She wanted to be more than the college girl who screwed her professor, got knocked up, married, and then lost a baby. All those things had made up the storyline of her life, a life she had not planned.

At twenty-six years of age, she had lived more than most young women. The loss of their son had been devastating to her, and she still had nightmares about it. There had been so much blood. Sometimes she awoke at night, still feeling that pool of warm death around her. She would be shaking and finally wake up enough to know it was just a nightmare.

That was all in the past now. As she walked into Sotheby's, she was greeted by several other young women who seemed eager to have her there. One of them, named Alice, was especially thrilled. "Oh, you are going to love it here! We get to be around some of the most priceless art you have ever seen! Let's get your paperwork finished up and show you around."

Lilly was now in the docent program and would be

gaining some amazing training here. It was the beginning of a new life for her and Alexander, and maybe they could try again someday to have a baby. She wanted to have a family with him. She came from a big family and was eager to have one of her own. "Thank you, Alice. I am very excited to be here."

Lilly followed Alice into a large office filled with huge paintings. Mostly abstract works. Lilly was wearing her best dress, a periwinkle blue dress she had bought at a boutique in Arizona, today for her first day at work. Her red hair looked stunning against the shade, and she felt confident when she wore it. Even kind of pretty.

A television was on in the back of the office, and Lilly could hear the news anchor talking about the body of that missing kid. Seemed like that story was always on the news, like there was nothing else going on in all of Miami.

Alice sat down in front of Lilly and handed her some papers to sign. "This is your employment packet. Sign the ones marked with a yellow tab. We will start you on some small accounts, and we have an auction this weekend. You will need to be there to shadow me and Teresa."

"Sounds great," Lilly said. "I have always wanted to work for Sotheby's. This is very exciting."

"Your husband is the new associate dean at the university, right?"

"Yes, he just started."

"He must a bit older than you to be an associate dean." Alice smiled.

"Yes, he is thirty-six."

"Older man? Love it!" Alice giggled. "He lucked

out. You are a beauty!"

Lilly blushed. "Thank you, but I don't really see myself that way."

"Are you kidding? Holy shit. You are a knockout. Seriously, you are going to sell a lot of expensive art with that face. The rich men always like it when we look the part, you know."

"Oh, no, I guess I never thought about that." Now Lilly was embarrassed and just wanted Alice to stop talking.

"Oh, yeah, for sure. Old rich guys like pretty young women showing them the auction items. We have a system to up the prices, but I'll teach you that later." Alice winked, making Lilly feel even more uncomfortable. "I will leave you to it, and after you're done, we can tour the galleries and get you up to speed on the docent program. Welcome aboard, Lilly Lane!"

"Thank you. I am very happy to be here." Lilly pulled her hair back into a ponytail and put on her glasses. Somehow that made her feel a little less easily objectified.

After four hours of paperwork and following Alice around as she explained every piece of art, sculpture, jewelry, and curiosity they had to auction, Lilly's feet had begun to hurt. She wasn't used to wearing such high heels and wanted desperately to go home, take a bath, and rest.

****

Alexander wasn't at the apartment yet when she arrived, so she started making a light dinner of grilled chicken and a salad. While the chicken was cooking, she took a hot bath, and let the bubbles chase away the screeching sounds of Alice's voice from her head.

As she was digging through their messy, still partially packed closet for an old T-shirt and shorts, she noticed a metal box with a lock on it. Now that's curious, she thought. She had never seen the box before and certainly did not know where the key to the padlock would be. She decided to ask Alexander about it once he got home. The buzzer for the chicken went off in the kitchen, so she went back in to prepare their plates.

Alexander walked in and smelled the air. "Ah, a home-cooked meal! Just what I need after this nightmare of a day!" He walked up to Lilly and kissed her on the head as she flipped the chicken onto a plate.

She turned around and kissed him. "I wanted to make you a nice dinner. How was work?"

"It was busy, but my plans for the semester and some of the faculty adjustments are coming along. Forget me. What about you, my little auctioneer?"

"Very funny. It was, well, kind of strange. Good at times. Then strange again. There seems to be a certain amount of whoring oneself to sell art."

Alexander was taken aback. "I'm sorry, what did you say?"

"The girls there, they are very particular about what we wear and how to dress. How to approach the male art buyers. It's all very scripted, really."

"Huh. Well, that doesn't exactly seem like your style. Are you sure you want to work there?"

Lilly raised an eyebrow and pouted her lips a little. "On the contrary. I think I will sell a lot more art than the others." She gave a sexy smirk and flipped her long red curls over her shoulder.

"That's the girl I remember from my office on campus in Arizona. And from my desk. And the closet.

And that time in my car in the parking lot." Alexander smacked her ass and grabbed his plate of chicken and a bottle of wine from the fridge. "I like this sassy version of you. She's been MIA for a while."

"Well, she's back, baby. I'm tired of being so subdued. After what happened, I kind of shut down a little. This is a new place, and I want to be myself again. You have a new office now. Let's break it in."

Alexander took a big gulp of the white wine. It's cool, tangy flavor felt nice as it went down. "My office is so much bigger now."

"Yes, it is. With a couch."

Alexander let a quick flash of January sitting on that couch penetrate his mind, and he pushed it aside. "Yes, a nice, big couch. Good chicken, babe."

Alexander and Lilly ate their dinner quickly. Then they polished off the rest of the wine. Sitting on the couch, Alexander flipped through the channels on the television while Lilly began to feel drowsy.

"I think I need some sleep. This whole moving to a new town and starting a new job thing is taxing." She yawned and got up from the couch.

"I might stay up awhile longer, catch the news."

"See your college girlfriend?" She laughed.

"What? January? We didn't date. I told you, barely knew her." His face was red, and he could feel his palms begin to sweat. Alexander had never been good at lying.

"I'm kidding, geez. Hey, I meant to ask you earlier, what's in that locked box in our closet? I found it when I was going through stuff to unpack."

"Oh, that's just a firebox to keep important documents safe. Marriage and birth certificates, that kind of stuff."

"Oh, it felt much heavier than that. Anyway, good night, Alex. Love you." Lilly left the room.

Alexander knew he would have to get rid of what was really inside the box. A locked box looked suspicious. He should have known better than to keep all of January's letters in that. He just wanted to make sure they were safe during the move. Safe and unattainable.

Guilt swept through him. Even with everything going so well, he was still hiding January from his wife. He was still coveting her. He just couldn't stop.

Sometimes he thought he might never be able to stop.

****

January woke up after sleeping only an hour, if that. They had made love and tried to talk more about what to do, but in the end, they still could not reach an agreement. She was going to take the job. He was going to move forward with the assignment, which he had, at some point, revealed involved Mexican cartels, only terrifying her even more. He had left already and gone in to work for some ops plan meeting. She called Gabby.

"Okay, when do I fly to New York?"

Gabby squealed maniacally into the phone, forcing January's already pounding head into a throbbing frenzy. "I am so happy! You will be fabulous! You talked to Zackary, and he is okay with all this?"

"Don't worry about that, Gabby. Just set it up. I'm ready to go."

Gabby explained she would call CBS right away and get the details sorted out. "What did he say when you told him?" Gabby was still curious.

"Let's just say he already has some big plans of his own. Undercover work."

"Oh, top secret stuff, huh? I get it. You had me worried you guys were splitting up or something."

"I don't know if that is the case yet. I still need some coffee and some perspective."

"All right. I will arrange everything and call you later. Congrats on the big gig, Janny. You deserve it."

"I think I do. I hope I am making the right decision. I will talk to you later."

January ended the call and lay back on the bed. She could still smell Zak on the pillows. He had been her love, her sanctuary, her friend, and her husband. She panicked at the thought of being without him. January didn't want to lose her husband, but she couldn't allow him to tell her what to do. She hoped he would return from work and want to come to a better conclusion. There had to be a way to make things work. They were married, and married people sometimes took other jobs and lived apart. Those married people probably were in stronger marriages than they were in to begin with. January sighed. She decided to take the day off work to try to figure things out. Going in to the office with these things swirling around her didn't seem like a wise choice.

She texted Alexander because she felt like his words would do what they had always done. Center her.

A.,

I am breaking apart, I fear. I need to talk or just sit with you and not talk. Something. Anything. Things are not well. I need your words.

Save me. Just for a moment.

J.

January lay back in the bed and pulled the blankets over her head.

The phone lit up with the promise of him and his words.

J.,

I, too, am struggling here. I lied about a box containing your letters to me. I need to focus on my marriage. Lilly needs me. I want to be there for you, but I am afraid of my feelings for you. I don't know what they are exactly. Deeper than friendship. I confuse it for love sometimes. Other times, I confuse it for nostalgia, but it's not that either. It's just...us.

Please forgive me for not being able to give you more. You are sacred to me.

A.

A.,

I like being sacred to you.

J.

J.,

I just don't know any other way to think of you. I think of you every single day. You are my North Star.

A.

A.,

I am lucky to be yours, even in whatever way this is, and I hope to keep you adequately illuminated. All the time. Even when I am feeling dim. I am going to New York for a meeting. It would seem I am network material. Big things happening. So we lived in the same town for a few minutes, anyway. No grocery story run-ins. No awkward double dates. You are in the clear. Maybe we could say goodbye in person. Or perhaps

*that would be bad. I don't want to complicate your life.
Or mine any more than it already is. All I know is you
are sacred to me as well, and I cannot lose whatever
part of you I am able to have. Keep our letters safe or
destroy them if it's better. Just keep me sacred to you.*

Always your baby. Always your friend.

J.

January turned off her phone and began packing a
bag for New York. She wondered if she should also be
packing boxes. Her marriage was falling apart. She lay
on the floor of her closet and cried for, at least, an hour
until she heard the front door open.

"Zak?" She called from the closet. She dried her
eyes and tried to pull herself together. "Zak?"

Zak walked into the bedroom and eyeballed the
suitcase on the floor filled with January's clothes.
"What's this?"

"I was packing for New York, for the meeting. I
still don't know when I am leaving." Her face was red
and puffy, and he just looked angry.

"So you have decided it's all or nothing?" he asked
flatly.

"No, Zak, I still want us to figure this out. I just
can't say no to this chance. It's an amazing opportunity
for me. For us. Did you talk to the chief? There has to
be a way we can make this work." January moved
closer to Zak and put her hands on his chest. "Please,
honey, let's figure this out." She laid her head against
him, but he pulled away.

"Listen," he began, "I talked to the chief at the ops
meeting this morning. There is only this job. It's
important what I do. I owe it to my boss. And to my
father. He would have wanted me to go."

"I know he would have. But would he not have also wanted you to stay married to me? Work this out with me?" January's eyes filled with tears again. They were uncontrollable now. "Don't you love me enough to fight for me, Zak?"

Zak lowered his head. "There's more, Janny."

January looked up, trying to meet his gaze. "What more? What do you mean?"

"I fucked up, Janny. There was this woman a few weeks ago. I met at some bar. I was drunk. I have no excuse."

January felt like she had been hit across the face. "You slept with her?"

He nodded sheepishly. "I have been in a pretty dark place since my father died and with work and everything. And there's something up with you. You get distant sometimes. Like you aren't really connected to me, and I just felt alone and angry. That's why I hurt you last week when we made love, I think. I was angry at myself and at you for being so disconnected. I mean, I messed up."

"I'm sorry. Did you just blame *me* for sleeping with some girl you met in a bar? Because that is kind of what it sounds like."

"No, Janny, it's not your fault. It's mine. I'm sorry I did it. I regretted it right away. I was worried Frank told you."

"Frank knows about this?"

"Yeah, he was there when she and I left the bar together."

"Oh."

"January?"

"Yeah?" She sat down on the bed, feeling like her

187

legs had given out. She was completely numb.

"Is there someone else? I mean, for you. Is there another guy?"

January was motionless. She didn't know how to answer him. "I have never cheated on you, Zak. I would never have done that."

"But there is someone. Right? I'm not an idiot, Janny. I can see it in your face. Fuck, I'm a detective. I know when someone is lying to me."

"Good for you, Zak, because I didn't know you were sleeping with other women. Perhaps, had I been a detective, I would have figured it out."

"Just tell me."

"Are you trying to find some way to vindicate your actions?"

"Tell me."

January looked up at Zak, his dark eyes filled with emotion. More than she had seen on his face in a long time. His beautiful brown eyes. Those same eyes she once got lost in and trusted. The eyes she faced when she promised her life to him.

"Zak, there is someone. But I have never cheated on you. He is just a friend and always has been. But I have kept him to myself because I didn't want to hurt you."

"I knew I wasn't crazy. You love this guy."

"It's not like that."

"Sounds like it to me."

"Well, a long-term friendship is not the same thing as fucking a girl in a bar that you just met. I think you win in the adultery category here." January could see her plans fading away. The trips they would never take. The children they would never have. The growing old together. It was dissipating like fog on a mirror.

"I know. I won't leave you uncared for. You can keep this apartment, if you need it. I will make sure you have money, Janny. But I think we are finished. I leave for Mexico in a couple of weeks. And the girl. It was more than once."

"Zak," January stood to face the man that had been her husband for five years. "I did love you, you know. I just couldn't help you cope with your demons."

"I know. You wouldn't have been able to, honey. This married life business wasn't meant for us. I am so sorry I hurt you. I should have just told you about the mistakes I made."

"Mistakes? There were others?"

"Does it even matter?"

"I guess not anymore."

He held out his hand to her and pulled her close. "I'm sorry, January. I never wanted things to end this way. Or end at all."

They stood there locked in an embrace for several minutes as January felt her skin against his chest and listened to his heart beating. Something she knew she would never do again as she had done every night for years as he slept beside her. Over his shoulder, their wedding photo gleamed in the sunlight. Two people, smiling and in love, with nothing stopping them from taking over the world.

Broken.

Zak let go first. "I will pack up some stuff and take it to a hotel. Feel free to stay as long as you need. Or permanently if you decide not to take the job. It's up to you. For what it's worth, I did love you, too, Janny. I just couldn't stay true to you. I tried. I just kept finding reasons to stray." He kissed the top of her head and left the room.

January curled into a ball and lay in the middle of what had been their bed. She felt as though she might fall through it as despair and anger piled on top of her like bricks.

From the other room, she could hear Zak tossing things into a bag. Then, the door opened and closed hard.

Just like that, her marriage was over.

****

When January turned her phone back on, she had multiple messages from Gabby demanding a response and with dates and times for her flight to New York. She would be flying there in two days and would stay there for training and prep work before pairing up with a photographer, who would be flying with her to Afghanistan. They planned to debut her on the air in New York first for a few stories and then send her overseas, setting her up as their newest embedded correspondent covering the war on terrorism. She would return home to Miami for a week to tie up loose ends and then fly to Bagram Airforce Base. One week to pack an apartment and start a divorce. It all seemed like too much to deal with.

January responded to Gabby that she would be at the airport and ready to go to New York at the scheduled time.

Alexander had also texted her.

Happy for you and the news of your big chance. You have worked for it and deserve it. I will make time to celebrate with you, despite my fears of touching you or looking into your eyes for too long. These are real problems I deal with in your presence. That is why I worry for my marriage. Because when I am around you, I get lost. We get lost. I can't risk getting lost around you because I will completely disappear in your eyes and your skin. My God. Maybe it's best we are once again going to be separated by geography. Meet me tonight, if you can, at Fadot's downtown. 8pm. Let me see you. Let me call you baby. Call you mine. Smell your skin. Just one more time.

Always yours,

A.

January decided she would go to him. Say goodbye. For good this time. She would have a drink and let his words fill her up one more time. She would tell him about Zak. Not to burden him, but so he would understand why she was so shaken up. "I'll keep it short and sweet," she muttered to herself as she took the elevator down to the lobby.

Then she planned to tell her bosses tomorrow she was leaving Miami for CBS News. Pulling out a small mirror from her purse, she cleaned up her face and put on a fresh coat of lipstick and pulled herself together. How to start over? She didn't even begin to know but knew she had to get the hell out of this apartment.

****

She decided to take a cab to the restaurant, a dimly lit pub located downtown but with tall, private booths. At least, they would have some type of privacy. She arrived a little after eight, and he was already there, waiting in a booth in the back. He had a beer in front of him, and it was half-empty.

Alexander looked so very handsome. He was freshly shaven, and his hair had been trimmed, although it was still a bit long at his shoulders as usual. His glasses were not on tonight but lay on the table beside the beer. January stood in the middle of the bar, her feet high in the red heels she had chosen to wear to greet him. The pair he had bought for her. Music played in the background, a soft, Irish lullaby, only increasing the weight upon January's emotional state. She stared at him as he sipped his beer, a look of distress in his eyes. She knew he was ridden with guilt by even being there, waiting for her. He was torn, just like she had been for far too long.

January decided this needed to be quick. Rip it off like a bandage. Her marriage was ending. This, whatever it was, needed to end, too. She would abandon this life she had come to know and do what she had always planned to do. Become a correspondent and live her life to tell the stories she wanted to tell. Her own story had become too cloudy, and she much preferred being the vessel for other people to share theirs.

Then, he looked up at her. Her Alexander. The flash of numbness filtered through her body, and for a moment, the walls around her disappeared, and it was only him and her. It was only this moment and their unspoken words. The waves rushed invisible between them, ripples of years and time and moments never experienced. The weight of a few moments over fifteen years pushed down upon them, and they held on to each other without touching. They moved through one another without moving. They understood without having to try. The magnetic pull between them reverberating as though their very souls were fiercely reaching across the space to touch.

January stood there, feeling naked among the

crowd, every word and emotion they had ever shared and not shared but thought about was there, glittering on her flesh for him alone to see. She considered walking over to him as he sat there, expecting her to, waiting for her, calling to her with his eyes, pulling at every part of her with his mind, but she just couldn't. Her pain kept her still. Unsteady but still. She stood locked onto the wooded floors of the old bar, as the dulcimer-laden lullaby played on.

Then, she raised her finger to her lips and blew him a kiss. Mouthing the word "goodbye." She turned around and walked out the bar, deciding it was best to just let it all go. All of it. He would not run after her, and she did not want him to. He had given her everything he was ever able to, and it just had to be enough. What they had shared, indescribable and the depths of which they could not understand, had to be enough.

It simply could not be sustained. Someone had to make the choice to stop it. To end the connection, break away from its desperate pull. Its interruption. Its never-ending distraction.

It was an unfilled and unspoken promise. Years of hanging on to something that was too unreal to ever be real. It was time to stop drinking the wine. Stop partaking in even a sip of what was not hers to consume. It was never hers.

After all, wine made her judgment hazy, her mind heady.

And she had always been more of a whiskey kind of girl.

While You Were Away

She sensed there was something more to the locked box in the closet than Alexander was letting on. Something about the way he talked about it and how she had never noticed the box in their previous house. It was just sitting there in the back of their closet, mocking her, as she unpacked boxes. He was working late, and there the box was, just staring up at her, almost begging her to open it. Lilly had been drinking, and after another long day of walking around and following the other women at Sotheby's as they droned on about each piece up for auction, she was feeling a little exhausted and a lot curious. Where would he have put the damn key? She first looked around the desk in the second bedroom which had become more of an office. His desk was filled with disorganized papers ranging from mortgage paperwork on their old house to graded and never returned papers belonging to his students in Arizona. "My God, you are a packrat," she muttered. Alexander had never been highly organized, but his intense level of intelligence seemed to overpower his lack of a filing system. He would easily have known where each of these seemingly random things were located if she had asked.

She opened drawers and cabinets and boxes but could not find the key to the locked box. Frustrated, Lilly sat back down and finished her wine. "You're being crazy," she told herself. Lilly looked at the clock. It was already past eight, and he still wasn't home. Long day for him, she thought. With a new job came new responsibilities as she was quickly learning at Sotheby's.

"Fuck the key," she said and pulled a pin from her hair which had been tied up in a high bun. Lilly attempted to open the lock with the pin and laughed to herself when it didn't work. Things like this always worked better in the movies. She struggled to remove the pin which now seemed to be stuck in the lock. "Great." Then she heard a click and the lock opened. She pulled the box, which was about the size of a shoebox, out of the closet onto the bedroom floor, so she could see it better. Checking her phone, a text from Alexander revealed he was on his way home. *Unexpected delay,* he called it.

She opened the box and set the phone down on the floor beside her. It smelled odd inside the box, like dried flowers. Lilly did not find it altogether too pleasant, but it was familiar somehow. There were countless letters in the box. A few old photos of Alexander and some of his friends from college. And a girl. She was in many of the photos and some of the pictures were just of her. One particular photo, dated '95, showed the blonde sitting beneath a tree. She was reading a book, leaning back against the tree, wearing all black. She had a blue streak in her hair and appeared to have a cigarette in one hand while clutching the book with the other. She was looking into the camera, a coy smile on her stunning face. Her eyes were piercing. "Oh, my God." Lilly felt her stomach turn. It was the girl from the news. A younger version, but it was her.

The letters, as Lilly pored over them all in a ridiculous pile, were all from her. January Morgan.

Love, Janny. Miss your face, Janny. Come see me, stranger, Janny. The stomach turning grew worse by the second. Lilly noticed the letters seemed to stop sometime around the time Alexander and she started seeing one another. She couldn't find any dated after that. Perhaps he had stopped talking to her. The letters were not that of a brief friendship from college as he had described; however, they were angsty love letters filled with secrets and references to things Lilly had never been told. Private jokes. Private stories. Private everything.

She loved him. That much was obvious. Her responding letters to him indicated he felt the same way, if not felt even more strongly for her. Lilly felt the tears stinging in her eyes. Why would he lie about this? Did he still talk to her? Was he with her right now? She couldn't handle it. Her hands were shaking from anger. The letters covered the floor. Hardly a speck of carpet was even visible. When Lilly closed her eyes, she could see January's handwriting. It was lovely and full of ridiculous curlicues. She had put a lot of effort into each word; that much was painfully obvious. Lilly looked for the letter dated most recently.

My dearest Alexander,

I do hope all is well with you and we can move forward after my visit to Arizona. I am truly happy you have found someone to be with who loves you as you deserve to be loved. I believe I have found that with Zak. You know what you are to me. There isn't really a word for it, but you feel it. You understand it. We own it. It won't go away just because we have found other people to be with, but it certainly must be contained and altered. Let's be friends. We've always been friends above everything. We can do that, right? I can feel you reading this as I write it. How strange is that? And it just started raining here. Seems like a good stopping point.

We are fools. You know that, right? Damn fools.

Yours always,

Janny

Lilly folded the letter and placed it back in the pile. That smell. It was all over the letters. Like some floral assault on her already wavering senses. They were in love. This girl had visited him in Phoenix when Lilly was dating him. This girl, this woman, this damn news reporter lived here. Now her husband could see her whenever he wanted. Lilly was seething. She thought about calling Alexander to confront him immediately about his lies. She packed up all the letters and put them back into the box, relocking it as best as she could. Then she took a deep breath. Maybe he just didn't tell me because he was worried about how I might feel living near his old girlfriend, she thought. "He should have told me. No matter what. He should have told me he dated her. Or wrote letters to her. Or whatever the fuck they did!" Lilly kicked the metal box, knocking it into a corner. She wanted to cry, but her anger kept the tears at bay. Lilly wanted to break something.

Then the front door opened.

"Lilly, I'm home. Sorry so late tonight, long day." Alexander put down his bag and paused by the door. It was silent. "Lilly?" He ran his hand through his hair, which was hanging slightly over his eyes. He was still reeling over his awkward experience at the bar. How could January have just stepped in front of him and then waltzed out of the bar like that? No words. Just her silent goodbye. What was going on with her? Alexander was confused and worried about her. The look in her eyes suggested something terrible had happened.

He entered the bedroom where Lilly was sitting in the middle of the floor, cradling her knees and leaning back against their bed. Her eyes were red, and her hair was hanging loose from the bun. "Are you okay?" he asked as he sat down beside her, placing his arms around her. "Lilly, what's the matter?"

Her eyes flared at him in anger as she pushed him away from her. "The news reporter. You know her much better than you said."

Alexander's eyes fell. "Yes. Yes, I do." He wouldn't hide January any longer. "We were pretty close."

"I found your letters. You were close right up until you met me. But what about after? Have you been close after?" Lilly stood up and began pacing.

"It wasn't the same after I met you, but yes, we have kept in touch."

"Do you love her? Is that why we moved here?"

"No, Lilly, no. We moved here because I have a job here. That's the only reason, I promise you. It's just a coincidence she lives here, too."

"Have you seen her? Since we moved here?"

"Yes. She was doing a story on campus the other day and stopped by my office to say hello."

"That smell. That fucking perfume, I could smell it in your office that day. That was her?"

Alexander nodded. "Yes."

198

"She was in your office? Alone with you? Did you fuck her?" Lilly was angrier than Alexander had ever witnessed.

"Absolutely not. We have never been together like that."

"You mean to tell me, in that whole box of love letters, you two never managed to find time to screw?"

"That's exactly what I am saying. We have never been together like that. Ever. Lilly, I am sorry I wasn't more up front about January. I should have been honest with you."

Lilly wasn't accepting this. "You know she's married, right? To some cop. I heard it mentioned in a news story that another TV station was doing. They suggested she could get all her news from her cop husband. She's married and so are you."

"I know. His name is Zak. They have been married for about as long as we have. I have never met him."

Lilly was twirling a tendril of hair around her finger as she paced. "Can you honestly look me in the eyes and tell me you don't have feelings for her?"

Alexander decided to lay all the cards on the table, as best he could. Describing his relationship with January was not something he had ever had to do. For one, it was almost impossible to put into words and because everyone would just simplify it to be love. It was deeper than that, a stronger connection than love. A species of love, perhaps. His scientific mind wandered. "Lilly, I do have feelings for her. We have known each other a long time and have kept in touch over the years. I guess you could even say I have love for her, but it's not the same as it is with you, my wife."

"Not good enough." Lilly walked out of the room,

grabbed her purse and keys, and left the apartment. The door slammed behind her, leaving Alexander alone and devastated. He regretted not having been more open about January to Lilly, but he just never knew how to talk about her. And when he tried to avoid her altogether, he could still feel her, and it pushed him to reach out to her every single time. It was like they couldn't avoid one another no matter how much they tried. Then again, he admitted to himself he never wanted to avoid her. He wanted to keep her close, his little indescribable secret.

"Cake and eat it, too," he muttered. He tried to call Lilly, but it went to voicemail. He knew, at this point, he should just give her some space. What he had done was unforgiveable, and even though he had not cheated in the physical sense, his mind spent a great deal of time hovering around January. Sometimes he would just feel her all around him out of the blue for no reason at all and lose himself for a second. That's when he assumed January was thinking of him, too. He could feel her right now. Trying to pull away from him. It was not a pleasant feeling, and he felt guilty that he was more concerned about that than Lilly walking out the door, but he had to be honest with himself. Sweet, young Lilly. He had never been fair to her. But January was gone or would be soon. Alexander decided to, once again, try to let her go and, when Lilly returned home, try to get her to come around to him. If she would.

At this moment, Alexander still knew it would never be over with Janny. No matter what he told himself. It seemed as though their blood flowed together in the same invisible vein which bound them together. Lilly was in pain, but it was January's pain he was feeling. What had been wrong with her? He had thought she wanted to celebrate her new job, but something was not right. Something bad had happened, and he really wished she had just talked to him. He hated the way she slipped in and out of his periphery, like something controlled by the desires of the wind. Sometimes he wanted to hold her down, force himself to stare into her steel gray eyes and make her say what they shared. Make her use a word to describe the connection they had. Other times, he just wished he could hold her hand. Their connection would never break, and he would never be able to fully live his life without knowing where she was or how she was doing, of that he was certain. Fifteen years had proven that.

Alexander sighed and leaned back into the couch. He just hoped Lilly would come home soon, so they could work things out.

****

Lilly was driving into the night with no exact plans as to where she was going. She felt betrayed and confused and was angry with Alexander for his lies. She thought about calling the television station to speak with January but then decided she would do something else instead.

She called the Miami Dade Police Department.

The line rang, and a desk officer answered.

"Um, yes, I am trying to reach one of your officers. His name is Zackary, I believe."

The desk officer, a female, sounded stressed. "I'm sorry, honey. A Zackary who?"

"He is an officer, maybe a detective, I don't know. Can you connect me to him please? It's important." Lilly knew she sounded harried but hoped that would accomplish her goal. She decided to take it a step further. "It's about a case."

The woman on the other end of the line took a deep breath and said, "Hold please. I'll send you up to major crimes."

Lilly parked the car in a strip mall parking lot while she waited on this Zak person to answer her call. If he was even there. Terrible elevator music played, crackling on the phone as she waited. Her hands were still shaking from the anger.

"Detective Tennent."

"Um, yes, is this Zackary?"

"I am Detective Zak Tennent in major crimes. Who is this?" His voice was firm and confident. He sounded like a cop would sound, she imagined.

"This is going to be a strange phone call for you. My name is Lilly Lane. I live here in Miami. Well, I just moved here actually. Wow. This is hard to say. My husband and your wife know each other. They are, well, I don't know what they are. But they are something."

Zak sat at his desk surrounded by papers, most of them profiles on drug dealers he would possibly be encountering on his undercover operation. He looked at the photo of January on his desk. "My wife? January?"

"Yes. They write to each other. Like letters and emails and stuff. I also think they see each other sometimes. I just found out about her tonight when I found my husband's box of letters. I, I don't know, I just thought you should know."

Zak had experienced such an awful day already, this was the last thing he needed. "January and I have split up. I am sorry about your husband's little box of secrets, but what Janny does isn't my concern anymore."

Lilly sobbed into the phone. "How can you be so okay with all this? I don't even know you or your fucking wife." The crying was too much for Zak to handle.

"Listen, calm down, Lilly, was it? I'm sure you and your husband can work things out. I don't think they ever screwed around for what it's worth. They were like pen pals or something. College buddies who flirted a lot." He knew it was more than that, but he wanted to calm the girl down, so he could finish his work and try to move forward from this wretched day.

Lilly continued to cry. "I really need someone to talk to. I don't know anyone here except my sister, and she is out of town. I'm alone and I am sitting in a grocery store parking lot in my car crying like an infant." She continued to sob. "Can you help me?"

"Help you? Darlin', I don't know you. Fuck." Zak rubbed his forehead. "Okay. Where are you exactly?"

Lilly gave a cross street and the name of the grocery store.

"Okay," Zak said, "There is a bar called Billy's Tavern, just across the street from you. Big silly yellow sign. Do you see it?"

"Yes, I see it." Lilly sniffled and wiped her eyes.

"Go there. Order a strong drink, and I will be there in fifteen minutes and we can talk. Only for a little while. I've got a mess of shit of my own to worry about and January is part of it."

"Oh, okay. I'll go there."

"Leaving now." Zak hung up and grabbed his keys and headed out the door. Frank stopped him as he was leaving.

"Hey, buddy, where you heading? Thought this was an all-nighter for you?" Frank was smiling and looked especially pleased with himself. Probably from all his television appearances, Zak thought.

"I have to meet a friend for a bit, and then I'll be back."

"How's Janny? They said she didn't go into work today when I stopped by for an in-studio interview segment."

"How's Janny? Not the right question right now, man. Not at all." Zak walked past Frank, slightly pushing him aside and headed toward the elevator. As the door closed, Frank could see Zak's face, and he looked broken down. He thought about checking in on January but decided it best to leave their business to them.

****

Zak arrived at the bar shortly after ten and removed his gun belt, placing it carefully in his glove box before going inside. He walked into the tavern. It was smoky and kind of loud from a bad cover band playing heavy metal from the late eighties. It was not his scene. Although he had spent so much time in bars lately, he didn't even remember what his scene was.

Sitting at the bar was a girl. Young and pretty and quite red in the face. She looked extremely out of place, so he assumed that was Lilly Lane. She is quite attractive, he thought. "Stop being an ass," he told himself. He sat down beside her. "Lilly?"

Lilly brushed her copper red hair out of her eyes and looked at him. "Yes. Zak? Nice to meet you." She held out her hand.

Zak almost laughed at this, but he shook her hand

anyway. "You, too. What are you drinking?" Lilly pointed to a glass of wine. "No, not tonight. Tonight, you drink whiskey." He held up two fingers to the bartender who nodded.

"I guess you and your wife split because of this, too, huh?" Lilly asked nervously.

"Nope. I fucked other women and just acted like a deplorable asshole in general. Her little letter writing campaign with your hubby was not something I really knew about until today, but I suspected she had someone on her mind from time to time. I'm not an idiot. She said they never fucked around, and I believe her. I mean, I told her I had been fucking around, and I am certain that would have been the right time for her to share similar information had that been the case. But it wasn't. Listen, Lilly, you seem like a sweet girl. Have a drink and go home to your husband. I don't blame him for wanting to keep in touch with my wife, but if they weren't screwing around, it's not worth leaving the guy over it." The whiskey was poured into glasses in front of them, and Zak drank his back quickly.

Lilly examined the glass cautiously and took a sip, making a face.

"Have you never had whiskey before?" Zak laughed.

"No, I am not a big drinker."

"Sling it back."

Lilly did as she was told and could feel the fire tear at her throat. She made a face again. "Ugh, that's awful."

"But it feels good, right?"

She did feel a little more warmed up. "I don't know. You seem like a pretty awful person, I have to say."

Zak nodded his head while he requested two more shots. "I didn't used to be so bad. I mean, the fucking around just recently started. Before that, I guess things were good with us. But Janny has been so focused on her big TV career, she just doesn't pay attention to me sometimes. I guess I got bored. Toss in your little letter writing spouse and she was just always so distracted."

Lilly looked right at Zak when he made that statement, his dark eyes heavy from lack of sleep. "Yes! Distracted. That's how Alexander is. Not all the time. But sometimes and when it hits him, it's like he's on another planet or something. Probably thinking dirty thoughts about your wife." Lilly drank the second shot more easily this time.

"How old are you? You look far too young to be all married and bedded down to some guy."

"Twenty-six."

"What? Why are you with such an older guy? Let me guess, he knocked you up? Or wait, he's rich?"

Lilly gave a slight giggle. "That is the rudest thing anyone has ever said to me."

"I told you I'm not a good guy."

"Okay, shit. At least, you are an honest one. Yeah, he knocked me up, but we lost the baby. I was his student, and we had a little affair, and I got pregnant and married and all before I finished my degree." Lilly drank a third shot.

"Okay, first, slow down on the liquor." He gave the cut-off sign to the bartender. "So this guy is older than you, follows my wife around like a lost puppy dog, and you are this hot, young chick who could have whoever she wants? Sounds like you have the power here, Lilly

Lane." He leaned in to her as he finished his drink. She leaned in, too, and kissed him as they sat at the bar. At first, Zak wanted to pull away, but she wouldn't let him. She just kept pulling his hair and thrusting her tongue in his mouth. "Whoa, sweetheart. I am not going to be your vengeance fuck. You seem better than that anyway."

Lilly raised her eyebrow and licked her lips. She finished the wine that had still been sitting next to her, untouched. "Take me to your car and let's play around."

"I think that is the absolute worst idea I have heard all day." Zak was feeling the whiskey, and she was clearly drowning in it.

Lilly felt good, warm and sexy, and she liked the look of this man. He was tanned, muscular, and looked quite nice in a shirt and tie.

"Do you have handcuffs? Since you're a cop and all?" Lilly's breath smelled of liquor as she leaned in and kissed him again. This time, she placed his hand between her legs. "Don't you want to touch me, Zak?"

"Yes, I have handcuffs." He tried to pull his hand back, but she was far too enticing to him. After everything that had happened, he asked himself, Why the hell not? At least, he would get one stab in against that guy his wife had pined after for so long. "Do you want to see them?" Suddenly it was Zak who liked the idea of a revenge screw.

"Yes. I want to feel them." Lilly moved his hand deeper beneath her skirt. He grabbed her panties and pulled at them. "Let's do this. They think they can treat us like fools with their insipid little love letters. Let's go play in your car, officer." Lilly couldn't even believe the words coming out of her mouth. She was attracted to Zak, but she was so angry with Alexander and that January woman she just wanted to do something bad.

Zak tossed some cash on the bar and walked out with this sultry young woman whom he did not know at all. It had become an all too familiar story for him. The fact that this was new territory for her was what excited him most. She sat down in the passenger seat of his unmarked patrol car, and he pulled the car around to the back of the bar. She grabbed her phone and positioned it on the dashboard, hitting the video record button. She raised an eyebrow at him as she did, and he laughed. "I think we are going to get along just fine." He couldn't keep from touching her. Her skin was so pale, and her yellow skirt was short and just far too easy to manipulate. "Give me your hands." She held out her hands, a lustful and drunken look in her eyes. She smiled as he put his handcuffs on her wrists. She smiled even more when he tightened them. Now that, he really liked. "You like a little pain, huh? Good." He picked her and sat her down on his lap in the drivers' seat.

He pulled her down on his sex hard and pulled her deep into him as he told her to move on him. Her hands bound, she was unable to touch him. He moved his mouth over her breasts, which were ample. "You are so sexy, little Lilly." She moaned as he let her ride him to ecstasy.

"Oh, God, Zak, I'm coming!" Her body shook, and he held on to her, pushing himself even more deeply into her as she came.

"You make yourself feel good on me, honey. I want you to feel good." He slapped her on the bottom, and she moaned again. That was quick, he thought.

Clearly, she needed something a little more irregular. He smiled to himself.

He unlocked the cuffs, and she put her hands on his face and kissed him as she moved off his lap. She grabbed her phone and tossed it in her purse. Rubbing her wrists, she turned to look at Zak and gave a coy smile. "That was fun. I think I needed that."

"I can drop you off at your house, if you like? I don't want you driving after drinking so much."

She rolled her eyes. "I see how you work, officer. Love em' and leave em'. No wonder your wife is writing letters to my husband."

"Now don't get a tone. This was just for fun, right?"

"Of course, it was. I was bored and angry. You took care of that issue for a few minutes, at least." She placed her hand on his cheek and kissed him again. "It was fun, Zak. Maybe we can fuck in your car again some time. And don't worry about me. I can drive myself home. I'm a little better at holding my booze than I let on." She winked at him and exited the car. Zak couldn't help but feel a little nervous after that statement. At this point, though, what harm would having sex with her do? He had already messed up his marriage. Janny was moving away.

He didn't really care about Lilly or her teacher husband. He sighed as he zipped up his pants and hung his cuffs back up on the hook near the steering wheel. He didn't want to go to the apartment because of January, so he decided to head back to the office and maybe crash there on the break room couch for a few hours.

Lilly Lane had been an unexpected turn of events

in his night. He licked his lips. A tasty one, at that.

****

Returning to the apartment was a sad state of affairs. January considered going to a hotel herself, just to avoid being alone in the place they had called home together. She looked around at the photos of happier versions of her and Zak and felt like it had all been a lie. Like the photos were the ones inside of the frames you purchase at a department store. It was time to accept what Zak had done, but she just couldn't understand it.

January knew their marriage had been going through a rut, but for him to make the choice to cheat like that and with strangers was a side of him she would never have expected. It was like he was living another life she knew nothing about. She wondered how long he had been behaving that way and how he could be so callous, so cruel. A divorce would be the next obvious step, but she didn't even know where to begin. She was about to formally accept the job of a lifetime and now had to hire a lawyer to begin the divorce process. It was just too much to wrap her mind around. The one thing she was grateful for was that they did not have children to worry about through all of this. January had wanted a child with Zak. She thought she could be that woman, the working mother and doting wife. Now the idea of all that seemed ridiculous, as though it was never a wise choice to begin with. She had her secret friend, but Zak was hiding something far more sinister, a self-destructive side that she could not compete with or help heal. If anything, she could see why she had held on to Alexander and his precious words for so long. She had an emptiness inside of her, and his words, even the simplest of the them, helped fill that void.

There was some regret about leaving Alexander at the bar like that. It wasn't one of her prouder moments, but when she saw him sitting there looking all conflicted, she just couldn't add to his torment. January was finished being the victim of her husband's bad habits, she was finished hiding her friendship or whatever it was with Alexander, and she was most definitely finished with being the woman who could destroy Alexander's life simply by being in it. She fell asleep easily, but her mind remained awake, keeping her dreams lucid and, at times, devastating. She woke up crying twice. Finally, she reminded herself she could survive this. Somehow, some way, she would get past it and find happiness again.

****

The next morning, January headed to WSVN to drop the bomb on her boss that she was quitting and going to CBS News. Her contract still had a few months left, and she hoped he would be willing to let her out of it, considering the nature of the offer she had in front of her.

Sitting down in Nate's office, January suddenly felt very nervous. She had worn her favorite gray dress and the red heels Alexander had bought for her years ago. She hoped they would be good luck in some way.

Nate walked in and closed the door behind him. "So." He sat down behind his desk. "January, my dear sweet news breaker. What brings you here on your day off?" Nate was a large, balding man in his mid-fifties, and he had worked at the station for a long time. He knew why she was there.

"Well, Nate, I have been offered a network

position with CBS. It will involve a move to New York, and they will very quickly send me to Afghanistan to embed with some troops fighting the Taliban. It is, I think you can understand, the job I have always aspired to have."

Nate sighed deeply and crossed his arms over his chest, making his suit jacket look far too tight. "I know about the offer, January. I happen to be good pals with the management staff over there and a buddy of mine is the VP of CBS News. I told them you would be a good get."

"You? You are responsible for this?" January was stunned.

"I don't want to lose you, of course, but I was in your shoes once. A reporter around thirty years of age, trying to decide if I would take the network job as a news director. I declined because of family reasons. I have regretted it my entire career. Not that my life is a bad one. It has turned out to be quite fantastic here in steamy Miami. But the 'what if' has haunted me my whole life. I know you and Zak are having some issues. Newsroom chatter and all. Take this opportunity and don't look back." Nate leaned over his desk and put his hand on top of January's. "You will be great on the front lines, Ms. Morgan. Do us all proud. Don't worry about those three measly months left on your contract. I would gladly pay it out to you just for hard work and dedication here."

January shook Nate's hand and thanked him. She almost started crying but was able to keep her business face on. "Thank you so very much, sir. I want this job more than most people could imagine. And after…well, some changes with Zak, I have to leave."

Nate nodded his head. "I don't know what he did to you, honey, but go. Do what you were made to do. Everything else will work itself out. And if he doesn't want to support that, take it from a man married thirty years, he shouldn't be with you. Good luck to you, Janny. We will all be rooting for you down here in the Magic City."

January stood up, as did Nate, and she couldn't help but hug the man. "I will bust my ass overseas. I think the job was custom designed for me." With that, she headed out to clean out her desk and inform her producer and Lenny.

Nate watched as one of his finest reporters floated away into the hallway. He had helped orchestrate her departure and was glad to have had a hand in helping a good reporter make a difference in this world. A reporter like Janny didn't come along often. He had held on to her for as long as he could. He sat back in his chair and began going through applicant reels to find her replacement. "Easy in, easy out," he muttered. Television was, after all, a revolving door.

January walked out into the newsroom she had called home for four years. Looking around, everyone was typing furiously on their computer keyboards as the five o'clock deadline approached like the grim reaper. No one made eye contact with her because it was not the time of day to make conversation. She decided she would wait until the news started to pack up her desk. Everyone would be busy. She didn't like goodbyes. Never had. The hardest ones had already happened anyway. The rest were superfluous. She would call her closest friends, of course, tell them she'd see them later. She would be coming back to Miami one more time before heading to Afghanistan and planned to make that the big farewell moment. Maybe even a little celebration at one of their favorite bars. But for now, she wanted a quick and clean getaway, so she could get on the plane to New York.

Lenny walked up and sat beside her. "I know you are ditching this joint, and I can't say as I blame you." He smiled, his age showing in the lines around his eyes. "I'm going to miss you, Janny. You were one of the easiest reporters I have ever worked with. Efficient and never needed my babysitting. And damn, were you fast at getting those interviews. Shit. I will miss that."

January gave Lenny a big hug. "I will miss you, too, Lens. You always knew what to shoot without me asking. We were a yin and yang out there. I wish I could take you to Afghanistan with me. I have to admit, I am freaking out a little."

"Babe, you are going to kick ass. You were meant for combat boots, sand, and heat. More importantly, you really care about what you do, and this is a big sacrifice for a reporter."

"He left me, Lenny. He fucking left me. He was, he was with other women." January felt the tears start to fall.

"I know, honey." He hugged her again. "He just wasn't cut out for monogamy. He should have told you that sooner. But, hey, it's a clean break. No kids. Just a fresh start for you in a fresh gig. A network gig, at that. You know I am not a religious guy. But I believe God has a plan for us all. This is your plan. It would seem Zak was only supposed to travel with you on your journey for a short distance. Remember the good stuff, Janny. Don't hold on to the anger when you go. Let him go but let him go peacefully. Be the bigger person. Trust me, it's the best thing you can do." Lenny gave a sympathetic grin. "I believe you will be just fine once it's all said and done."

January held on to Lenny's hands. "Thank you, friend. For everything. You better email me while I am covered in sand and dodging bullets."

"You know it." He handed her a box. "Can I help you pack up?"

January nodded and began to empty out her desk as reporters hurried around to leave for the five o'clock live shots or get into the studio. Four years of awards, pictures, scripts, and notes all fit neatly into one box. A big box but they all fit. Lenny placed her three Emmys on top. "You never took these home?"

January shook her head. "Nah. Just metal statues."

"Hardly. At least, they make nice paperweights or shelf décor."

They both laughed. Lenny hugged her once more and walked her to her car.

"You know," he said, pointing to the GTO, "I can always babysit Layla for you while you're gone."

January laughed. "Over my dead body. I plan to be buried in this car. See you in two weeks? I will be back to tie up loose ends before flying to Afghanistan. Make sure my party is all planned and ready to go."

Lenny laughed. "Already in the works, my dear."

January gave a little wave and placed the box filled with her memories of WSVN in the backseat. Red pumps to the gas, she sped away from the place she had called her work home for four years. Big changes were coming so fast she felt like she was already in a war zone.

As she was driving home, her phone buzzed. It was a text from Alexander.

J.,

We need to talk. NOW. It's extremely important. Call me or meet me somewhere. Either way, don't wait too long.

A.

This made January immediately feel nervous. What more could she possibly endure? She
called him.

"Janny." His voice melted her right away. The numbness returned instantly, and she had to pull her car over. Not only because of the fear that now coursed through her body but because he was coursing through her, too, as he always had.

"What's wrong? You're scaring me."

"My wife knows about you."

"Okay. What's to know?"

"She found my box of letters from you. She was quite understandably angry."

"That's bad, Alexander. I'm so sorry. Did you explain we are not together and I am not even staying here?"

"I did but she was much too angry to hear my sad excuses. I fucked this one up on my own. I should have told her about you. I should have backed away from you as you have chosen to back away from me. I would not even have called had something else not happened because of all this."

January clutched her steering wheel in the parking lot of a gas station near her and Zak's apartment. "What else?"

"I don't even know how to tell you this."

"Just tell me."

"Lilly was out of her mind with jealousy and anger. She apparently went out last night and sought out your husband."

"What?" January began to shake. "What do you mean 'sought him out'?"

"She met up with him at a bar or something and they, my God, I can't even say it. They ended up together in his car."

"Oh. Did he know who she was?"

"Yes."

"And they did it in his car?"

"Yes."

"She told you this?"

"Not exactly."

"He told you?"

"No. She sent me a video via text on my phone of the two of them screwing in his car, including a message telling me she was moving in with her sister and we were finished."

January could hear the pain in his voice. The disbelief. She was feeling sick, like she might throw up. "Oh, my God, Alexander. I am so sorry. Zak isn't a good guy these days. He probably just used her to make me suffer more."

"Yes, that is for certain, but I think this was almost one hundred percent Lilly. She played him a little and then filmed it just to mess me over. And mess you over. She said she would ruin you and put the video out there for all to see. She wants to 'end your career,' as she put it."

"No, she can't do this. She will ruin more than my career. She will ruin yours and Zak's. She will ruin her own. All of us will suffer because of a decision like that." January was terrified. Everything she had worked for, up in smoke, because of a scandal like this. Everything Alexander had worked for. All of it. Gone with the press of a button. "I will call Zak. Tell him. He is the only one who could possibly fix this. What she is doing is against the law, and maybe he could use that to keep her from making the decision to publish the video. Listen, I don't know her, but she has no idea what this could do to *her* future. I'm angry with her and with Zak, but you love her, and that means I owe her the respect of making sure she doesn't make another stupid choice. Give me a little time. I'll call you back."

"Okay, Janny. I am so very sorry, baby. This never should have happened."

"Zak and I decided to split up last night. Not because of our friendship but because he has been having extracurricular women for a while now. I'm sorry to say, but Lilly was just a nightcap for him. I'll make him fix this. He owes me that much, at least."

"Okay. Call me soon."

"I will. I'm sorry, too. So very sorry."

January tried to collect herself as she dialed Zak. It took a while, but he finally answered.

"Yeah?"

"Zak, we have a serious problem. Meet me at our apartment. We need to fix something before it gets out of control."

"Fix what? Our marriage? Because I think that's…"

"Zak. This is something else. Please. You owe me this. Just meet me at home please."

Zak tossed back the rest of the coffee he had been

drinking. "Okay. Okay. I'll head over there now. I'm leaving right now."

January ended the call and pulled her car into the parking garage. She practically ran to the elevator to get to their top floor apartment. The apartment was in disarray. Apparently, Zak had come by to get some of his things and had not done so in a very organized manner. Add in the mess of January's attempt at packing for New York, and it was quite the disaster. Decker meowed from a pile of laundry.

January took off the red heels and tried to put away as much as she could while also pouring herself a glass of wine. Zak arrived about twenty minutes later, looking rugged from what was most certainly a rough night and possibly an even more difficult day coping with the previous night.

"Okay, Janny. I'm here. Listen, I know we need to talk about things, but I just can't do that today. Can we talk when you get back from New York?"

January sat down with her wine and just stared at Zak for a moment. He was so good looking and had always been just a joy to be around. Sometimes she would just stare at him while he slept and feel grateful he had chosen her to be with. Staring at him now, she could see a different man. A man she had always felt like she was working to maintain. Now she knew why. He was never really hers. Not completely. "You know, Zak, I loved you. I loved you so very much. I understand that, somewhere along the way, we went off track and just continued to derail while we both occupied ourselves with work. We used work as an excuse to avoid facing our bigger issue. That issue being us. I can accept the fact that we are no longer going to be together, and part of me, at least, eventually, will be able to accept that you found other women to occupy your time with rather than just telling me you didn't love me anymore. But here's the issue. Lilly Lane." January crossed her legs and sipped her wine.

"Okay, so you know about that. I guess your teacher boyfriend filled you in after little Lilly went home and confessed?" He looked more irritated than sorry.

"Not exactly like that. Zak, at any point during your little car interlude, did you happen to notice Lilly was recording your sexual exploits with her phone?"

"Well, I guess I did, but I wasn't really in the position to put too much thought into it." He gave a slight smirk, which only made January's stomach turn.

"Lilly is threatening to publish the video online so that she can ruin your career, my career, Alexander's career, and basically just blow us all to hell."

"What?" He looked shocked. "She seemed so naïve."

"Well, I guess someone finally pulled one over on you, detective, because she is a woman unhinged and is preparing to take us all down. I asked you here because I want you to talk her out of it."

"What makes you think I can do that?"

"I don't know, Zak, maybe because you allowed this to happen? Because you do love your job and wish to keep it? And maybe, just maybe, a little part of you still has a modicum of respect for me and the love we once shared and understands how something like this would kill my job offer?"

"And you're worried about Alexander, of course."

"Zak, at this point, I'm worried about all of us. I just want to get on that plane tomorrow and fly to New York and try to start my new life as best as I can. I do not need a sex tape of my husband floating around out there to hinder my plans. I guess you will need her number, so I have written that and her sister's address on this piece of paper for you." January handed Zak a piece of paper with the information she had gotten from Alexander. "Just make her change her mind. Tell her it's illegal. I don't care which one of your cop methods you use but use one and put this little girl in her place. Do it before she ruins us all, including herself. She's young. She could ruin her entire life, too, you know."

"Shit. Okay, okay. I'll call her. You're right. This is bad news, and it would really put me..." He looked up at January. "...and you in a bad spot." He took the piece of paper and put it in his pocket. "I'll take care of it right now and let you know what happens."

January sipped her wine again, feeling the slight intoxication medicate her pain even just slightly. "I would thank you, but this is completely your fault. Just fix it."

"My fault? You should have seen that poor girl crying at the bar. She found letters you had sent to the good professor and was a mess. Her whole life ruined, she said, because of you and the way he pined after you. You let this continue. You are the one that wrote letters to her husband. She ran to me for comfort. Maybe for a little vengeance. I don't know what the hell is wrong with any of that. I don't blame her. I cannot allow this video bullshit, but as for the other stuff, no, that is on you." Zak stood up and walked toward the door to leave.

"Just fix it, Zak. My lawyer will be calling you tomorrow to begin the divorce. Let me know when Lilly has deleted the video and come down from her rage."

"Done." He walked out the door and slammed it behind him.

January turned off the lights and finished her wine in the dark. She needed the darkness right now. A silent blanket of darkness to hide her from the madness that surrounded her. Alexander entered her mind as he always had when she felt weak. He had always been a calming thought in the past, but right now, he was right there swirling along with the madness. Part of it. Inside of it. Just another element of something she could not explain or control.

Lilly and Zak

Zak was struggling with how to handle this. Either way, he drove as fast as he could to the address January had given to him. He tried to call the number, but it went straight to Lilly's voicemail. When he thought back on his night with Lilly, he could not believe he'd allowed the phone thing to continue. He was slightly drunk, and she was so completely into him; he just lost focus. Clearly, she was far less child-like than she let on. He had to respect that a little, but she had no right to screw with his life. It wasn't his fault their spouses had a thing. Not to mention, she had wanted him, and he had wanted her. It was a fair exchange of need. Satisfied needs. The more he thought about it though, the more he began to see it for what it truly was. She had used him. Quite effectively.

The house was a modest one located about thirty minutes outside of Miami in a suburb. There were cars in the driveway, including the one he recalled as being Lilly's. "Time to get this sorted out," he muttered. He walked up to the front door and knocked hard. The cop style of knocking. Lilly answered the door wearing a pair of short white shorts and a tank top, her hair long and curly over her shoulders.

She did not seem too surprised to see him. "Ah, detective. I wondered when you might try to come by and have a little chat with me." She held the door open, allowing him inside. "My sister isn't home. We can play around a little, if you like?" She laughed a cocky laugh.

Zak turned to face her. "Listen, little girl, I'm on to your game now, and I should have been more attentive the other night, but here I am now, asking you to stop doing this. Don't make me tell you again."

"Or what, Zak? You going to handcuff me again? Give me a good spanking?" She bent over a little bit as she spoke. "I have been very bad after all." She laughed again.

"You think this shit is funny? You could ruin my job. Do you want to ruin your life, too? Having yourself all over the Internet is not a great way to land a job, unless you are shooting for porn or the pole."

"I've done some creative editing to blur out my face, but yours is visible. I just texted a clip to your wife a few minutes ago. I thought she could use a little sampling of our front seat romp. It was fun, wasn't it?" She walked up to Zak and put her arms around his waist. "Do you want to touch me again, Zak? No cameras this time?" She put her hand on his jeans and began rubbing him until he became hard.

"You are a sociopath."

"You love it. Admit it. You like this."

"Listen, I am about to begin an important undercover operation. This could jeopardize my entire career, Lilly. I don't deserve this. They might. But not me. Not you. Now if you want to mess around, I'm totally in, but I need you to refrain from plastering that video all over the place. Please."

She leaned in closer to him. "You smell good. Like sweat, cigarettes, and guilt." She kissed his neck and continued rubbing him with her hand. "I like it when you say 'please' to me." She pulled him closer to her by his jeans. "Let's move into my room."

Zak was losing his focus again as he felt her breath hot against his mouth and her hands strong against his sex. He wanted her again. "Wait, no, not until you delete that video from your damn phone."

"How about we watch it together first?"

He followed her into the bedroom.

"Are you kidding?" Zak had to admit he was interested and amused by this little girl with deviant behavior, and it was driving him crazy.

"Uh-huh." She turned on her laptop and pressed the space bar. "There we are. We look pretty good like that, I think." She lay back on the bed and opened her legs to him as he watched the computer screen, dumbfounded and completely entranced. "Come here and touch me, Zak. Like you did the other night. Maybe a little rougher if you want."

Zak lay down beside her and handcuffed her hands to the bedposts. He kissed her stomach and grabbed her breasts. Then he backed away and deleted the video from her laptop. Grabbed her phone from the nightstand and deleted the video from there, too. "Is it anywhere else?"

"Not that I'd ever tell. Get over here, detective."

He couldn't fight it. He lunged at her and ripped her shorts off, and he pushed himself inside of her. "Stop manipulating me, Lilly." He lifted her hips and pulled her legs around his waist. "Go back to your husband and stop fucking around with my life."

She thrashed around as he took her and kicked at him. "That ship has already sailed, don't you think?"

She moaned and called his name as he used his teeth on her breasts and her hips. "Besides, I kind of like you now."

"Don't get too attached, little girl. I'm leaving town. Now one last time," he thrusted into her again, "is that all of the video?"

"Oh, God, Zak, yes, that was it. I sent it to Alex and January. I only wanted to mess with them. Oh, Zak, you were just a way for me to do that."

He slapped her thighs and kissed her as he released her hands from the cuffs. "I'm leaving. Lilly, this is it for us. Get yourself together and figure shit out. No more videos." He cupped a hand under her chin and lifted her gaze to meet his. His eyes were fiery and stern. "Leave Janny alone and don't ever fuck with my job again. When I get back from my operation, maybe we can have some more fun, though. I kind of like your spunk."

He walked out of the room, and Lilly watched his car pull out of the driveway through the bedroom window as she put her shorts back on. She felt like crying but remembered she had done enough of that. She was tired of feeling sad, victimized, and lied to. She turned on the laptop and located the hidden file on her desktop. For a moment, she considered uploading it to the Internet. Her finger shook over the return key.

"What are you doing, Lilly?"

She turned around to see her sister Jennifer standing by the bedroom door. She had come home early from work. "Lilly, don't. Don't do that. No matter how much he has hurt you, this will only make your life a living hell. Even more than it already is. I can't imagine what you're going through, but don't make it worse. Just please, listen to me and get rid of that video."

Lilly could feel the tears returning as she ran into her sister's arms. "How could he do this to me?"

"Lilly, he's a guy. They are not perfect. Just as we are not perfect. He did a lousy thing. But seriously, did you really still love Alex? I mean, after you lost the baby, you became a zombie. Then you came out of that and just weren't the same. Alex used to call me all the time asking how to get you to come back to him. He was terrified of losing you. Not just emotionally but losing you as his wife. No matter what stupid thing he did, he loved you. You had already checked out on him, and I think he could feel that." Lilly's sister sat beside her on the bed.

"You're defending him."

"No, his little TV girlfriend is not defendable. But admit it, you have been over this marriage business for a while. He knew it. He told me he knew it three years ago and then told me he wanted to help you and be there for you and he blamed it all on the baby. He was in a bad spot. Not nearly as bad as you, but he suffered, too, when you lost your little boy. Then, he had to deal with losing you, too. He never really got you back."

"I know." Lilly cried as her sister held her and rocked her back and forth. "I don't want to be married anymore."

"I know you don't. Now you have the perfect reason to say goodbye. And stay away from that cop. That is not helping matters."

Lilly kind of smirked. "I think I needed to do something chaotic."

"Well, you certainly accomplished that. I cannot

believe you, but I am also kind of impressed." Jennifer laughed. "I mean, wow. He's also quite sexy in a bad boy cop kind of way."

"Yeah. He's bad all right. Kind of good, too." She laughed a little as her sister continued to hold her.

"It's going to be okay, Lilly. Just let Alex go and move on with your life. I will be here to help you through it. Every step of the way. I love you, sis."

Lilly allowed her sister to hold her as she cried and tried to imagine a life without Alexander. Surely, there could be a life without him. At this moment, she just needed her sister.

****

January stared in shock at the video on her phone. She tried to look away but couldn't. Lilly's face staring at the camera as she writhed on top of Zak in his patrol car. It was overwhelming. She called Zak.

"Did you handle it?" she asked pleadingly.

Zak cleared his throat. "Yeah, it's taken care of. She said she sent the video to you and to the good professor but no one else. I deleted the video myself. We should all be in the clear now."

"Good. I just want to leave here knowing I can leave this in the rearview."

"Just go to New York, Janny. I took care of it. And for what it's worth, I'm sorry you had to see it."

"After being stabbed in the gut a hundred times in less than forty-eight hours, another stab or two really doesn't make a difference. Goodbye, Zak. My lawyer will be in touch. Good luck in Mexico. Stay safe please."

"I will. And, Janny?" He sighed as he ran his hands through his hair. "Do good work out there. You will be amazing, I'm sure. I know it doesn't mean much now, but I am proud of you. I can always say 'I remember her when.'"

"Yeah, you can say that, I guess. When I was just a lowly beat reporter in Kentucky."

"You were always meant for this. Go show the world what you can really do. Take care, January. I'm sorry it didn't work for us."

"Me, too, Zak. Me, too." She ended the call and texted Alex.

A.,

It's taken care of. She sent the video to me, too, of course, but it's deleted and finished. Don't ask how. Just know it's done. I'm so sorry about all of this. I cannot even face you to tell you in person. I'm leaving tonight, as I had my flight bumped up. I will return in two weeks to empty out the apartment and finish things here in Miami. Then, I'm leaving for Afghanistan. Take care, my beloved friend. My True North. My sacred thoughts. Ours was quite the thing.

Always your baby,

J.

January took a cab to the airport for her red eye flight to New York City. CBS had set her up in a nice hotel in Manhattan, which was within walking distance to the news station. As January took her seat on the plane, the weight of everything just took a seat right beside her. It would not be so easy to let go, and she had to learn how to carry it with her until she could make sense of it all. She popped a sleeping pill to assuage some of the anxiety she was feeling, and she desperately needed sleep. As the plane took off and she began to drift off to sleep, Alexander's face obscured her dreams, and it was his arms she could feel wrapped around her. It was so real she felt herself lay back into him and dissolve.

****

"Ma'am, ma'am, we have landed."

January woke up to a stewardess pushing her on the shoulder.

"Oh, I'm sorry I must have been sleeping…"

"Yes, honey, we are here. Welcome to New York." The stewardess smiled and glided away quickly. Most everyone was already off the plane.

January grabbed her bag from the overhead compartment and sluggishly walked off the plane. It was around six in the morning, and it felt every bit like it. "Ugh." She went to baggage claim to obtain her other bags, her head pounding from the sleeping pill and the awkward way her neck was positioned on the plane. A man was standing beside the door with a sign that had her name on it. "That's kind of cool," she muttered.

"Hi, hey, that's me. January Morgan."

"Follow me, miss. I will have someone take your luggage to the car."

When she made it outside, the cold autumn air hit her in the face. It had been 90 degrees in Miami. It was in the fifties here. She was wearing jeans and a T-shirt. No coat. There would need to be some serious shopping to make up for the lack of winter clothes. As she hugged her body and tried to protect it from the cold air, the man led her to a stretch limousine and opened the door for her. "Miss Morgan."

"Why thank you, sir. I am going to the Hilton in Manhattan."

"Oh, no, ma'am, your husband, a Mr. Zackary Tennent, said it is with his best regard he puts his wife up in the Plaza. A much better choice, if I do say so."

"Oh, okay. The Plaza it is, then." January was stunned. Guilt must have inspired Zak to open his checkbook.

"Your meeting with Mr. Browning at CBS is at two pm today, so you will have time to rest up before I return to the Plaza to take you to the station."

"That sounds perfect. I could use some more sleep. And some food." January could feel her stomach grumbling. She considered room service and a long nap and decided that was just what she needed. The city was alive, noisy, and smelled of coffee, bread, and car exhaust. She slid into the buttery leather seats of the limo and looked at her phone. Zak had texted.

I will never be sorry enough for what I have done to you. Please enjoy the Plaza. Spend some money on yourself. Allow me to give you something, even if it's just a fancy place to stay. I loved you, Janny. I'm so sorry I couldn't love you as you deserve to be loved.

January felt the tears welling up in her eyes as the limo zoomed past the tall buildings, the hundreds of people all walking hurriedly to their destinations. Zak was gone and the reality of it was killing her. She still loved him, and she probably would have stayed with him had he not strayed. Despite her connection to Alex. Even still, Zak had once been good to her, and when he was good, he had been wonderful. Now he was a text message. A wispy memory from behind her wedding veil and a strong lover in the dead of night. A protector and all her hopes and dreams for the future, faded. As quickly as he had entered her life, he had vanished.

Leaving her to suffer the wounds. Zak was gone. She leaned against the cold window and sobbed.

The plaza was just as busy as the rest of New York City with people fluttering in and out of the front door at high rates of speed. The cold air hit her again when she exited the car. "Wow, it's cold here."

The driver stood beside her and motioned for the hotel concierge to take her bags. "You will find a selection of clothing more befitting the temperatures in your room, Ms. Morgan. Again, courtesy of your husband." He smiled and tilted his head. January tried to tip him, but he told her it had already been taken care of. "I will see you at 1:30 in the lobby to take you to your meeting."

"Thank you, sir." January stood in front of the massive plaza doors. They were gold and green, and the building itself was jaw-dropping. She walked inside, and a man greeted her with her luggage on a cart. "Follow me, miss."

"Should I check in?"

"No, ma'am, that has been taken care of. Breakfast will be brought to your room in thirty minutes. Your husband said egg white omelet with vegetables and coffee? Is this acceptable?"

"Um, yeah, it's perfect. Thank you."

They were on the elevator for a long time, it seemed. Seventeenth floor. He opened the door to her room and the view of Central Park made her gasp. "My God."

"Yes, this is a superb room." He placed her luggage on a rack inside the closet. "Is there anything else, ma'am?"

"Um, no, I am good. Thank you." Again, a denied

tip.

The room was extraordinary. Everything seemed to be gilded in gold with a tall bed and a high backboard. It was elegant and very antique. Crisp white sheets, flowing white curtains, and large, plush couches. It was almost too luxurious to be real. January went into the bathroom, and it was huge, filled with beautiful stark white tile on the walls and octagonal blue and white tiles on the floor. The claw foot bathtub was like something from a movie, and the shower could have housed a football team. There were, at least, eight shower heads, including two that rained down from the ceiling. "My God, this is living!" January felt a surge of excitement that she had not experienced in quite a while. She opened the closet to find, at least, ten outfits for her. Each one made for the weather. Some suits, a coat, tops, dress pants, and a couple of sexy dresses for evenings out. On the closet floor, multiple pairs of heels and boots and a very large, beautiful Louis Vuitton bag. "Oh, Zak, you have outdone yourself." She ran her long fingers over the clothing and breathed in the fragrance of the newness of all of it.

There was a knock at the door. January opened it and a man brought in her breakfast, on a silver platter. Other people came in, each carrying a vase filled with white gardenias and magnolia flowers. In all, there were thirty-two vases brought into the room. The fragrance was staggeringly wonderful. They were January's favorite smells. One of the maids laid down the final vase. "This is the last one, ma'am. Mr. Zackary Tennent says one vase for each year you've graced this planet."

January was overwhelmed. Zak had really gone out

of his way to apologize. She sat down and ate the perfect egg white omelet and downed the mimosa that accompanied it. Then, January hit the giant bathtub, filling it with expensive-smelling bubbles and hot water. She lay in it for an hour, just enjoying the warmth of the water and the peacefulness of a quiet space. She planned to take a short nap before heading over to CBS, but for now, she had all of this to enjoy.

The stress had taken its toll and the chance to just give in to something relaxing was so desperately needed. She sipped a little more of the mimosa and allowed her body to sink deep within the bubbles. Her mind was fuzzy from the champagne, the warmth of the bath, and the exhaustion from minimal sleep on the plane. She found her hands moving the bubbles over her body and the scent of her favorite flowers penetrating her senses like a drug. January moved her hands over her flat stomach and her round breasts, which were so full in the water they floated above the water. Her nipples were hard, and she grabbed them softly at first, but then pulled at them, the way Zak once did. Moving her hands to her thighs, the water warm and the soap making them slippery and soft. She leaned back into her pleasure, allowing herself to truly feel her own body for the first time in months. Her body was smooth and firm, and she had always felt good in her own skin. January moved her hands to that special place between her legs where she knew she could easily make herself come. As she did this, her mind drifted to Alexander. His mesmerizing eyes, the way he had once submitted to her will in the college library, the way she felt every time she read his words. It was a beautiful torture, the having and the not having of him. The way his words dripped into her soul like the water was now dripping from her breasts. A terrible torture she could never overcome. I am just in your mind, she thought, hoping the thought made its way to him wherever he might be at this very moment. "We have only ever been in each other's minds," she murmured. "Ahhhh, oh, Alex, my love." She moved her fingers in and out of herself until her body quivered in ecstasy, and she felt sated. Thoughts of Alexander's lips on her sent her own fingers to her lips where she shook again, quaking inside at the thought of him. Coming again without even touching herself. It was his eyes, his face in her mind, the need of him and his words. Ever present, ever there. Always hovering over her and winding its way through her and penetrating the very depths of all that she was. Letters and words, and thoughts, and ideas, and moments never attained. Here in the hot water, surrounded by opulence and soap, January felt spent and at peace. She emerged from the tub, wrapping herself in softs towels and more thoughts of Alex and his unending hold on her. She lay down on the bed and drifted off to sleep, content and with a pulsating pleasure continuing between her legs. That pulsating lulled her into dreams of words on paper, black ink dripping onto parchment, and Alexander's hands all over her softened, fragranced body.

****

When she woke up for her meeting at CBS, she was in physical pain from the lack of Alex. The ache inside of her had not gone away during her slumber. Instead it had remained, rendering her body and mind in a state of longing and need. It was noon and she lifted herself from the exquisite sheets and realized she was still naked, except for the towel she had somehow shaken from her body as she writhed in her sleep. Her dreams, lucid, vivid, and filled with his hands ripping into her soul as though her flesh would never be enough to sate his need for her.

"Oh, my," January shivered for a moment as she dressed herself. Zak had purchased a sexy collection of La Perla lingerie for her, and she smiled to herself as she put it on. "Zak." He had gone a bit overboard with his well wishes. Guilt had really done a number on his credit card.

She wanted to look professional, so she settled on a nice soft light brown skirt suit, black heels, and a stunning green pea coat. She moved her belongings from her worn-out black purse into the Vuitton. She chose to wear her long blond hair straight and smooth and kept her makeup minimal. Except for her red lipstick. "Okay, Janny," she said to her reflection, "let's go to CBS News."

January looked around the amazing room one more time and sighed. If only Zak had wanted to do things like this with her before, they might have survived. Now it was a new day. "Onward and upward," she told herself.

Entering the lobby, the same driver was waiting for her. "Miss Morgan, your car awaits."

She looked at his name tag. "Thank you, Jamie."

"Much more appropriate attire, I must say." He smiled as he opened the limo door for her.

"Yes, I had a bit of Miami to wash off first."

The streets were more alive than ever, and people walked fast as glittering buildings towered above them, intimidating and astounding all at once. The CBS building, also known as Black Rock, was located on 52nd Street. Windows were open on the ground floor, so the bustling activity could be seen inside by the tourists, and the morning show set was also visible from the street. Amazing. January had to catch her breath for a moment because she simply could not believe she was here. She entered the building with confidence and checked in at the front desk in the main lobby.

"January Morgan. Here to meet with the VP of News."

"Why hello, Ms. Morgan. We are expecting you. Can I have someone bring you a coffee, water, anything at all?"

"An espresso would be amazing right now."

"You've got it. I'll have that to you. Just have a seat, and Mr. Ramsey's assistant will be down to escort you momentarily." The lady at the desk was very formal and nicely put together. She was young, maybe early twenties, and stunningly beautiful with a short bob of dark hair.

The espresso was delivered to January within minutes, and she drank it down fast. The nervousness was only exacerbated by the sudden jolt of caffeine.

Her phone buzzed. It was Alexander.

J.,

I know you wanted to keep your distance, but I could not allow you to walk into the greatest moment in your career without letting you know I am with you. Good luck, baby. They will adore you, just as I always have.

A.

January could feel him digging into her again. She turned off the phone. No, no more distractions. Not today.

Another young, attractive woman walked up to January. "Ms. Morgan, please follow me to the elevators. Vice President Ramsey is ready to meet with you now."

"Wonderful. Let's do this." January took a deep breath.

"Don't worry. All the new hires are nervous when they meet Jack. But trust me, he's harmless, and if you are here, you already have the gig. This is just so he can assess you in person and get you out there reporting here in the city. Get your face out there. Don't worry. It will be fabulous. Just breathe."

January smiled and felt like hugging this tiny girl as they stood in the elevator. "Thank you."

"No problem. My name is Mary, and I am sure we will see each other quite a bit over the next couple of weeks. There is a lot to do, not only to get you acclimated to the network but to prepare you and your team for Afghanistan. Expect eighteen-hour days. I hope you are comfortable at the Hilton?"

"Well, I am actually at the Plaza."

"Jack, put you up at the Plaza?"

"No, my husband. I mean, my soon-to-be ex-husband did. It was kind of a good luck present."

"Wow, that's some soon-to-be ex-husband! Are you sure he doesn't want to stay your husband?"

"Mary, not for all the Plazas in the world would I allow that to happen."

"Ah. I understand. Philanderer."

January sighed. "Just a little bit."

"Sorry, honey. Hey, but look at you now! I think you will find you are the true victor in all this."

With that, January did hug the girl. "I just met you, Mary, but I think you are pretty fabulous. Thank you."

Mary was clearly uncomfortable with the hug but still smiled. "I have that effect on people, January. Okay, this is our floor, and Jack's office is straight back and to the right. The big one with the big doors. Oh, let me take your coat." January handed her coat to Mary and headed down the hall. She walked with confidence as the power of the new red-soled shoes pushed her into her future. The door to Mr. Ramsey's office was open, and he sat on a large leather couch, waiting for her. There were several others in the room, two women and another young man, who was dressed very casually.

Jack Ramsey stood up and greeted her. "January, welcome. I hope you are enjoying your first morning in the city."

"Yes, it has been lovely."

Jack Ramsey was tall and appeared to be in his mid-forties. He had silver hair and bright blue eyes. He was also very tall, and January found herself looking up at him, mesmerized by his stature. He smiled widely and looked over at the others. "Please have a seat and let me introduce you to the team. First, we have Susannah. She will be your voice back here, as she is the director. Then we have Alayna, who will be your producer. She will be going overseas with you. And finally, this rugged-looking man is Jesse. He is your photographer. He has twenty-five years of experience and has been embedded multiple times. He will be your guide, your protector, and your direction when you feel overwhelmed."

All three waved their hellos and offered meager smiles. Jesse had dark skin and his long hair was tied back. He appeared to be Middle Eastern. As though hearing her thoughts, Jack quickly clarified Jesse's heritage. "Jesse is from Israel but speaks four different languages. He is also highly trained in Krav Maga, among other things, so don't let his camera fool you. It is not his only tool. Am I right, Jess?"

Jesse looked uncomfortable with people talking about him. "Yes, sir." He held his hand out to shake January's. "It's nice to meet you, January. This is going to be an adventure. Are you ready?" He smiled, revealing his dimples and bright white teeth.

"I think so. I look forward to working with you."

"Okay, boss, I'm outta here. I have some footage to edit for my series." Jesse waved to everyone as he left the office.

Jack looked at January for a moment, sizing her up. "I think we can keep your look the same. Maybe cut your hair a little. Your writing and live shots are solid. How are you at adlibbing?"

"It's my strongest ability," January stated confidently.

Jack smiled. "I would also think breaking stories falls into that, too. Now I want to get you on the air tonight. I know it's soon but trial by fire, right?"

January felt the nerves return. "Yes, yes, of course. What story did you have in mind?"

"Well, Alayna is working on that. Susannah, you can head back to master control. I just wanted you in here to meet January."

Susannah dutifully stood up and walked over and shook January's hand. "Nice to meet you. Welcome to CBS." She was wearing large-framed eyeglasses and a black suit. She seemed like the epitome of what January imagined New York to be.

"Nice to meet you, Susannah."

Jack continued, "So, Alayna, work with January on a piece for tonight. We will have you live in the field, maybe fronting something we already have slated for another reporter. We just need to get you on camera and out in front, so people know you are here. You'll have to deal with human resources at some point but focus on your piece for now."

Alayna stepped in. "I just edited a story about the national lottery craze. Powerball is up to four-hundred million. We can have her front that from some busy gas station or something, just to give her some exposure?"

"Not hard enough, but it's a start. After today, I only want her attached to hard news. She is a hard news reporter. Not a fluff piece girl. I want her marketed as hard news. Let them know in marketing. Her image, photos, everything, even her bio on the website. All hard news. We want to present her as tough as nails before we send her to be embedded." Alayna nodded and wrote down notes.

Jack paused and looked at January again, his bright blues eyes piercing. It was beginning to make January feel odd. She raised an eyebrow and smiled at him. "Yes, Mr. Ramsey?"

"Oh, nothing, just taking you in. My new face. I am just thinking of how and where I will fit you in our little world."

Alayna chimed in, "This is just the way he is January. Don't let him freak you out." She laughed. "Jack, don't freak out the new reporter, or she'll high tail it back to Florida."

"Okay, okay. January, you are extremely beautiful.

Your eyes and lips stand out, so I want to see them. Keep the lipstick more nude. I know the instinct is to show them off with red like you're doing, but I want them to be a lighter pale pink or nude shade. Your eyes, however. They are astonishingly gray and really pull me in. Alayna, have makeup play up her eyes like no one's business. I want them to entrance our viewer like they entrance me. Even on a mundane lotto story."

"You got it, sir." Alayna wrote down more notes.

"Now, January, let Alayna here get you acclimated and hit the ground running. My hard news beauty, my desert angel who isn't afraid to get dirty and be bold in her storytelling, go forth and make news!" Jack stood up and sat down behind his desk. "Oh, and welcome to your new home, Janny." Jack smiled and shuffled them out the door.

January was speechless. "What the hell was that?" She laughed and so did Alayna.

Alayna rolled her eyes. "He's a bit eccentric."

"A bit?"

"Well, a lot. That's his vibe. He likes doing this to new people. He must really like you because he usually asks questions. Like, what is your writing style, and how would you handle an international crisis? He was different with you. I take that as a good sign. I've seen new reporters leave his office crying before." Alayna had a look of seriousness on her face. "Okay, let's get you into the news room, assign you a desk to use until you depart with Jess and me. You will need to get a physical and get vaccinations, too, but I'll arrange that for you. For now, sit here. Take a breather. I'll have someone bring you coffee, and then we'll get you into the sound studio to voice your first package, which I am finishing up right now."

"Wait. You mean I don't write the story?"

"Honey, this is the network. I am your producer. I will do most of your writing, interview-getting, and editing, along with Jesse. Now the live stuff, January, that is all you. Make sure your live interview skills are strong. Adlibbing, strong. Everything in the desert will be fly by the seat of our pants on most days. I can write shit all day long, but if there's an attack or a bomb goes off, well, it's all you all day. No script."

"Got it. Okay. Yes, I need that coffee please." January took another deep breath and felt a sense of relief that she had been allowed a moment to think.

So this is CBS, January thought. Wow. She leaned back in her chair and looked around the massive newsroom. So busy. It was like New York City all packed into one space. "But I'm here." January smiled, and for the first time, it hit her just where she had arrived. "I'm here."

Caught Between New York and Miami

Alexander stood a few feet away from Lilly as she packed her stuff into boxes. Her sister Jennifer was also there, helping to cart things away. "Lilly, can we talk, in private please?" He begged her and reached for her arm as she walked by him, box in hand.

"I have nothing more to say. You love someone else, and I fucked someone else. We are finished, Alex." Her face was like stone.

"Can we, at least, try to separate on more amicable terms? We have both made mistakes here, but that doesn't mean I don't still care for you. I love you, Lilly. Please let me help you. Just talk to me."

She turned to face Alex, her eyes red from crying. "Listen, I'm sorry about the video. That was pretty shitty of me. But you hurt me. I didn't know you had someone else in your life. A friend, a lover, a…a…January. Whatever she is to you, I didn't know about her. You kept her from me because you knew it was a betrayal. Even if it was a small one. And, Alex, I stopped loving you some time ago, I think." Her eyes filled with tears. "I wanted to make this work because I thought we could. But after the baby, things just weren't the same."

"I know, sweetheart. I know." Alex leaned in and held her tightly in his arms. "Hey, we were pretty great together there for a while, though."

"Yes, we were. I'm so sorry, Alex. I never should have come to Florida. I knew back in Arizona this wasn't working for me, but I thought a fresh start would help somehow. I wanted to believe it was just the memories of what we had endured."

"Lilly, that was a horrible experience. For both of us. You are young and have your whole life ahead of you. I will not hold you back from being the amazing person I know you are. I love you too much to be that guy. I'm sorry I didn't tell you about January. It's hard to explain what I don't even understand myself. I made a mistake by keeping her locked in a box like that."

"Alex, there's nothing to understand. Don't try to put a label on it anymore. Just love her. It's okay to love her and it be that simple. Really, it is." Lilly touched his face and lifted his chin, so he would face her. "I know you. You feel deeply and think deeply, and this woman is a bigger part of you than you are willing to admit to yourself. Face it. Deal with it in whatever way you can. I think it's safe to say Zak Tennent won't be getting in the way of that. They are getting a divorce."

"I suspected as much."

"We will need to do that, too, you know. But let's keep it as easy as possible. I can't handle any more trauma. I just want to start a new life. Here, maybe or somewhere else. I don't know. But let's do it quickly, so we don't torment each other needlessly." Lilly held on to his hands. "I did love you very much."

"Please let me know once you have settled in at Jennifer's house, so I know you're safe."

"I will. Call her, Alex. Make her yours. I can see it in your eyes. You need her."

"Lilly, she is gone. I think that ship has sailed even before it was ever built." Alex shook his head. "I have my job to focus on. Please, call me when you can." He kissed Lilly on her forehead and then watched as his wife of five years left their apartment and his life.

He went to the fridge and opted for a beer because it was easiest. Sitting alone in the apartment, he truly felt empty. Lilly was gone. He didn't know how to move forward. The one person in the world he would have reached out to for solace was gone, too. January seemed to really mean it this time, when she said they needed to stay apart. After everything that had happened and that damn video, he could only imagine what she must be feeling. He just missed her. He needed her. More than he had ever needed her before. Alex thought about that day in the rain in college. Her face, so pale and damp from the rain, glowing from her youth. That kiss in the backseat of his car in 1995 that he could still feel sometimes in the dead of night, even all these years later. How could he just let her leave like this? How could he stand by and let her slip through his fingers again? No! "Not again, Janny. No." In that moment, he decided he would fight for her. One last time, he would try. They had nothing left to lose. Alex needed to smell her and taste her. He wanted her back in his life now. Even a few days apart was too much. He had always needed her mind, her heart, and her soul. Now he wanted her body. She had always told him he had three out of four. He had always responded with, "You know I will never ask for the fourth." Now he wanted the fourth. He wanted all of her.

From the television in the living room, he could hear her voice. "The Powerball is effectively up to 400 million dollars, and that has people filling up the stores and gas stations for their chance to win. There have been multiple fights at area gas stations as a result of the lines, and the police are out in full force to monitor what is quickly escalating into unexpected drama. As for winning, it's a slim chance, but that isn't stopping these people you see around me, desperate for their chance at a carefree life. January Morgan, CBS News."

He stared at her in awe. She was already on the air? He had no idea it would be so fast. She had just left last night! The world of academics never moved quite at that speed. She had looked amazing and sounded strong and confident. He could also hear the excitement in her voice. She was happy. Alex so loved seeing her happy like this. He sat down on the couch and decided to give her a little space, just until she could return to Miami for a few days. She had mentioned she had to come back before going overseas. He would hold off and let her breathe and focus on her new career. That was best. It did not change how much he wanted to go to her and kiss her on the streets of New York. It would not change how he barely slept at night because he could feel her with him even when she wasn't. Sometimes he woke up and expected to see her sleeping there beside him. Even now, he could sense her nervousness after the live shot.

"My January. The first. My last." He thought of the library and how she had wrapped herself around him and demolished his world with her kiss. He had not gone a day without thinking of her for fifteen years. In some way, at some point, every day, she was there. Like a distant rain that always fell, but when it moved in close, it pounded on the roof like a fury and then stopped. He had hated the silence. When the letters would stop. Alex knew now he needed her words just as much as she said she needed his. "Feed me," she used to say to him. "I need your words to get through the day. Feed me." He would oblige her, of course, because he wanted her to feel fulfilled and inspired. He felt lucky to be the one who inspired her. Her muse, she had called him. Just as he had always called her sacred. She was sacred to him, and he wanted to make her feel just how much.

****

January was exhausted. She had worked every show, every day since her arrival to New York City two weeks earlier. They had featured her on morning show live shots and evening news lives. Late news. She was sleeping an average of four hours a night. Jack said it was the best way to saturate the country with her name before they sent her abroad. January had also been given orders to go to Virginia for five days before heading to Bagram Airforce Base for a specialized training called Centurion for embedded journalists. She was told it would be like real life war training, and it terrified her. She knew the mock scenarios would be useful as she had never been in a war zone before.

Fortunately, she was able to convince Jack to let her take a quick trip back to Miami first. Zak had filed for divorce, and they needed to meet to finalize everything. Zak had decided to sell the apartment and promised to split the sale with her which she accepted. He offered her more money, too, but she declined the offer. He would be leaving for his operation in Mexico soon and was awaiting instructions from his team commander. Going home to Miami also allowed her to make sure her car and her cat would be in good hands. So much to do and she was already functioning on caffeine and adrenaline alone.

Alexander never called. Never texted. No emails. Nothing. He had done as she had asked, and she was grateful. She needed to get her head straight. Now she was better, had her bearings, and loved the pulse of New York City. Of course, Zak's little parting gift of two weeks at the Plaza made for a pretty amazing place to lay her head at night. She was sure to take advantage of the room service, too. She figured it was a small price for him to pay after all he had done. Especially that damn video with Lilly. Her stomach turned when she thought of it. January wondered what Alex and Lilly had decided to do after that. She assumed they were separated, too, but she dared not ask while in New York. Instead, she had worked. Hard. She had improved her look, her voice, and her writing.

Alayna ran up to her as she packed a few things from her desk. "So here is your itinerary. You fly to Miami for two days, then to Virginia for Centurion training. Got it?"

"Got it. Wow." January took the stack of papers from Alayna.

"I have also included a list of what you should and should not pack clothing-wise as it's much different over there. Your fancy high heels won't fly, sister. You'll need combat boots, BDUs, that kind of thing. Good luck at Centurion. It's kind of scary at first but just stay focused and remember the training is necessary. So, when a guy pops out from behind a wall and puts a 9 millimeter to your head, just go with it. It's only an exercise." Alayna gave a coy smirk.

"Okay. What now?"

"Work out every day, if you can, and stay strong. Eat protein. Run. Endurance is important. Oh, and good luck with the whole divorce thing."

"Thanks. I'm sure that will actually make Centurion seem like a walk in the park." January hugged Alayna and then took the elevator to the lobby. Jamie, the driver, was waiting for her, dutiful as ever.

"To JKF, Ms. Morgan?"

"Yes, Jamie. Thank you. And thank you for everything for the past two weeks. It has been nice having a familiar face to guide me through the concrete jungle." She smiled and he nodded as he closed the door of the limo. Inside was a bottle of chilled champagne.

Jamie looked back, pointed to the drink. "That's from me. I thought, after the whirlwind you've experienced, a nice pre-flight drink was in order."

"Oh, Jamie. You are my hero." January leaned back into the soft leather and sipped the champagne, slowly at first. The second glass she tossed back. The champagne was dry and bubbly. Perfection. She decided to text Alex to let him know she was returning for a couple of days. She hoped it would be a welcomed text after not speaking with him for so long.

A.,

I am about to board a flight to Miami. I will have two days. Maybe you can give me an hour to just see you. I need your words.

J.

He texted back right away.

J.,

I am waiting for you. I thought it might be time for

us to really talk. Unencumbered.

Always yours,

A.

January smiled. Maybe it was the exhaustion or the champagne or just the fact that she had missed their conversations and little exchanges so dearly, but she felt the ache and the need for him return like a bolt of lightning straight through her soul. The flight home would simply not be fast enough to get her to Alexander.

****

Her plane landed three hours later, and she checked into the Fontainebleau Hotel on Collins. The heat was still very present in hot Miami, and bikini-clad women ran around with drinks in their hands.

January's phone started ringing. "Hey, Zak. I just checked into the hotel. What time shall I meet you at the lawyer's office?"

Zak told her to be there at two pm. "I've been watching you on the air, Janny. You're doing a great job up there."

"Thank you, Zak. And thank you for taking care of me up there. I mean the hotel, the clothes, the driver, all of it was a bit excessive but very much appreciated."

She could hear people talking in the background and assumed he was at the police station. "Janny, I just wanted to do something nice for you. After what happened with us, and especially with the whole Lilly nightmare, I just figured I owed you. And more than that, I wanted to take care of you, something I have not done very well."

"Well, I appreciate it. It was quite luxurious. I will see you at two. Bye, Zak."

"Goodbye, Janny."

January entered her hotel room and changed into a sundress and sandals. "From one weather extreme to the next," she muttered.

****

After taking a cab to the meeting, January sat across from Zak's attorney. Her attorney was there, too, and she looked irritated that Janny had arrived so close to the scheduled time. She's probably banging Zak, too, January thought. Zak gave her a sheepish smile, and she returned it with a similar expression. "Hello, Zak. Are we ready to do this?"

Zak's attorney laid a few pieces of paper out to be signed. "As neither party is seeking spousal support, it has been agreed they will split the money from the sale of the condo. January will keep her car. The cat will stay with a friend until she returns from abroad, and that will be the end of it. Are we in agreement?"

January's attorney whispered in her ear. "Are you sure that's all you want? He has millions. Take more."

January shook her head. "No, that's all I want. Just the condo money and to keep my car. Zak can have the rest. It was never mine to begin with. Even the stuff in the condo, he can keep it. I'm leaving the country and will have no use for it."

Zak's attorney pushed the document in front of her with an ink pen. She took the pen and looked up at Zak one more time. "We had fun once, you and me. Take care of yourself in Mexico, Zak. Please."

He got up and walked over to her and held her hands lifting her up to face him. "I did love you, and I am so very sorry. For everything. Go do your thing, Janny, and be the star I know you can be." He leaned in and kissed her lips softly and then bent over the table and signed his name. January did the same, and they walked out together.

"Oh," he said, "I had Layla stored in a car garage for you. She will be safe until you get back to her."

"Thank you, Zak. Goodbye."

He smiled, his white teeth contrasting with his tanned skin. "See you around, Janny." That smile that had once made her melt.

Lenny had sent January a text earlier, telling her to meet up with some of her WSVN colleagues at a local bar, where most of the news reporters frequented. She told him she would stop by after the news for a beer and to properly say goodbye to everyone.

****

It had come down to this moment. She was leaving in two days for Virginia and then the Middle East with no return date to New York even set. It was November and still hot as August in Miami. The sky was turning a lovely shade of pink and purple as the sun began to set along the beach. Alexander sat on a blanket, staring out at the ocean, waiting for her.

He just wanted to see her one more time before she left.

Just one more time.

A breeze picked up, warm on his face. The salty air smelled exhilarating. He looked down at his hand, the white skin where his wedding ring had been, still not tanned over.

January could see him in the distance, sitting along the shoreline. This part of the beach had been deserted since November because it was not a touristy time of year. And this beach was local; tourists didn't even know it was here. It was January's favorite. It occurred to her as she stood just feet away from Alexander, and this might be the last time she would ever see him. Maybe even ever see this beach. She would relocate to New York after returning from her assignment overseas. CBS News had already made arrangements for her to have an apartment there upon her return, which was unknown. Her bags were packed, and she planned to check out of the hotel first thing in the morning and fly to Virginia for training and then to Atlanta where she would fly to Bagram Airforce Base in Afghanistan. She was wearing a long, blue maxi dress and carrying her sandals. Around her neck, the lapis necklace Alexander had sent to her.

In the distance, at some beachside bar, Jeff Buckley's version of "Lilac Wine" was playing.

She walked slowly through the warm sand, always astounded at the beautiful sunsets in Florida. They were like a living painting every evening. More than fifteen years had passed since she had first seen Alexander. So much had happened. So many mistakes had been made. She needed to apologize. She needed to finally close this chapter in her life's story. It was time to, once again, say goodbye to Alexander. Goodbye to Florida. And goodbye to the mess she'd left behind.

She sat beside him and stretched out her legs. Leaning her head on his shoulder, she whispered, "I am so sorry, Alexander."

He fought back the emotions filling him. "Don't be, baby. We just got lost is all. Really lost. We do that with each other."

"There were so many times we could've…"

"I know. It just wasn't meant to be for us. You are

something sacred to me, something that just slides though my hands the moment I hold you."

"We destroyed our marriages."

Alexander put his arm around January and pulled her close as the sun dipped deeper into the horizon. "I think it's safe to say they already were suffering even before Lilly found your letters. You had already left Zak. Lilly, well, I have to take ownership on that one. I betrayed her, and she paid me back. She's so young. She will find someone else, someone who will love her and her alone. I was never fair to her because it was always you in my heart. Always you in my mind. For more than a decade, it has been you in my head, heart, and soul. Fifteen years, and it has always been you, January." He turned to face her. The glow of the sinking sun lit up her face with a golden hue so beautiful it was like honey. "It always should have been you. I should have fought harder."

January looked up, her eyes filling with tears, and they were no longer gray but now the shade of aquamarine. "Alexander, what are we to each other?"

He sighed. "The real thing, I suppose."

"But I have to leave. I can't stay here. I have my job, and there's just too much sadness here. I just can't stay." Tears were streaming down January's cheeks.

Alexander wiped them away. He looked at her like no one ever had or could, like he could see the very deepest parts of her soul. Like he had been living in those parts already for years and knew them better than anyone. Better even than she knew them herself. His hair had fallen into his eyes as usual, and she brushed it away. "You never cut your hair."

He smiled. 'Don't cry, baby. I know you have to

go. Don't be tormented by it. You have so much left to do in this world. I want you to conquer it. I fear I have held you back."

"No, you have been my muse. You have inspired me and filled me up when I needed to keep going. You never let me down, and you have always been there for me. Your words have fueled my soul, Alexander. You have no idea what your love has meant to me or what it has done for me. You are mine." She laid her head in his lap and sobbed.

Alexander ran his fingers through her hair and along her shoulder. The last flickers of sunlight reflected on her neckline. It was one of Alexander's favorite parts of her. He touched it and felt his entire body quiver as did she. He leaned down and kissed her there on her neck, filling his senses with magnolia and sea salt. Her skin was soft and inviting, just as he had imagined it to be. He kissed her neck again.

"Alexander, I don't want to leave you."

"But you have to. This is a once-in-a-lifetime job. And hey, maybe you will invite me to New York to see you when you get back."

"Alexander, there is talk about keeping me out there for a year, at least."

"Baby, our timeline has never been an easy one."

She muffled a laugh through her tears. Sitting back up, she leaned in to face him, his dark green eyes and tousled hair looking just as it had on that day in the library back in 1995. "You look the same as you did back in school."

"And, baby, you just got prettier. And smarter. And more mine."

January leaned in to kiss him. She kissed him hard

and kissed him deeply. She didn't want to stop kissing him once she started. He pulled her into him, and she let him wrap his arms around her. "Oh, Alexander, please don't stop this time."

"I wouldn't dream of it."

They kissed on the beach as the sun set in front of them and the air became cooler. From a distance, a band played, and they felt like they were the only two people left in the world. For just a moment. A moment after fifteen years of letters, phone calls, texts, emails, brief meetings, and unfinished advances. He touched her everywhere he could put his hands and couldn't touch her completely enough or fast enough. It was territory he had wanted to explore for so long, her skin, her body was finally his to experience.

"I need you, please, I just need you." January allowed him to lay her down, and he looked down at her.

"You are the most beautiful thing I have ever seen. I will love you until the day I die. I am going to make love to you now."

"Yes." January breathed softly as he put his weight on her. He felt so right there, cradling her from the world around them. "So much yes."

He leaned in and kissed her mouth, her face, her neck, her arms. He kissed every part of her. As the sky turned dark, the desolate beach belonged to them. He lifted her dress and pulled her down to meet his hips and then lifted her onto his lap. "I want to look into your eyes when I am inside of you. I have waited too long for this."

She wrapped her arms around his neck as she moved against him. Unzipping his shorts and pulling her panties aside, he entered her, pulling her down onto him slowly. Her moans were like music as she breathed into his ears and covered his mouth with her own. She moved with him in perfect rhythm. His hands were on her face, in her mouth, and his eyes looked into hers. He lowered the top of her dress, so he could put his mouth on her breasts. They were perfect, full and round. He licked each one, tasting her, kissing her, sucking her, biting her. The more she moved on him, the deeper into her he went, and the more he forgot where he was. He was lost in her. January was in ecstasy. She had never felt like this before, every part of her was numb and alive at the same time. There was no more resisting, no more dancing around the need. It was being fulfilled at long last. "You are mine," he whispered into her ear as his hands grabbed her hips and pulled her down onto him.

"Yes."

She kissed him again and ran her hands down his back as he pushed into her and pulled her back into him. She kissed his eyelids, his forehead, his hands. They pushed into each other so hard it was like they were trying to become one person. It was a soft, unyielding violence, pulling them into each other. The ache within January was so deep, almost inside of her bones, and it moved all through her, rattling her senses and exploding into an orgasm that made her body shake as he wrapped his arms around her. She muffled her screams by burying her face in his chest. "Oh, my…"

They held each other, still writhing, connected but sated.

"I love you, Janny. I have loved you since the moment I laid eyes on you that day in the rain. I have wanted to make love to you every day of my life. I wish I had fought harder for you."

January laid her head on his chest, and he held her there beneath the stars with the ocean crashing onto the shore. She was everything he had every wanted and needed.

"I have always loved you, too. It has just never been the right time for us. This, though, wow. This was truly worth the wait. I am carried away, and I want you again." She kissed him long and slow and lay against him. "Can we make love again in a…" She felt herself drift asleep in his strong arms, the ocean breeze cool on her tingling skin.

Alexander felt some pride in having pleased her so completely. He could taste her skin. He could feel her inside of him and, for the first time, in his arms and not just in his mind. He felt, at that moment, she might try to stay. But he knew he couldn't let her change her mind about going to the Middle East. He had to push her if she tried to argue about it. They would have to figure it out somehow because he couldn't live another day of his life without having their bodies intertwined this way again. That would be worse than death.

He pulled the blanket around her shoulders and let her sleep. At least, he could watch her sleep while he held her, even if it was just for a while.

In the distance, he could see lightning over the ocean. The sky was lighting up a brilliant shade of purple and the only love of his life was leaving him.

Again.

Alexander looked down at this beautiful woman in his arms. The woman he had known as a girl. He had watched her grow from a distance and become this unstoppable force, this amazing human being. As thunder rolled softly across the water, he reimagined that day in the college parking lot, the day they were both leaving campus. In his mind, he kissed her and refused to let her go without showing her how much he loved her. Then the timeline would have been so different. So very different. Or maybe it would have still ended up exactly like this, with January sleeping in his arms on the beach. Either way, he reveled in the perfection that was this night. The perfection that was the two of them together.

January awoke to the sound of waves crashing against the shore. They were so close she could feel mist hitting her on the legs. "Oh, Alex, wake up. We slept on the beach!" She started laughing. "This has never happened to me before." Alex was still holding her tightly, as though he was afraid she might disappear in the middle of the night. The sun was just beginning to rise, and the sky was turning a beautiful pink. It must be just before six am, January thought.

"Alex, honey, wake up."

He opened his eyes, groggy for sleeping outside and in such an uncomfortable position. "Morning, baby." He wiped the grains of sand from her cheeks and kissed her. "I got to have to you last night." A huge smile spread across his face.

"Yes, you did."

"I think I might want to have to you again."

"Okay, but let's go to my hotel. We are lucky we didn't get arrested last night for that little public display." January tried to stand and immediately felt dizzy. Alex caught her and took her hand.

"I get to hold your hand now."

"Yes, you do."

Alex moved his fingers along her palm. "I want to hold your hand as much as possible. First, breakfast. Then, more hand holding at breakfast. Then, I want to lay you down on a bed and make love to you as many times as my physical body will allow before you get on a plane and leave again."

"Alex." January stopped walking and looked into his glittering eyes, alive from the fire of their union. "Maybe I shouldn't…"

"Nope. You are going to do this job because it is everything you have worked for, and I refuse to be the guy who keeps you from that. But today, I get to spoil you. A lot." He pulled her across the sand to his car. "Come with me."

In the car, they still held hands. January found herself glancing over and staring at Alex as he drove to the Fontainebleau. The wind from the open car window blew his hair back, and he appeared to be more tanned than when January last saw him. He was wearing sunglasses and his clothes smelled of ocean and of her, which he loved immensely. Sensing her gaze, he turned to look at her.

"I think I want to make love to you, now actually. Can you wait for room service to bring the breakfast?" His smile was cocky and self-assured. January could see joy in his face, and it illuminated him.

They started kissing in the hotel lobby and continued kissing down the hall. Alex pressed her against the hotel room door, and she struggled to open it with her key card as he pressed against her, still kissing her. "Alex, I need to open…" The door clicked and fell open as they made their way inside the room.

She jumped up and wrapped her legs around his waist, exploring his mouth with her tongue and digging her long nails into his back. He tossed her onto the bed and took off his T-shirt, revealing his toned, firm body. He was so tall and lean and, January felt like she could eat him alive. He pulled her dress over her head and kissed her breasts.

"I'm going to start a nice shower for us, baby." Alex left the room and left January on the bed, practically panting from desire. She walked into the bathroom and joined him in the shower. The water was hot and steamy, and she could feel the sand falling from her skin. He poured soap in his hands and washed her, moving his hands all over her slick, wet body. He wanted to worship her. He got on knees and pulled her close to him, letting his tongue explore the space between her legs.

"Oh, Alex, yes," she whispered. Her head tossed back, and she had to brace herself with the wall and moved his mouth all over her, sending her into a fit of pleasure. He stood up and kissed her again, allowing her to taste herself in his mouth.

"I love the way you taste. It's better than I imagined. And, my God, January, did I imagine." He lifted her up and entered her as the hot water flowed down over their bodies. Pressing her back to the shower wall, he moved in and out of her slowly. It was calculated. A slow burn that built up inside of her, the more he teased her with his thrusts. He was so strong. She didn't know he was so strong. "You feel so good, Janny." He kissed her again and lifted her up a bit higher as he moaned slightly. Then he released himself inside of her, filling her with his warmth. Filling her with himself.

Alex washed her hair and pulled her against him. "I love you, January."

January felt the words cut through her like an icy wind. It was as though she had been hearing them in her mind for so long, but this was real. No longer was it in her mind and then gone without a trace. Her secret. There he was holding her beneath the falling water and telling he loved her.

"I love you, too, Alexander. I have loved you for fifteen years." She laid her head on his chest, and he wrapped his arms around her, kissing her on top of her head. Never in her life had January felt more at peace, more like she was where she needed to be. It was an all-consuming fire from which she would choose to remain right where she was, burning alive and taking pleasure in its destruction of her. No more reasons, no more excuses, no more second thoughts, just finally absolution.

Alexander carried her to bed and lay her down, staring in awe at the beauty of her body. "You are almost too glorious to behold." He kissed her stomach and then her mouth. "I'm going to order us room service, and then I am going to make love to you some more." He smiled and walked toward the table with the phone. January enjoyed watching him walk away.

"You have a nice ass," she said. He laughed and turned around and jumped back on top of her.

"At some point, we are going to starve to death." He began kissing her again, and she felt the need building once more. That ache, that need she had just accepted as part of her life for so long, now was being remedied. He entered her again and nibbled at her breasts. "I just can't get enough of you."

January was becoming dizzy from the rush she was experiencing. The two of them together was ferocious and made her want to disappear inside of him and hide there. He wasn't as slow as he had been in the shower; this time, he really pushed her hard. "Oh, Alex, I can't take anymore."

"I won't let you deny me anymore, Janny. You're mine. We are meant to be like this. Can't you feel it?"

"Yes, I feel it. I feel you. You're trying to tear me apart." She was breathing so hard she could feel the vibrations starting again, this time in her stomach and then down her legs and around her inner thighs. Finally, the bolt entered her deep, like he had, and it shook her whole body. It was an amazing electrocution that reverberated for minutes after it started. She feared she may not walk for days. He released her again, sweat dripping from his forehead into her mouth. Apart, they had been angst and unrequited need. Together, they were starting a fire. January's body was spent. She lay against Alex and ran her hand over his chest and down his chiseled stomach. "You feel right. This feels so very right. Why didn't you take me in college? We could've known about this so much sooner."

Alex pulled her close, taking in the feel of her flesh and the smell of her hair, all intoxicating. "Baby, you were so young. I was worried I might taint your innocence or something."

"Taint my innocence? Wow. You do know me, right?" She laughed. "I am fairly certain I came on to you first. Library? Remember?"

"Oh, I could never forget that day. You were so chic with your little black dress and your black finger nail polish, straddling me in my chair. Interrupting me while I was trying to be a good senior and finish my paper on Nietzsche. You were a bad little girl." He slapped her gently on her behind. "I wanted to jump into that ocean so much, but you made me feel like I was a dirty old man taking advantage of a little girl."

"You were twenty-two."

"But still, I just can't explain it other than to say it was like I had too much respect for you to just have sex with you in a library or the back seat of a car or my dorm room. Even then, I put you up higher than that. Now, having tasted you, I wish I would have, at least, put my mouth between your legs back then. It really would have done wonders for my self-confidence."

January punched him in the chest. "Seriously, I wonder if we had just made love then, maybe we never would have separated at all. I love you, and I want to be with you. Stay with me."

Alex was getting up. "I'm just going to order food."

"No, I mean, don't ever leave me. Now that I've had you, it's only going to be worse. I think I secretly hoped making love to you would just get it out of our system and we would be able to finally move on from each other. Break away clean, you know? Now I cannot imagine ever going a day without being in your arms." January sat up in the bed and clutched a pillow to her chest. Her hair, still damp, hung loosely over her shoulders.

Alex walked back over to her and kissed her gently on the lips. "Baby, we were meant to be. We'll figure it out. I promise you."

Centurion

January had a hard time getting on the plane for Virginia. Alex practically pushed her into the check-in line.

"Write to me," he had said.

January would be able to use her phone only intermittently and would have access to email only at very special times. Centurion training would last five days and was supposed to include real-life shoot/don't shoot scenarios and mock attacks. Reading the manual she had received from the program director made it sound like going through boot camp. Alayna would be meeting her there for the same training, and Jesse was already en route to Bagram Airforce Base.

After looking down at her boarding ticket, she glanced back at Alex one more time and felt a piercing in her heart like a thousand knives over and over again. He was smiling his kind yet sly smile, but she knew inside he was fighting not to show what he truly felt. She had already cried twice and, for a moment, thought she might jump out of line and back into his arms. To have come this far after fifteen years only to say goodbye again was just more than she thought she could handle. She mouthed the words "I love you" as she blew him a kiss. Her heart was beating quickly, and she could feel his was, too. She could feel him more than ever before. For years, it had been that way, but now, it was like he was always pressed up against her. When she didn't feel him there, January quickly brought him back with her mind and her longing for him.

****

The flight landed in Richmond on a rainy and cool afternoon. As she made her way to the taxi, January pulled the green pea coat Zak had bought for her tighter around her body. The training would be cold, as most of it was going to be outside. Richmond, Virginia was almost too close to North Carolina, where she and Alex had first met. First kissed. First fought. And first been friends. January held on to those days with all of herself. Those days had sustained them and held them together for so long, even when they were apart. Now that she had her Alexander, she would hold on to their new days now. The past thirty-six hours had been nothing short of magical. She leaned her head against the window of the cab as a gray fall day in Virginia displayed the last leaves flying through the air. Being with Alex was even more wonderful than she could have imagined. She had lost track of how many times they had made love, but the soreness between her legs reminded her it was a lot. She embraced the soreness. He left his mark on her, and as she ran her fingers over her lips, she closed her eyes and imaged his lips on hers. There had been so much kissing, kissing like they were running out of time. They never had enough time.

****

The Centurion building was a large brick facility which appeared to be highly secure with tall fences lined with barbed wire. There was an obstacle course on the grounds and multiple military vehicles placed in various spots and in different conditions. Some were Jeeps, which were overturned; there was a tank and a couple of Humvees. In the distance, January could see an area for shooting targets. Surrounded by woods, there was nothing else out here, except the facility and a very long dirt road leading to a tall gate. January entered the building after someone buzzed her in, and a lady at a desk took her press pass and driver's license to ensure she was who she claimed to be.

As the lady was creating a badge for January to use, she checked her phone, eager to see a message from Alex. There was nothing yet. The woman returned and reached out, handing January a badge with her name and CBS News typed below her photo. "I'll need to take that, too, ma'am."

"My phone? What? Why?"

"It's a security risk. We cannot have you using your personal cell here and taking photos of this facility. You will get it back on Friday before you check out." The woman was wearing brown military fatigues and did not seem to have much patience for people like January.

"Oh, okay. Here you go, I guess." January, with great reluctance, held out her phone, her only link to Alex. It would only be her lucid dreams of him to keep her warm as she waited five more days for his words. His words, she needed to survive, like she needed food. Right now, she was starving. She hoped the soreness from their lovemaking would hang on just a few more days. The smell of him in her hair. The lingering tingle of his lips on her thighs.

"The phone, Ms. Morgan?"

"Oh, sorry, yes, here it is." January sat down on the

couch in the lobby with her bag at her feet and nervously bit at her red nail polish. A tall, very muscular man also dressed in tan fatigues came out and introduced himself to January.

"Good afternoon, Ms. Morgan. My name is Kevin, and I am going to help get you oriented to your new home for the next five days. I know we have a few others coming and a few have already checked in, so I will take you to the barracks, so you can get settled. We will meet for a briefing at 1400 hours."

January shook his hand and smiled. He towered over her and maintained a very stern facial expression. "Follow me, Ms. Morgan."

January picked up her bag and followed the intimidating man into a room with six cots. Not beds. Cots. "Um, Kevin, sir, this cannot be where I'm sleeping. I was told there were beds."

Kevin pointed to the cots. "Those are beds, ma'am."

"Oh, Kevin." January laughed. "Not exactly. I guess, if you mean, it's this or the cold ground outside, these would be considered beds."

"January," he said with a glint of sarcasm in his eyes, "it is this or the cold ground outside. You seem a bit too delicate for that, so I would recommend picking out one of these non-beds to be your bed. Oh, and you will need to start referring to me as Corporal Winslow from this point on. Casual chit-chat ends here in the non-bedroom." He winked at January and walked out of the cold, white room.

"What the hell was that?" January muttered to herself as she placed her back on one of the very thin blue striped mattresses. "It's like prison in here."

Alayna walked into the room wearing a tan T-shirt and brown cargo pants. "Janny! You made it! What do you think of our accommodations here at Chez Prison Hole?" She laughed hysterically. "This is just awful."

January laughed. "I was so sure this was a joke, but it appears they really want to scare the shit out of us at this training."

Alayna nodded. "Yeah, Jesse said it's very real the whole time, and no one breaks character, except for the classroom sessions."

"Breaks character? They are not actors."

"No, they are Marines. But they never un-Marine themselves." Alayna rolled her eyes. "Needless to say, we are screwed. But hey, it might be harder here than Afghanistan."

"I have a feeling you might be right about that." January sat down on the cot and could feel the coils through the mattress. "God, this is going to kill my back."

"Listen," Alayna began, "every major news organization sends their embedded reporters through this program. It's a necessary evil. As weird as this is, I know it will be better for us to know some of this stuff than not know it. I don't know about you, but I have never been to a war zone, so I'm cool with a week of pain."

January pointed to Alayna's clothes. "Where'd you get those fancy duds?"

"Oh, these? Follow me, recruit, and I will take you shopping in the worst store in the world. Everything in there is the color of sand. Hope you like sand!" Alayna giggled as January followed her into a closet with shelves of the same outfit she was wearing. "See? So many choices."

Both women laughed as January picked out a few shirts and two pairs of the cargo pants. "Okay, so what's next?"

Alayna showed January the bathrooms and showers and then the mess hall for meals. It was just like being in the military, January imagined. "I guess I will dress for our orientation. Who else is here?"

Alayna said there were reporters from the Associated Press, Reuters, CNN, and a couple from NBC. It was a relatively small group of people, but Alayna said they ensured reporters and photographers received their training separate from other entities, which used Centurion for training. Because embedded journalists had a specific function, their training was specialized to their tasks abroad. January just wanted to talk to Alex. Just hear his voice.

Alayna noticed January looking forlorn. "Hey, what's on your mind? Are you freaking out about the journey ahead? I know I am."

"Yeah, I am nervous but exhilarated at the same time."

"So, Janny, I didn't want to pry, but I know part of your trip to Miami was because of your divorce. Everything go okay?"

"Yes, it was almost too easy. I didn't want anything of his, and he wanted nothing of mine. No kids involved, so it was pretty cut and dry. It was still pretty awful, but we had reached the end of our road together."

"I'm sorry, Janny. You'll find someone else! And hey, being around hunky army men for months might have its privileges." Alayna was clearly very excited about that part of the job.

"I just hope they keep us out of the line of fire. Plus, I already have someone."

"Damn, Janny! That was fast!"

"Well, we have known each other since college, and it's been building for a very long time. We just were in other relationships and would never have acted on it. But we acted on it this weekend. A lot." January couldn't stop the wide smile from spreading across her face. She felt like she was glowing when she talked about Alexander. "We really fit. Like he was meant to be mine or something. I know it might sound silly to you."

Alayna shook her head, "No! I've read about stuff like this. It's your twin soul."

"My what?"

"He's your twin soul. Your soul mate. So, like, do you have the same thoughts? Think about each other at the same time? Have dreams about each other on the same nights? Stuff like that. Oh, and one of the books I read said you can feel each other, even when you are miles apart. Like your souls are communicating, even when your bodies and minds are not."

"Wow, that's some pretty intense literature you read, Alayna. And I thought you were just a news-reading kind of girl." January thought about what Alayna was saying, and while she would never admit such a personal thing to her new friend and co-worker, Alayna was absolutely right. About all of it. "Twin souls, huh? I like the sound of that."

"Seriously, you should read about it. It's very cosmic and very rare. He might be your other half, literally."

"I never really thought of it that way. But maybe. I mean, we do connect in a pretty intense kind of way." January was filled with that numbness that only arrived when Alex was thinking of her. She could feel it everywhere. "I just want him and not only in a sexual way. I feel like I need him to breathe."

Alayna laughed. "Dependent. Just kidding. No, that sounds like the real deal, honey. Let's knock out some kick-ass news, so we can get you back to this guy before you stop breathing."

"Yeah, I wouldn't want that to happen." January was happy to have Alayna with her during this experience. She knew, if Alayna had not been there, she might have become too introspective and separated herself from the rest of the trainees. Inside, she felt the ache returning with a vengeance. She needed Alexander so badly; even the thought of him, which was once a longing gone when she opened her eyes, had grown into a full-fledged physical need. She wanted to feel him around her in the real world and not just in her mind, as it had been for so many years before. January hoped he was doing okay because, without him, she felt like she might break in half. The tingling in her body asserted his need for her. She held on to that as the first five days of their separation began. There would be many more days. Months. Maybe longer. She didn't want to think about it. It hurt too much. The longing was worse now that she had experienced him. "Looks like we have an hour before our briefing. I think I might lay down and take a short nap on the ridiculous mattress."

"I'm exhausted, too. Sadly, I don't think our sleeping situation will be much better in Afghanistan. This might be a five-star resort compared to sleeping in a dusty tent."

January closed her eyes while the metal coils of the thin mattress pushed uncomfortably into her side. Even with the bad bed, she still fell asleep quickly, her mind hazy and filled with memories of Alex's hands and mouth all over her body.

When January awoke, it was to the sound of a foghorn. She shot up in bed so quickly she banged her head on the metal bunk above her head. "Ow, shit!"

Kevin, the man in fatigues from earlier, was standing beside her. "Ms. Morgan, I am going to need you to report to the briefing room right now please. You are running late."

January looked at her watch. "Oh, I am so sorry. I overslept."

"Damn right you did. Get yourself together and meet us in there. I have a table with your manual ready to go." Kevin winked at January, softening a bit of his tough exterior. Clearly, he enjoyed messing with civilians.

As she was walking down the hall to find the briefing room, the power went out. Emergency lights came on in the dark hallway, but January was still struggling to see as she walked forward, passing closed-off rooms, hoping to hear some activity from one of them or see a sign indicating which room was the training room. There were no windows, and the security lights were dim and making a slight buzzing sound. Suddenly, January felt more like she was in the middle of a horror movie than at a military-inspired training. The whole thing was just strange.

"Hello? Anyone around? I am looking for the training room." January walked forward and pulled her hair back into a ponytail. She thought she heard a noise behind her and turned around but didn't see anyone or anything. It was as though she was in a completely closed and deserted building. "Kevin? I mean, sir? Where the fuck did everybody go?" January nervously chewed on her chipped nail polish.

Her heart raced, and she could feel fear moving through her body. The fear stopped her from moving, and as she turned to look behind her, an arm grabbed her and pulled her in. The masked man was holding a handgun to her head and had his left arm holding her to him. She screamed and tried to kick and fight back, but he was so strong; he stayed perfectly still. He whispered into her ear, "Bam, you're dead." Then he laughed, and the hallway lights came on. January, still terrified, could see her group of fellow trainees at the end of the hallway, and they were clapping. January thought she might cry, but instead balled her fist and, out of pure reactionary anger, punched the man who had grabbed her right in the nose.

"Fuck!" he shouted as he tossed the mask to the floor and grabbed his nose, which was bleeding quite profusely all over the tile floor. "Kevin, you said you had briefed her on the exercise. That was not the response of someone who saw this coming. Asshole!"

Kevin was laughing as he stood beside the other trainees who all had looks of complete shock on their faces. Alayna's jaw was nearly to the floor, yet she was still stifling a laugh. January was breathing so hard she fell to her knees. "I'm so sorry I hit you, but you attacked me!"

The bleeding man placed a cloth to his face. "Seriously not your fault. This is on Kevin. It's his stupid practical joke. Nice right hook by the way. Damn."

January looked over at Kevin. "You suck at practical jokes."

Kevin ushered everyone into the training room. "This is just the beginning. In a war zone, that kind of thing can happen to you at any time. I want to make sure you guys are prepared and know how to respond to an active shooter. While you do have a nice right hook, there are a few other options that might have been more favorable. Let's go talk about them and get you ready to go to war, January Morgan."

January offered to help the bleeding man stand up. "So sorry again. I'm Janny."

"I'm Robert. Robert Hartwood. Retired Army, now a cop who occasionally helps here at Centurion. But after today, I might reconsider that."

The two of them entered the training room to uncomfortable applause. Kevin motioned for January to take a seat. "Welcome to Centurion. We cannot make you fighters here, but we will show you how to protect yourself, how to be aware of your surroundings and people's behaviors, and we will speak in-depth about where you are going and the type of culture you will soon be surrounded by. In a war zone, a gun pointed at your head could very well happen. An IED explosion could happen. Sexual assault could happen. We are here to train you on how to stay with your assigned unit so that you are as protected as the United States military can ensure. Now that Lieutenant Hartwood is no longer bleeding and Miss Morgan seems to have regained her faculties, let's introduce ourselves."

As everyone went around the room and gave their

name and media affiliation, January felt like she might never reclaim the air that had been ripped from her lungs.

****

The next several days were a blur of early morning obstacle-course runs, classroom trainings, simulated shooter incidents, and simulated physical attacks. They learned a great deal about Afghanistan and how the military was working with the civilians there, as well as the safe places to go in the event of a bombing. The days were long, and the nights were short and filled with fitful sleep and sore muscles and tired minds. January missed Alexander and would have given just about anything to just read a few words from him, but they had been denied all communication during their training. It was supposed to prepare them for the lack of communication when in the desert because the computers out there were not always in the best working condition and chances to call or video call home would be few and far between. January learned a little bit about how to shoot a handgun, which she had never done before. She also learned a little hand-to-hand combat and a few interesting tricks with knives. If anything, January thought she might enjoy learning more about self-defense once she returned to the states and had some free time again. She now fully understood the value of the training she was receiving, and despite her need for sleep and a decent cheeseburger, she felt ready to tackle the long road ahead. One more day at Centurion and then she would be flying to Bagram Airforce Base in Afghanistan. From there, she and Alayna would be taken, via military vehicle, to Kabul to meet up with Jesse, who was already there, and members of the military unit they would be assigned to. It was finally almost here. The day she had been waiting for and working for. January Morgan would be filing reports from the front lines as a correspondent for CBS.

Kevin knocked on the dormitory room door. "Come in," January said as she sat up straight on the edge of her cot. She had been reading her book about the geography of Afghanistan during the twenty-minute break they got in the middle of the day. Kevin walked up to her and smiled. "Hey, kid, I just want you to know how proud I am of your progress these past few days. I know I sort of used you as an example-victim back on day one, but you handled it like a professional. Since then, you have shown a lot of promise. I feel like you will be able to handle yourself pretty well out there." He was wearing all black today, which was a departure from the sand-colored fatigues. "Good luck out there."

"Thank you, sir. I really appreciate it."

"And, Janny, if someone ever comes at you with bad intent, let your gut lead the way and remember those movements I showed you with the blade. Knives are best when someone is right up on you. By then, the gun might not help. Trust your gut. Trust the blade. I'll make sure the guys over there outfit you with a good one." He smiled and walked out of the room.

January lay back on her pillow and held the book close to her chest. Trust the blade, she thought. The words rolled over in her mind as she drifted into a brief sleep.

Embedded

When Alayna and January could finally see the Centurion facility in the rearview mirror, they high-fived each other. It had been a brutal experience. Useful, yes, but it had physically and emotionally wrecked them both, and they felt it. "I cannot wait for this flight, just so I can drink," Alayna said, sounding exhausted. "I just want one strong drink and a pillow, and I will not wake up until Bagram, I swear to God."

"I will raise your drink by two drinks, my friend. Once we get to the airport, let's have a drink and a meal there before the flight leaves. I'm thinking something greasy and with fries on the side." January had become so tired of the cafeteria food at Centurion. While it was healthy, it was the exact same choices every day. January was dying for something unhealthy. "Let's also get ice cream or pie. In fact, I might eat two slices of pie with my whiskey."

Alayna was laughing hysterically. "You are nuts, Janny! But, yes, pie and whiskey does sound like a winning combination."

****

They arrived at the airport in Richmond, and the air was getting colder. It was easily in the forties now. Alayna shivered. "It just occurred to me we will be spending our Christmas in the desert. That might suck."

"Christmas is overrated anyway. If anything, it will

save us from having to buy each other really shitty gifts at the last minute from a drug store." January tipped the cab driver, and they both walked quickly into the airport, pulling their coats high around their necks to fight the cold wind. January felt a jolt move through her body, which immediately pushed the cold away. It was so strong she could hear his thoughts. I'm here, he said inside of her mind. She stopped and turned around, and there, by the check-in counter, was Alexander. She ran to him. Dropping her bags onto the airport floor and leaving a confused Alayna standing near the pile. January jumped into his arms and kissed him fiercely. She was grabbing him and kissing him so hard a security guard came up to them and asked them to "cool it." "You're here! Why are you here in Virginia? I'm about to board in two hours."

Alexander smiled, his beautiful face lighting up as his dimples revealed themselves. He wasn't wearing his glasses, and he had cut his hair. He looked more professional, regal even. He seemed taller somehow.

Alayna walked up to meet him. She blushed as she looked at Alex. "So you're the guy?"

"I'm him."

"I'm Alayna. I'm your lady's producer." She shook his hand. "Nice to meet you, Alexander. I will give you two some time. Janny, I'll meet you at the gate, pie and whiskey in hand."

"Sounds perfect. Be there soon." January wrapped her arms around Alex. He was wearing a long black coat and black gloves. He was wearing jeans, of course, and a soft gray sweater that Janny immediately buried her face in. "You smell good. I missed you so much, Alex." Her head fit perfectly right at his chest, and he wrapped his arms around her.

"I've missed you, too, baby. I couldn't stand it this past week without even a message from you. I had to use this chance to see you in person."

"I was just about to call you and here you are!"

"Follow me." He pulled her hand, and she grabbed her bag and followed.

"Where are we going?" January was slightly concerned he might have decided to kidnap her to keep her from leaving the country. Then she smiled at the thought and decided she would willingly stay just to feel him against her.

"I know it's not the most comfortable place in the world, but I think it will work for our current needs." He brought her back out into the cold and to a black car with darkly tinted windows was parked along the curb. "Get in and let's drive to the back of the cell phone lot."

"Are you out of your mind?"

"Well, I was looking at a picture of you last night from one of the parties we hosted in the dorm, and you were wearing a black bra and a pair of black leather shorts. Not sure why you were dressed that way or how I still even have the photo, but I kind of lost my mind a little bit when I saw it. So that was all the incentive I needed to fly here and make passionate love to you in the backseat of this rental car in the cell phone lot. So get in."

January was speechless but did exactly as she was told. After she hopped into the car, they drove through the crowded parking lot to the cell phone lot, which was not nearly as crowded. The window tint was dark enough to give them privacy, but Alex still parked as far away from every car as he could. They both got out and got into the backseat.

"Okay, Alex. You are insane. But I am completely irrevocably in love with you, and it would please me greatly if you would make love to me in the backseat of this rental car right now." Alex took off his coat, as did January and they kissed frantically, as though they needed each other to breathe. "Oh, Alex, I need you so badly." She pulled at his sweater, revealing his pale, firm stomach. She kissed him there and then on his chest while he pulled her sweater over her head.

"I missed these." He placed his hand behind her and lay her down on the backseat as he unhooked her bra. "They are so perfect. So beautiful and perfect." He ran his mouth over her breasts and nibbled at them, causing her to squeal in pleasure. "I'm so glad you are wearing a skirt and these knee-high boots. I will keep that image in my head until I get to see you wearing them again." He lifted her skirt and pulled her panties down.

His skin was so warm against hers, despite the freezing temperatures just outside the car. She unzipped his jeans which were hanging low on his hips, which she had so desperately missed grabbing on to. She pulled his hips down as he entered her. Slowly at first and then quickly. He was pushing into her so hard the back of her head was knocking into the car door. "Sorry," he murmured as he pulled her down and kissed her head. "You are everything to me." He moved in and out of her until she could feel his warmth filling her up, and the waves of pleasure coursed through her body as they came together. He lay on top of her for a moment, running his long fingers over her breasts and her lips. "I don't want you to leave. I admit it. I will, of course, force you onto the plane, if I have to, but I will miss you and think of you every second of the day."

"Alex, when I come home, we need to figure all of this out."

"There's nothing to figure out. There is only us now. Just us, baby. It'll be okay."

They kissed long and slow as tears rolled down January's cheeks.

"Thank you for meeting me at the airport and making love to me in the backseat of a rental car."

They both laughed.

"Anytime, my love."

Alexander drove her back to the curb, so she could check in. Her hair was disheveled, and she was sure her sweater was on inside out. He kissed her again, brushing her hair from her bright gray eyes. "As soon as you can, let me know you have arrived safely. I love you, Janny."

"I love you, too, Alex." She got out of the car and walked in a near dream-like state to the check-in counter. She could feel some of Alexander dripping down from inside of her onto her right thigh. The woman at the counter gave her the once-over and shook her head. "Your identification and passport please, ma'am?"

"Yes, here you are, and I think I might need to freshen up before I board. Where's the ladies' room?"

The woman motioned with her hand. "Honey, that must've been some goodbye because you look like you were manhandled!" She laughed in such a way that made January embarrassed.

"Something like that." January smiled and headed to the bathroom to straighten herself up. When she met up with Alayna at the terminal, Alayna was holding a box and a small bag.

"Cherry pie and a small bottle of whiskey from the duty free." She smiled and handed the goods over to January. "Hey, so how was your time with Mr. Wonderful?"

January started eating the pie right out of the bag. "Interesting. Nice. Unbelievable."

"So what happened? Did you stand outside and kiss in the cold and say your farewells? It's so romantic that he showed up here." Alayna had a dreamy look in her eyes. "I wish I had a guy who would do that for me. Maybe I do." She gave a shy smile.

"I knew there was someone. You better spill it. This is a very long flight." January smiled. "My relationship with Alex is unique. Yes, there were goodbyes in the cold, but we also made mad, passionate love in the backseat of his car in the parking lot." January gave a coy smile and raised her eyebrow at Alayna.

"You didn't?"

"We did."

"I am fairly certain you violated multiple post nine-eleven laws. Wow, you guys don't mess around! Or you do. Either way, I'm impressed."

"I feel like I cannot breathe without him, Alayna. I feel panicky and like I am leaving part of myself behind."

"It's the twin soul thing. This trip will be tough for you and for him. Just stay busy and that will help you cope. I mean, we are going to be crazy busy, not to mention the whole 'being in a foreign country and war zone' element. Just write to him. Email him. Video call him. We will have the technology to do that. In fact, our military unit is probably looking forward to our arrival because we will give them better access to their families back here in the states."

The loudspeaker blared. "Flight 345 to Los Angeles with connecting flight to Kabul is now boarding."

January and Alayna looked at each other. "Well," January began, "this is it. Let's do this!"

The two young women got in line to board the plane, both slamming back their small bottles of whiskey before they boarded, giving each other a little high-five. The time had come, and January Morgan was on her way to Kabul.

****

The flight to Los Angeles was roughly four hours. It was smooth and both Alayna and January could sleep for most of the fight. Transferring to the next leg of the journey was a much different story. While the plane was not crowded, the flight was turbulent and very long. Nearly sixteen hours in the air, and January found herself walking the aisles, just to feel the blood moving in her legs. Alayna had taken a couple of sleeping pills, but January couldn't allow herself to relax enough to do that. She tried to read, watched a few of the in-flight movies, which were all terrible, and ordered a few cocktails. After the tenth hour in the air, time seemed to slow down, and she found that she was the only one who was still awake in a darkened airplane while everyone around her slept. Alexander was on her mind, but so was Zak. She realized he would be in Mexico by now, embarking on the undercover job. She could not imagine the people he was going to have to associate with and, even worse, pretend to respect. His Spanish was okay, but she wondered if it was enough for him to effectively communicate. There was still so much left between them, and even though their marriage had failed, January still loved Zak very much and wanted him to be safe. Being surrounded by members of a drug cartel was certainly not safe. Finally, after thinking herself into a state of near panic, she decided to take a few melatonin tablets and chase them with a glass of wine. It allowed her to sleep for a few hours, which was all she could hope for under the current circumstances. As she drifted off to sleep, she thought of making love to Alex in the car. It gave her mind a certain peace and filled her with a sense of security as the plane landed in the middle of a country ridden with dust and danger.

****

The flight was bumpy toward the end and landing at Bagram was unlike any landing January had ever experienced. When the plane finally came to a stop, things seemed to move in fast forward. The airplane door opened, gushing in a blast of sandy air, while stairs were moved so passengers could exit. Two men in army uniforms boarded the plane carrying automatic rifles. They waited as each person exited, and then asked January and Alayna to come with them. There was very little discussion, and the men seemed to be in a hurry. "We will ensure your bags are brought to the base camp. Your photographer is already waiting for you and has been gathering video. He also has received your satellite equipment, laptops, and any other technology you will need to conduct your operations. I am Lieutenant Phillip Bellamy, Third Infantry Division. This is Staff Sergeant Billy Radcliffe. You will be with us during your time here, ladies."

"I am January, and this is Alayna, my producer. Wow, it's freezing here."

"Yes, ma'am. Winter in Afghanistan is no joke. Please get in that Jeep, and let's head to base camp. Are you both ready?"

Alayna looked terrified, so January took her hand. "Yes, sir, let's do this." January was also afraid but decided to remain strong and remember her training. To appear afraid inferred weakness, and she didn't want to seem weak, especially not now.

"Oh, and, January," the lieutenant began, "I have this for you." He handed her a fairly large knife with a leg strap. "A friend told me you earned it." January smiled. Kevin had made good on his promise.

"Do I get a weapon?" Alayna asked.

Lieutenant Bellamy laughed. "Yes, ma'am. You get the entire Third Battalion. I think we make a nice weapon. Oh, and you, ladies, will want to cover your heads with those scarves. Women aren't exactly respected that much here. And then there's all the sand in the air." Both soldiers laughed as they barreled down a dirt road, heading toward the base camp. Dust was flying in January's face, so she pulled her scarf up a little higher, covering her head.

****

Roughly an hour later, they arrived at what appeared to be a city, or, at least, what was left of one. "Welcome to Kabul," one of the soldiers said flatly. "Not exactly the lovely streets of Manhattan." There were children running and playing in the streets and people selling produce and textiles. The buildings were in bad shape, and there seemed to be an equal number of soldiers to civilians. As they drove past, the children tried to chase the Jeep and waved. Some of them shouted words in Pashto, a language January had been trying to study but had been failing miserably at her attempt to pronounce words in the dialect. The soldiers tossed some candy out of the Jeep, and the children clamored for it, screaming sounds of gratitude. Sergeant Radcliffe shouted over the engine and the screams. "So it's good to see the kids and to hear them because, when we don't see and hear the kids, there's a good chance someone is waiting in the wings with an RPG. Kids are always cleared out when they are ready to fuck us up or blow up another building."

As the Jeep rolled through the bumpy city streets, civilians flew past them on scooters. It seemed as if there were no road rules or even lines to divide lanes. It was chaos, pure and simple. Buildings had crumbled from explosions, and the ones that were still somewhat standing were exposed. January could see women averting their eyes, cooking over makeshift stoves. Their walls were gone, but they remained in whatever was left of their homes. It was cold as ice, and these people wrapped themselves in burlap blankets and still stood inside their wall-less houses and tried to cook for their families. Seeing this hit January hard. "My God," she said, "I can't believe people are living this way."

"You think the city is bad, you should see the river they toss their trash into. Then they have these horrible pumps to filter out the water from the same trash river for drinking. Even if the Taliban had not robbed these people of their freedom, the living conditions and illiteracy would have done enough damage." Lieutenant Bellamy shook his head. "All in all, we are making progress here, despite what you are seeing. The war has been going on for nine years already, and we have helped rebuild a great deal of infrastructure. The Taliban does try to destroy most of it, but some of it will remain if we guard it well enough."

With the bustling and crumbling streets of Kabul now in the rearview, they approached the base camp which was lined with what the soldiers called CHUs. This meant containerized housing units. January was quickly learning the military loved its acronyms, just like cops.

"Welcome home, ladies," Bellamy shouted. "Let's get you inside to meet with the squad leader and assign you to your quarters." The Jeep slid into a space beside two Humvees. January and Alayna realized they had been holding on to each other during the entire drive. For one, they were so cold they could no longer feel their toes, but they were also terrified and astonished at the living conditions in Kabul. Neither one of them was emotionally prepared for what they would see, and January knew she hadn't even seen the half of it yet. Going inside of the largest CHU, January relished in the warm air that hit her in the face as she entered. She felt like it might be hours before she truly felt warm again. The room was spacious, and there were multiple desks and a hodgepodge of computer equipment and radios, none of which appeared to be organized or assembled in an orderly fashion. There were, at least, twelve other people in uniform walking around the space, each one looking busy and respectfully acknowledging the two young women as they walked by. Bellamy escorted them over to an office, and he knocked on the door. "Sir, sir, the CBS crew is here."

The door opened, and a very tall man in camo was standing before them. He was older, probably in his mid-fifties with graying hair. He smelled of cigars, and his office was filled with books and papers. "Well, hello there, ladies! I am Lieutenant General Mason Holloway. Welcome to our little slice of heaven." He smiled broadly. "I suppose the boys took you on the scenic route through Kabul's thriving downtown?"

"Yes, sir," January began, "I cannot say that I look forward to returning there."

"Well, that's understandable as it is a certifiable shit hole. And thanks to the Taliban, it is a bombed and broken shit hole to boot. So here's the plan. You ladies have been assigned to one of our units just a few buildings down from this one. There are other reporters staying in that unit, and your photographer is already settled and has your editing equipment and cameras all at the ready. He's clearly been here before. Before we send you out into the war zones, we will need to help you with some roll over training."

Alayna chimed in. "Oh, we had that in Virginia."

"Not like this you ain't." Mason's laugh was more of a cough mixed with a bellow followed by more coughing. Clearly, he was enjoying his cigars a little too much. "All right, ladies, we will ensure you get the video you need, the interviews you need within reason, and we will do our very best to keep you safe at all times. More importantly, we will ask you to do exactly what we say when out in the field as these men and women know when an attack is coming, and their instructions are for your personal safety. Got it?"

"Yes, sir." January shook Mason's hand and tried to offer a small smile, but she felt it was forced. Her fear must have been just as clear as day on her face. Mason looked down at her in a somewhat fatherly way.

"Listen, you two will be just fine. I will personally see to it that you not only get some good stories but get the hell out of here as safely as you arrived."

Bellamy and Radcliffe led Alayna and January back out into the cold, arid air. Looking around, January was taken aback by the beauty of the mountains that surrounded her. Snowcapped and stunning to examine. If it weren't for the large military presence and the recent trip through Kabul, she would swear she was in Colorado. This was, of course, not Colorado.

Jesse was waiting for them in containerized housing unit number nine, reserved for press. There were plenty of tables filled with editing equipment and video tapes. It looked just like a newsroom without the studio. There were lights set up in corners for reporters needing to record intros to their stories indoors, and in the back of unit nine were beds, showers, and a small kitchen. Alayna ran up to Jesse, and he picked her up in his arms and held her.

"Oh, wow." January didn't realize the two of them were a thing. They had never gotten around to that conversation on the plane, but now it was quite clear.

Alayna flushed. "I know I should have told you, but Jess and I have done our best at keeping our private life out of the newsroom. I trust you, Janny, and quite frankly, we will be here a long time. I don't have the energy to hide my relationship with Jess all the way in Afghanistan."

Jesse kissed Alayna on the head. "I thought you guys took the long way to get here, but I am glad you made it safely. I was worried."

"No, we made it here fine," Alayna said, "But this place is not exactly pleasant. I mean, I knew it would suck, being a war zone and all, but it's beyond my wildest dreams."

January sat down at one of the desks. "I still think the mountains are beautiful. I have never seen anything like that. Do we have Internet access out here?" She was more than eager to send an email to Alex, assuring him of her safe arrival.

Jesse turned on the dated PC. "Yes, we do. It's slow and lags a bit, but you can access email, and we can even feed video. We even have the ability to go live with the new TVU backpacks. They have provided us with plenty of equipment to turn the daily story, if needed, and of course, they will also want the long-form pieces. We will be busy, January, but at least, we know we have the technology to do our job. Unless it all breaks, and then we are screwed." He stifled a laugh. "I talked to the assignment desk today, and they want a live shot from you tomorrow with just some basics. You know, just asserting our presence out here, maybe toss in some sound with our squad leader, that kind of thing. It's not like coverage from Kabul or any other town out here is anything new, but they want to remind our viewers CBS has not left, and they want fresh content. Let's find some good people stories, too, not just the basic war recap stuff."

January was overwhelmed. "I need food. I need a drink. And I need a nap. But first, I would really love to email Alexander."

Jesse logged into the computer. "There you go! As for food and drink, we eat with the soldiers and dinner is in an hour. Or 'chowtime,' as they call it. I have some protein bars and water bottles inside that desk if you need something now."

January wasted no time rifling through the drawer to find one of the bars. She ate it so fast it made her stomach hurt. Finally, the screen lit up with the promise of her email account and possibly a letter from Alex. She needed to read some of his words right now because she had never felt as out of her element as she did at this moment. She hoped Alex would be able to share stories of his mission trips to help offset her first experience of seeing a third world country face to face. The email from Alex was short but filled January with warmth.

Baby,

Hope you are there. Wish you were here. Proud of you for everything and looking forward to more of us.

I love you,

Alex

With fingers still chilled by the icy air, January typed away at her response.

My dearest love,

So the one that got away is officially mine now. I cannot tell you how unbelievably happy I am. Even here, in the middle of what I can only describe as complete destruction, I feel joy in knowing you are on the other side of the world waiting for me. I am safe. I will be on the air tomorrow. And, Alex, I love you, too. We can say that now. Over and over again. Freely.

I love you.

Your January. Your baby. Just yours.

The first night on base was a challenge. The time change and jet lag made for a feeling of dizziness that

January just could not shake. All the soldiers were friendly, and the other news reporters were extremely helpful. Many of them had been embedded before and, over dinner, spoke often of their previous experiences. One reporter named Ernest with NBC told a startling tale about watching a landmine go off not far from his convoy the year before. While the story sent shivers down January's spine, it seemed to create laughter among the other reporters and soldiers in the room. Clearly, danger was everywhere, and while it was taken very seriously, it was also a point of humor. One soldier jokingly responded, "Sometimes their bombs aren't exactly on the roads. Not sure if that one was poor digging skills or just someone who had limited eyesight." The laughter roared again.

Alayna was leaning against Jesse, her arms wrapped around his waist as they ate. January needed sleep. "Good night, guys. I'm going to turn in. I will see you both in the morning, and we can hit the ground running." More laughter. "Shit, guys, I didn't mean it like that!" January laughed a little, too. It felt good to laugh because it made the fear a little less overwhelming.

Crawling into her bunk, January could feel the jet lag hitting her once again. Sleep. Sleep would help. She drifted off quickly, despite the scratchy green blanket and the rock-hard pillow. Her dreams were erratic and unceasing. This was not a restful sleep, but a fitful one in which her mind did not catch up with the exhaustion of her body. Still, she remained asleep for nearly fourteen hours until Alayna was shaking her.

"Wake up, sleepy head! Sheesh!" Alayna was already dressed and appeared to have been awake for quite some time. "You talk in your sleep."

January allowed her eyes to adjust to the blue fluorescents of the room. "I've been told I also sleepwalk. Don't let me do that here. What time is it?"

Alayna looked at her watch. "Well, almost noon here. Still yesterday back home. But you need to get moving, have some lunch, and get prettied up. We are heading out with our unit in one hour to collect a few elements for the evening news. They want us live for the evening show, which means going live at night, around 9:30 Kabul time. This gives us a good full day to make some news." Alayna was bouncing around excitedly.

"You're awful chipper today." January covered her eyes with the pillow.

"Well, I am here in a place to cover the news I have always wanted to cover with the man of my dreams. From where I'm standing, Kabul ain't so bad. Now get up, reporter, and let's get moving!" Alayna practically danced out of the room, leaving January alone in the barracks, which could sleep up to eight women.

Sgt. Radcliffe assembled with Jesse, Alayna, and January after January had eaten and finally made herself presentable. He had a map and gave them an overview of the days' plan. "All right, we will be heading back into the city today. I will say there is more security there than you might have thought after yesterday's quick tour because the embassy is there and right next to that is the supreme court of Afghanistan." He pointed to two buildings on the map. "The problem is this; the Army Corp of Engineers keeps rebuilding, and then the Taliban will destroy what is rebuilt. This happens over and over again. Kabul used to be a vibrant city, and I can only imagine what it once was like before the Taliban took hold. Now we can see a firefight lasting well into six hours or longer with RPGs and AK47s. Even children carry these weapons. Today, we will be going to a village in Kabul where we have been working alongside the Corp of Engineers to help rebuild what we hope will be a water filtration unit to improve the water quality. You guys noticed the sewage water yesterday, I'm sure, or, at least, smelled it. So, your first story as an embedded journalist will be about the toilets, January." Radcliffe smiled. "Hope that works for you and your TV leaders back home. We leave in thirty."

January stifled a laugh but knew the story was important, despite the topic. It was a start, and every day there would be a new story. Be it human interest, cultural, death, or destruction, each day would be filled with multiple stories and multiple angles. Water quality would only be day one. Jesse loaded up a backpack with gear while Alayna and January filled their packs with water, snacks, makeup, hair ties, and wet wipes. Sunblock, bug spray, CBS baseball cap, and a scarf. January knew she would need something she didn't have but tried not to make the pack too heavy, just in case there would be some walking. Or running.

After another bumpy ride in another Humvee, the crew, along with two other armored vehicles, arrived at a small village, just on the outskirts of Kabul. Children were running around the dirt road, many of them wearing only diapers or underwear. Some just wearing shirts and no bottoms at all. They all appeared unbathed, and their mothers looked on from small

square buildings that barely looked tall enough for
someone to stand in. Each structure appeared to be
made of the same sand-like material that surrounded
them. Everything was the same color. Tan. The houses
blended in with the ground and with the mountains in
the distance, but the sky was blue today, making a nice
contrast to the dusty poverty below. Alongside the
ruddy, earthen homes was the river, which had lost its
movement and rather, seemed to be stilled by the
weight of the contents within it. January knew what
those contents were, and her stomach turned as she
watched a small child of about three splashing in the
acrid water. January found herself wanting to run to the
child and hose him down, but she planted her boots in
the sand and leaned back against the vehicle. Soldiers
from the other vehicles got out and moved toward an
area near the water where some people were taking
water samples. They were also wearing fatigues.
Sergeant Radcliffe motioned for us to follow him and
the other soldiers to talk to the men eyeballing the water
samples and holding jars of the murky water up to the
light. The water was not clear. It was not even slightly
brown. It was pure darkness. Alayna gasped.

As we walked, another crew of soldiers unloaded
gallon jugs of fresh water and protein bars, handing
them out to families. Mothers and fathers and children
smiled awkwardly as they accepted the kindness.
Another military truck pulled up with bags of rice and
more water. Jesse was already getting video of all these
things, as well as shots of the river turned sewer.

Radcliffe waved to one of the men testing the
water. "Hey, Jonathan! I bring news people!"

Jonathan, a member of the Army Corps of

Engineers, seemed happy to greet the sergeant and equally happy to see media. That was not something January was accustomed to. "Well, we appreciate the coverage. More coverage means more food and water donations and hopefully more funding to help clean up some of this mess. Nice to meet you." Jonathan extended his hand and shook January's and Alayna's hands. "I wish I had better news, but what you are seeing is about as bad as you can imagine. E. coli and about a hundred other issues that make this not safe to drink or to play in," he said as he pointed to the little boy who waddled back to his mother officially covered in human feces. The smell was worse this close to the water. January felt her stomach lurch.

"All right," January began, "I would like to interview you, sir, if that's okay, and talk a little more about the work you are doing here to help these villagers."

"No problem." Jonathan smiled and straightened his round eyeglasses. He was quite tall, so January decided to stand on a nearby rock to better reach him with the microphone. A tripod could always be raised, but a reporter could only look so tall when standing next to someone who was over 6'5".

January conducted her interviews, and while Jesse worked on video, Alayna sat in the truck and began writing the story. This allowed January a moment to walk around and really take in the surroundings. It was unbelievable people could live like this at all. Suddenly January understood why Alex had made a point of spending so much time in Haiti, helping people. She hugged herself as a cool breeze swept down from the mountains which towered into the clouds high above the small houses and what once was a lovely river below. But the Taliban had built dams and rerouted the river water, leaving only a motionless black lake for these families. Their source of purity and life, taken from them. It was not a bomb but a slower kind of death. January felt someone pull at the back of her shirt, and she turned quickly, a feeling of fear running through her body. A small girl wearing a dirty blue dress stood barefoot and smiling before her. The child was possibly nine years old, and she was quite lovely with dark hair and brown eyes with flecks of green. "Hello, sweetheart." January bent down and smiled back at the child who was now holding out her hand. "Oh, I see. Well, I have a bottled water, a candy bar, and I have this." January took the silver bangle bracelet off her wrist and handed all three items to the child. The little girl smiled again, revealing a few missing teeth, her baby teeth. She placed the bracelet on her wrist, and her eyes widened. She was dazzled. Then, from one of the houses, which looked more like a hut, a man came outside, walking at a rapid pace. He picked up the little girl and removed the bracelet, tossing it to the ground. He allowed her to keep the water and candy. He spat on the ground and glowered at January. As he carried the child back to the hut, January could see the little girl's eyes fill with tears.

Radcliffe walked up quickly. "I should have said something to you about that kind of thing. Remember when I said women are not respected here? Well, especially American women. And even more especially, American white women who give seemingly expensive items to their daughters. Had that been a little boy, it might have ended a bit differently." He picked up the bracelet. "Don't take it to heart." He patted January on the back as he walked back to the other soldiers. It was time to head back to the base to set up for a live shot. January stood motionless and speechless for a moment still staring at the hut with the now loudly crying child inside. Something inside of her crumbled.

Back at base camp, January prepared for her first live report from Afghanistan. Jesse had set up the lighting, and Alayna had written an amazing story about the Taliban's efforts to destroy this village by stealing the once-flowing, clear river. All January had to do was voice the package and introduce it live on the air. She hoped Alex was watching. After taking a deep breath and going over her script for the tenth time, January felt ready. She placed her earpiece in her right ear and straightened her hair. The dessert air was getting cold, and she was wearing a scarf around her neck and a light jacket. In her ear, January could hear the news anchor setting her up.

"Tonight, we lead the news with the ongoing war against the Taliban in Afghanistan. Correspondent January Morgan is live tonight at Bagram Airforce Base with the latest on how one village is suffering a different kind of attack by the terrorist group, an attack that does not involve bombs, rather, destroying the river they once depended on for food and clean water. January?"

"Good evening, Brian. It was once their source of food, water, and a place to bathe, now the level of sewage and bacteria is so high, even the Army Corps of Engineers is saying it's too late to save the water. That is, unless the dam built by the Taliban is destroyed, allowing the water to run freely once more." January could hear her story start to play in her ear. Jesse held his hand up until she was to be back on camera. As the story wrapped up, Jesse pointed to January and mouthed the word "cue."

"So, Brian, as you can see, there is a lot of work to be done here, and the Taliban is still quite active in certain areas, trying to fight the efforts of the Army Corps of Engineers and the efforts of our military as they work to improve the conditions here for the Afghani people. Live in Bagram, January Morgan, CBS News."

"And you are clear, Ms. Morgan. Good work!" Jesse turned off the camera and began wrapping up the microphone cable.

"Thank you. I was more nervous in that live shot than any live shot I have ever done." January felt the sweat on her palms, even though it was freezing outside.

Alayna walked up and hugged January. "Nice job."

"Your story was great, Alayna. You are an amazing producer. I think we make quite the team. Day one in the books." January let the air escape her lungs, and it felt good. A relief to have finished the first one. There would be plenty more. But for tonight, January felt accomplished. She planned to email Alex as soon as she could and take a moment to sip a glass of wine. One of the soldiers had a bottle he had picked up in the city of Bagram, and she was curious about how it would taste. Jesse, Alayna, and January had agreed to meet up in the mess hall for wine and food a little later to celebrate their first full day of news.

The Two Wars

January had been in Afghanistan for two months. Every day, she had turned in a different story, and she had received good feedback from her news director. The two months had gone by in a relative haze as January and her crew were driven to various parts of Afghanistan from small villages to war-torn towns that no longer housed anyone, except the possible sniper hiding in the shadows. Women were scarce, and men walked the streets with a look of distrust in their eyes, still not certain the American soldiers were there to help them. January watched as infrastructure was built by the engineers and then destroyed by the Taliban. She felt weak from the long days in the hot sun and the late nights in the icy cold air. But it was at the end of the second month on an especially overcast and chilly day in Kabul when the biggest story so far for January would happen. She had been at the American Embassy in downtown Kabul, visiting with some representatives there to discuss American relations with the Afghan people. On this day, what started off as a typical Monday in the broken yet still bustling city, ended in two devastating events. After January and Alayna wrapped up their interviews at the American Embassy, Jesse had suggested they get some coffee at a café nearby. There were plenty of American soldiers around, and they had never felt unsafe near the embassy. Taking their seats inside the café as they had done many times before, they were greeted by a kind man, who was the owner and barista there. The coffee was strong, and for January, that was perfect. In fact, January had come to believe she had to come all the way to Afghanistan to drink the best coffee she had ever tasted. Toss in the amazing bread, rice, and sweet cakes they served, and January was certain she was gaining a few pounds. The food in Kabul was simply amazing. The café smelled heavenly, and they ordered their individual favorite drinks. Alayna sipped an espresso; Jesse preferred chai tea, and January just ordered whatever the coffee of the day would be. It was always perfect.

Jesse had been very pleased with the embassy interviews. "I'm glad they let us in to finally tour the building and actually talk to someone. I mean, we are Americans, after all."

Alayna agreed. "Yes, it makes sense on the surface, but they are so highly secure, I guess they never found it necessary to allow media in to do a story. At least, not in recent years. I think this will make for a nice piece, although I am not exactly sure where to fit it in with all the other stuff we've collected. I mean, aside from a story a day, we have collected enough extra b-roll and interviews to have stock stories, in case we ever decide to actually take a day off!"

Alayna was right. They had not slowed down for a second. These short coffee breaks were a welcomed moment in what had, otherwise, become a job that did not seem to stop. Everywhere they turned, it seemed there was a story to tell, a new angle to address. As the warm coffee filled January's stomach and her senses, Jesse's cell phone began to buzz. Usually it was the station checking on their daily story progress. January groaned. "Won't they let us have one minute to catch our breaths?"

Jesse answered, and immediately his face lost color. "Yes. Um, okay. I don't think she...but how am I...okay. Okay, here she is." Jesse handed January the phone, and his eyes were filled with dread.

January took the phone with a questioning look in her eyes. Jesse just shook his head and gave Alayna a quick glance.

"Hello?"

The other end of the line was silent for a moment, and then January heard a familiar voice on the line. "Hello, Janny. It's Frank." January had not talked to Frank since Miami just before she and Zak split.

"Frank? How did you get this number? What's going on?" January was suddenly filled with panic. Why would Detective Frank Williams be calling her while she was working overseas? "Frank? What's wrong?" Her hands began to shake.

"Oh, God, Janny. I didn't want to be the one to tell you this, but I figured it should be me and not someone you didn't know well. Or worse, you didn't hear anything at all. Janny, Zak is gone. He was killed in Mexico by some members of the Sinaloa Federation cartel. Someone discovered his identity while he was undercover."

"Oh, Frank." January began weeping. She nearly dropped the phone. "How...how do you know he's gone?"

"The cartel, Janny, this is so difficult to say. Let's just say they sent evidence of what they did to the police department. Proof. Janny, I am so very sorry. We are planning a service for him. A proper law enforcement memorial service. He will be honored for his sacrifice. January, I am so very sorry. I know this is hard for you to hear, especially while being so far away." Frank felt terrible. He never wanted to be the one to tell her. "We have some planning to do and some more investigative things to work out before we can have the service. His death, for now, is not public record. I know how that sounds. Again, I feel like an ass."

"No, I understand. You still have an ongoing investigation. You can't bury my ex-husband yet. Not publicly without showing they won. I get it." January was sobbing now. "It's all about winning. Winning the drug war. Well, that war can't be won, Frank. Neither can the one I am living in. Zak is gone. He's gone." January laid the phone on the table and buried her face in her arms and cried.

Jesse picked up the phone. "Yes. Yes, sir. I'll make sure she knows. Thank you. Okay. Goodbye."

Alayna wrapped her arms around January and Jesse took her hand. They didn't know what to say. January felt nauseous. She needed to be home to bury Zak. To ensure he received the service he deserved. And now. Not later when the investigation was over. That was ridiculous. She was angry with their department for even considering keeping his death secret for any duration of time. Jesse spoke first. "Janny, I know what you're thinking. But you have to understand, Frank explained, if they make Zak's murder public now, other undercovers could be compromised. They don't want more blood on their hands. They just need a little more time." Jesse couldn't understand it either. He just knew that what Frank had told him made sense. Just holding off a little bit could make the difference in the lives or deaths of, at least, five other men.

January was crying so hard her eyes burned. Memories of their life together flashed in images, both good and bad, before her eyes. They had not been made for each other, but he did not deserve whatever fate had befallen him.

That was when the explosion happened. It was close, so close the walls of the café shook and even cracked. Jesse grabbed both women. "We have to get out of this building before it collapses!" They ran out into the streets and were immediately greeted by soldiers who pulled them inside an armored vehicle. Whatever had happened was at the supreme court building, right next to the embassy. January could see a van buried into the lobby through the front door. There were screams. The fire was burning hot and gun fire could be heard in the distance. This was the other war. The other unwinnable war.

"Stay inside this vehicle!" shouted the soldier. More machine gun fire. Another explosion. Finally, a soldier got into the vehicle with them. Jesse grabbed his camera.

"You have to let me get video of this. That's why we're here. Please. I need to get out of this truck." The soldier nodded and tossed a Kevlar vest at Jesse. He put it on quickly and barreled out of the armored car to get video. The soldier stayed inside with both women. He handed them Kevlar vests as well. "Just in case," he said with a slight tinge of fear in his voice.

January was in shock from the news she had just heard, but the explosion had taken the pain away for a moment as she went into a different frame of mind. The reporter side of her brain took over, shelving her grief. "What happened over there?"

The soldier shook his head. "It was a van filled with people. They were being taken to the supreme court, escorted by security, but the Taliban had attached an improvised explosive device to van. The driver was one of them. I don't know how they pulled it off, but there were probably ten people in the van. Not counting who was killed inside the building. I don't know how bad it is yet. But it's bad." Sirens in the background were drawing nearer as help arrived. Still more gunfire. There were Taliban on the ground, shooting at civilians and military. January wanted to jump out and get into the fire fight. She wanted to see it, just not through the window of the vehicle. "Ma'am, I cannot let you out. It's my instruction to keep both of you inside this vehicle."

Jesse got back in.

"Okay," Jesse exclaimed. "Got it. Let's get the hell out of here."

With that, they zoomed in a fury out of downtown Kabul. Heading back toward Bagram, the devastation and smell of sulfur and burning bodies fell behind as January lost consciousness.

****

When January woke up, she was in the barracks, safe in her bed. She tried to sit up, but the dizziness caught her, and she immediately laid back down. Alayna was there. "Honey, you need to stay in bed. You fainted in the car. Please, rest." Alayna laid a cool cloth on January's head.

"No, we have a story to do. What time is it? Let's

get the package together." January was standing up and trying to find her jeans.

"I called Alex for you. I thought he needed to know what happened. He wants you to call him when you feel better. He's so worried about you, Janny."

"I will. No time now. We have to get ready for the six. What time is it?" January could only think of a line written by Sappho: *"There is no place for grief in a house which serves the Muse."* This made her stomach turn and her heart ache. "Seriously, we have to get to work."

Alayna sighed. "The story is produced. Just needs your voice-over. We have two hours until the live, but I told them back at the station you might be…"

"Might be what? No. I am ready. Let's voice the story and get back to Kabul to do the live shot in front of the building. I am not doing another live shot here. Tonight, we go to the fucking scene." January was on auto pilot. She was burning inside. From grief. From shock. From the bare need to do what she came here to do. That was her salvation. Alex would have to wait. Grieving for Zak would have to wait. She had a job to do. "Is Jess ready? Let's go. Now." January pulled her hair back and walked out of the room, her head spinning and adrenaline fueling her every move.

Shrapnel and Other Shiny Things

Their story had been international. They had been the only embedded correspondents at the scene. They had everything. Jesse had the best video. Interviews. All of it. Two weeks of follow-ups and running on caffeine, all three of them had worked without speaking. No one dared mention Zak, and Frank had not called back. Alex had written fifty more emails and text messages. January wanted nothing to do with any of it. Work. Work was her medicine. It had always been her medicine. Her drug. The only thing that had not toyed with her. Hurt her. Let her down. Loved her and not loved her and loved her again. Work. Work was everything, and right now, despite how sick she felt every day from the stress of it all, she would work.

It was a Thursday and a soft unit special operation task force had invited them along for a trip to an area where the Taliban had been reportedly hiding out. The phrase "guerilla tactics" had been tossed around. They were in a convoy of six Humvees on their way to Jalalabad. January had since learned the bomber of the supreme court had taken a drug before driving the van of innocents into the building. The drug made them feel euphoric as they shouted "Allah Akbar" before dying for their god. January wondered what kind of drug it was. It sounded sort of nice. They drove past buildings without walls, people inside cooking food on a fire as though the walls were still there. No sense of direction. No street lights. Cars flying by with no sense of roads. Then, on the road to Jalalabad, there was a long stretch of nothing. It calmed January. Jesse and Alayna were holding on to each other. Alayna had grown more fearful since the supreme court bombing and had tried to break through January's barriers but had failed at every attempt. She was worried about January's mental health and had considered calling the station and asking to have her removed from the job, sent back to New York to cover regular crime. Mourn her ex-husband. Get home to Alex who was losing himself, too, without word from her. Alayna could only see blind intent in January's eyes. Intent. She was intent on getting herself killed or working so hard until it happened from exhaustion.

Once they reached Jalalabad, they stopped along the road. The battalion exited the Humvees and moved toward what used to be a town. It had been bombed so many times; it was hard to tell where buildings began and ended. It was basically a pile of brown rubble with the occasional wall somehow still standing, defiant to its attackers, unwilling to fall. January respected those few still-standing walls. They were all wearing their vests, and the soldiers assigned to them stood by, closely guiding them to a secure area but never too far from the vehicles. Jesse had his live remote backpack, so they could go live from the area. This was expected to be a good location for possible action and bringing the new backpack with live shot capabilities was expected by their bosses. This was what war correspondence was all about. Their predecessors who had covered the Vietnam War could only have dreamed of such immediate images, having technology to allow them to show the world what they were witnessing at that exact moment. Underneath her helmet, January already had her earpiece in and the receiver attached. This was going to be a quick turn if anything happened. Live while the gunfire was happening. No more shooting a story and editing it for later. It was time to be live during the mayhem. Show the world this war was not over. Not even fucking close. January gripped the microphone in her hand until it hurt. Alexander entered her mind for a moment. His kiss. The warmth of the safety of him.

No.

Not today.

A group of soldiers moved together in unison toward one of the broken buildings. One that still had stairs and part of a second floor. They were quiet and stealthy. A small blur ran through the wreckage of buildings and sand. A child. He was running toward the soldiers crying. January felt like running toward him. He needed help. He was alone. Lieutenant Bellamy was standing beside her. He shook his head, making eye contact with her. He could sense her worry. Her need to run to the child. "No," he whispered. The soldiers backed away from the child and pointed their guns at him.

"Stay back!" one of the men shouted. "You, little boy, stay right where you are. Show us your hands!"

He doesn't understand you, January thought. He doesn't speak English.

The boy ran toward them anyway. He couldn't have been more than five. The bomb went off quickly as the little boy got close. Someone had pushed a button. The child's body became like the buildings, pieces of what was once a whole. With him, two soldiers also suffered a similar fate.

January screamed. Or, at least, she thought she did. She felt the scream more than heard it. Bellamy shouted toward his comrades. "Get back! Get back!" Then sniper fire from that half-building with the second story. Four other soldiers hit. Bellamy moved Alayna, January, and Jesse behind one of the Humvees. "Stay here!" He took off toward the firefight.

January looked at Jesse. "Now. We go live now." She texted the morning producer who would still be at work and explained what was happening.

You have to let us cut in. Right now. Special report. Firefight. Happening now.

The producer responded right away.

Stand by. Give me two minutes.

That could be too long. Too long. January felt the blood hot in her veins. She could see Alayna shaking her head. "No, we can't go live now!"

"Jesse," January began, "this is what we have been waiting for. Let's go."

Jesse raised the camera to his shoulder and nodded toward January. He already had his earpiece in, as well, as gunfire rang out in the background.

In her ear, January could hear the anchor fumbling to the set. He was clearly unprepared. "Hello? January, can you hear me? It's Gregory."

"Yes," January shouted into the microphone. "I can hear you. We are ready when you are."

The opening news music was coming on. The one reserved for breaking news. More gunfire. Lieutenant Bellamy was back.

"Good. You're back. I need to interview you in just a few seconds!" January was adamant.

Bellamy was not happy but knew this was part of his job. "Okay, this way." He led them away from the Humvees, to an area with more soldiers. "They knew we were coming. I think we got the last of them. My guys are just clearing the area now."

Then the voice. The voice of the news anchor. Safe in his anchorman chair. Somewhere in the bosom of New York City. Nowhere near the unwinnable war. "We have breaking news happening right now, as we go live to war correspondent January Morgan in Jalalabad. January, I can hear gunfire. What's happening right now?"

"Well, Gregory, we arrived with this convoy to inspect an area that has been in question for possible Taliban hiding out. Maybe using this space as a headquarters or hideout. I am here now with the Third Batallion Lieutenant Phillip Bellamy. Lieutenant, please tell me what has happened here this morning and why ensuring these possible hideouts are checked often?"

Phillip Bellamy was nervous. Nervous about what was happening and clearly saddened he had lost some of his men. He was not ready to be on television. Yet, that had been part of his charge. He spoke loudly and with authority. "We have lost some men out here. This was a village that had been destroyed several months ago. We had some intel there might still be activity here and needed to check on it. We lost…" Bellamy became choked up.

More gunfire. They all ducked down. "Sir," January began, "this is still active. What can you say about the Taliban and their continued stronghold over the people of Afghanistan?"

"It's not over. This war is long from being over. Even if we defeat the Taliban, the remaining Taliban will just become something else. There is no clear way to defeat this type of terrorism. They fight to the death. They're happy to die. How can you ever defeat people who want to die, who think whatever is after death is better and deserved for their evil actions in life?"

January stood motionless, looking into Phillip's eyes. He's right, she thought as the bullets whizzed by so quickly January could feel the heat of them pass her cheek. And then enter her body. The warmth of her own blood oozing from different places. A bomb going off. Loud. Ears ringing. Alayna screaming. Then, no screaming. Then a body on top of her. Holding her down. Holding her as she drifted away. Gregory's voice in her ear. In her head? "January, can you hear me? January?"

Then, nothing. Just the hum of dying.

****

January lay in the hospital surrounded by noises she could not hear. Doctors rushing around her, nurses placing an oxygen mask on her face, IV in her arm, shouts of "more pressure" and "elevate her head." January could not hear these things as her mind hovered somewhere in the darkness, only the reverberations of the explosion still moving throughout her mind and her body clinging to life.

"We need to remove the shrapnel from her leg. It's too close to her artery. Let's rush her to surgery. Also monitor her concussion, please, nurse." The emergency room doctors were accustomed to dealing with war injuries, and this one seemed hopeful. "Watch the blood loss. She's a lucky young woman." They moved the bed as quickly to the elevator leading to the surgical floor as they could. Three hours of surgery, as doctors intricately removed pieces of the IED from January's inner thigh, her arm, and a few pieces on her face. There were two bullets, too, in her shoulder and leg. It was too soon to know how serious her concussion would be, but no bleeding in her brain had been detected so far. Her skull was in-tact, thanks to the helmet she had been wearing at the time. Her abdomen, though severely bruised was clear of injury, although she had two broken ribs. Her breathing was somewhat labored, and her pulse was faint.

A nurse ran up to the surgeon as he worked on January's wounds. "Doctor. This patient, she's pregnant." The nurse looked down at the woman on the table, exposed, covered in wires and tubes, and bleeding. "We need to check on the fetus. She can't be too far along." The doctor shook his head.

"After the trauma her body just experienced and will continue to endure, I do not see how a pregnancy survived this. But stranger things have happened. Let's just keep her alive, and then we will ensure the baby's safety."

"Her pulse is slowing, doctor. We need to get her fixed up here," another surgeon shouted.

Blood dripped onto the floor, and the buzzing of the explosion echoed somewhere within the lingering thoughts inside January's mind. She was slipping away. Alexander's face hovered within the darkness; he was talking, but she couldn't hear him. He was moving away from her.

"She's gone into D-Fib! Get the crash cart! Stand back, and clear!" January's body shook as waves of electricity passed into her heart.

Silence as the staff of nurses and doctors waited and watched the heart monitor.

The beeping returned, slowly at first and then rhythmically. A collective sigh spread through the room.

"Okay, let's get her cleaned up and have a scan of her brain to ensure swelling has not occurred."

January was then moved to another room she could not see as she remained in hazy unconsciousness. It only became deeper when doctors determined her brain did exhibit some signs of swelling. They placed her in a medically induced coma and moved her to ICU.

****

Alexander had just handed the cashier a handful of cash. "It's perfect." The lady at the jewelry counter smiled.

"Oh, yes, sir. It's exquisite. A beautiful antique from the 1920s. I've never had a piece in here before with diamonds and lapis. The platinum weaving throughout the band. It's extraordinary."

Alexander clutched the box. "It was made for her." A radio hummed low in the background of the little estate shop. He heard something about Americans killed in Afghanistan. "Ma'am, can you please turn up the radio?"

She did as she was asked. "Oh, dear," she said. "This is about that news crew that was blown up by the IED while on a shoot. I heard they were live on TV when the bomb went off. Some of them were shot, too."

Alexander felt his stomach turn and his knees go

weak. It couldn't be her, he thought. He ran back to his car where his cell phone was still sitting on the passenger seat. He struggled with picking it up as his hands were shaking and discovered he had nine missed calls. Several of them were friends who had left frantic text messages, telling him to watch his TV. He had a voicemail, too, from an unknown number. It was from a woman with a thick German accent, calling from a hospital in Munich. "Hello, sir? Mr. Lane? We have your lady here, January Morgan. Please call us." She left a number.

The other voicemail was from one of the commanders of the unit January was stationed with. "Mr. Lane, this is Lieutenant Phillip Bellamy. We have some terrible news about your, um, your January. Ms. Morgan and her crew, along with some of my men, came in contact with an IED. It went off just feet from where they were set up. We lost several people. I was injured but was able to cover her before the bomb went off. January is in surgery. She was flown to Munich after we gave her initial treatment here at Bagram. You need to get on a plane and head to Munich as soon as you can. When you arrive at the hospital, tell them who you are, and I will have a military member escort you to her side. And, Lane, she's in bad shape. Try to catch the next flight. I am so sorry, my friend."

Alexander could feel the tears stinging his cheeks. This man spoke as if she was already dead. He headed toward the airport. As he drove, he called the hospital in Munich. That took longer than he would have liked, and he went through four people before he finally got an English-speaking nurse on the phone. "Hello, my name is Alexander Lane. I am calling about my girlfriend, January Morgan. She was brought in after her convoy was attacked in Afghanistan. She is a news reporter. Please, help me. I need to know how she is." Alexander choked on his words as he whizzed around traffic.

"Ms. Morgan is in stable condition right now, sir. She is in a medically induced coma as we are monitoring a possible head injury."

"Okay, thank God. I am on my way to the hospital. Thank you."

The airport was buzzing with crowds. Alex parked his car in long-term parking and rushed into the airport to the first terminal he could see with Germany on a sign. The flight to Munich was not to depart for another two hours. After that, eight hours in the air. As Alex sat in the terminal waiting area, the televisions were all on, each one with a reporter talking about the live broadcast of the IED explosion. He stood up and got a bit closer to one. There, he could see January on camera, talking and pointing around her at some crumbling buildings. She had a man in fatigues standing next to her for an interview, and as she was asking him questions, the explosion happened. The screen went black as the sounds of the bomb going off and screams could be heard. Then, nothing. His love. His life. She was just standing there and then…nothing. Alex sat back down and placed his head in his hands. He couldn't feel a thing. His entire body was numb, and he could feel her slipping away from him, just like her image from the screen had suddenly vanished amid tragedy. "I'm coming to you," he murmured. "I won't lose you. Not after everything we have been through to finally be together. My baby."

The next hours were a blur. Alexander was focused on only one thing, and that was getting to January. He held the ring in his hand, gazing at its beauty. He hoped, more than anything, she would wear this someday.

****

Once he arrived at the hospital, he alerted a desk attendant who he was and who he was there to see. "January. I need to see my January." His face was red from crying, and the attendant looked at him with sympathy.

A soldier standing in the lobby heard him and moved in. "You are Mr. Lane?"

"Yes. Please, take me to her."

He was led to a room on the fourth floor. Outside, soldiers and German police were standing guard. They moved out of the way as a doctor approached.

"*Guten tag*. I am Doctor Fritz Herschberg, and January is my patient. She is sleeping now, but you can visit. She was placed in a coma to allow her body to heal. We pulled her out of the induced coma, and she is now resting."

Alexander's eyes were puffy with dark circles beneath them, and his right hand was sore from clutching the ring box for so many hours. He sat beside her. Her face was pale and marked with scratches and bruises. Her lips were dry. An oxygen mask helped her breathe, and a machine beeped away in the corner. He held her hand. It was warm. "Oh, my baby, I love you so. Please come back to me. I need you with me. Please come back to me, my love. I waited too long for us. We are just getting started, you and me." Alex laid his head on her stomach.

A nurse came in to check on January's vitals. "She is holding on quite well, sir. I think she will make it through. We are just trying to ensure the safety of her baby."

Alex sat upright quickly. "Her what?"

"The baby. She is about fourteen weeks along, we think. But it appears the fetus is still strong inside her. Tough little person."

Alex laid his hand on her stomach. "Oh, honey." Alexander was weeping now. Everything he had ever wanted was wrapped up in this woman and in those beeps on a machine. "Fight for him. He needs you, too. We both do."

January's eyes opened slightly, the light burning them. She felt weight on her. Someone was holding her down. Bellamy. He was saving her. She tossed around and opened her eyes fully and took a deep breath. This was not Jalalabad.

A hand was clutching hers. Alex. Alex was here. Where was here?

"Alex?" Her voice was hoarse. "Alex!" She cried his name, and he held her. He was real. This was real. He kissed her forehead.

"You are going to be okay, my love. Both of you."

January gave a slight smile and felt the pain of her damaged body. "You didn't call me 'baby.'"

Alex laughed through the tears. "I'm sorry, baby. I love you. And I love our baby. Oh, honey, why didn't you tell me?"

"I wasn't so sure myself at first. After I found out Zak died, I just thought I was sick from grief. Then I took a test. I started making plans to leave, but I had to get in one last story. Then, then...oh, God,

Alayna...Jesse." January was weeping. "My friends are dead."

Alex laid in the hospital bed beside her, cradling her and their unborn child. "I know. A lot of people died out there. I am so sorry about your friends. About Zak. About not pushing harder to reach you. I knew you were suffering. I just couldn't get you to come back to me. It's like I could feel you trying to separate from me somehow. Break our bond."

January wiped the tears from his eyes and pulled Alex closer. "I was. But I couldn't. I could still feel you. Just like I feel him." She placed Alex's hand on her belly. "Is he going to be okay?"

"Nurse says he is fighter. Sounds like his mom already. She also said you are around fourteen weeks. The car at the airport?"

January stifled a laugh through her tears. "Yeah." The pain was strong, but she was still here. And so was her baby. Their baby. "You are okay with all this? I'm broken, mourning the loss of so many people I loved, and pregnant. Talk about some baggage."

"Baby, you are alive. I have waited fifteen years to have you. Now I find out we made a little person who is growing inside of you? I am more than ready for all of this. I am so in love with you, broken or not. You are mine."

"I love you, too, Alex."

"It's you and me, January. It always has been. Everything in my life has led to you. You have always been my life. I wish I had fought harder for you from the moment I first saw you. You are going to get well. I will take you home, and we are going to begin our lives together. All three of us."

"I love us. I love the sound of the three of us."

Alexander pulled the ring from his pocket, a glistening diamond and lapis ray of light forged into a circle. He placed it on her finger. "You belong to me, and I will never let anything keep us from where we should have been all along. Marry me. Be my wife."

Tears were streaming down January's face, and with all the emotion and pain of everything she was consumed with, she knew this was forever. Her muse. Her love. Her Alexander. "Yes, Alex. I will always belong to you."

January Morgan knew she was exactly where she was supposed to be. After fifteen years of longing and missed opportunities, other relationships and loss, it was finally their time. Fifteen years, and the timeline had finally stopped wavering. January was united with her twin soul. She placed her hand on her stomach and smiled despite the pain. So many years and it was all, at long, last real.

They were finally real.

A word about the author...

I was born in Oak Ridge, Tennessee and am a dedicated lover of the Appalachian Mountains. I was a television news reporter and anchor in multiple markets across the country for 12 years. After TV, I became an associate dean for a college. I have a Master's Degree in Behavioral Psychology and am the mother of two boys. We live in Tampa Bay. I love writing, reading, baking, running, Crossfit, and spending time outdoors. Most importantly, I love being a mother.

Made in the USA
Columbia, SC
11 July 2019